The Bone Picker

A Sam Chitto Mystery

Lu Clifton

First Edition, First Printing April, 2017
Cover design by Robert Parshall
Cover image CC0 *Pixabay*

Summary: It's bitter cold in Oklahoma's Ouachita Wilderness when Detective Sam Chitto of the Choctaw Tribal Police takes on a thirty-five year old cold case involving a missing Vietnam vet and a murdered couple. The discovery of a man's skull in the murdered woman's casket, which her family had disinterred for further investigation, attracts the attention of the veteran's mother. Believing the skull to be that of her son, she tasks Chitto with becoming a Bone Picker. Because bones survived flesh, Choctaw of old preserved the bones of their deceased, believing their essence dwelled within. Honored people, called Bone Pickers, retrieved the bones for the family. When his preliminary investigation reveals former suspects in the old murder inquiry have a shorter-than-average life span, Chitto goes looking for the reason. As he unravels the mystery, long-held secrets that have kept residents living in fear the past thirty-five years begin to tumble.

1. Fiction—Indian reservation police 2. Murder—Investigation—Fiction 3. Choctaw Indians—Fiction 4. Oklahoma—Fiction Title: Sam Chitto Mystery

ISBN 978-0-9985284-0-3
ISBN 978-0-9985284-1-0 (e-book)

Two Shadows
P.O. Box 154
Davis, Il 61019
Email: info@twoshadows.biz

For my sons, Jeffrey and Christopher

ACKNOWLEDGEMENTS

I'm always jolted when readers tell me they recognize one of my characters as being someone they know, to which I can only quote Carolos Ruiz Zalon, who said, "Books are mirrors; you only see in them what you already have inside you." Though some of the characters in my books have clairvoyant abilities, I do not. The only malaise I suffer is an active imagination. Fiction is, after all, invention. In short, the characters are fictitious.

The same goes for setting. While Pushmataha County and the town of Antlers do exist, many of the places and settings depicted in the book do not. The same can be said for the events portrayed. Given this admission, thanks to Pushmataha County citizens, and especially its sheriff's department, for not taking what I wrote seriously.

A special thanks to Henry "Skip" Watson III, a retired Army Colonel who was an Army War College Fellow at the Fletcher School of Law and Diplomacy in the Boston suburb of Medford. Skip read the manuscript with a keen eye to military terminology and our involvement in Vietnam.

In understanding the Choctaw Tribal Police organization, I am indebted to R. D. Hendrix, Director of Law Enforcement for the Choctaw Nation. As fiction writers are prone to do, I exercised artistic license in developing characters and plot in *The Bone Picker*. If I have portrayed anything incorrectly in so doing, it is through no fault of R.D.'s.

I am also indebted to the Choctaw School of Language for help with Choctaw words and phrases. *Yakoke!*

PROLOGUE

As the helicopter ahead lifts off, he turns his attention to people below it, clinging to a ladder leading to the roof. A vertical queue of people, waiting for a ride to freedom. As the CH-53 he's on shudders to a hover over them, the troop ladder is deployed. It bows under the weight of people scrambling hand over fist to reach the safety of the aircraft. As the ladder is withdrawn, he watches more people appear below to wait their turn. They disappear from sight as the helo lifts off, the rooftop merging with another rooftop and another until a city emerges below. Squalid. Dirty. Teeming with miniscule specks looking more like rats than members of the human race. He thinks back to other missions where his job would've been to make sure those specks stopped crawling. But this day, he had not had to use the MA Deuce .50 caliber machine gun he mans.

He glances at the man opposite, also manning a 50. They catch each other's eyes, then turn their attention back to the open doors. The air swarms with planes, so many it's hard to tell which is friendly, which enemy.

Frightened people fill the helo's belly, saturating the heavy air with the sour-sweet smell of sweat. Fear. Men cling to small bags and rucksacks. Women cling to children. He watches faces mouth words of reassurance, not realizing words would be lost. The thropping of one Jolly Green's blades was deafening. Dozens of the heavies were enough to burst the eardrums. Like monster heatbugs stripping the ground of life, the copters are evacuating thousands of U.S. citizens and nationals from Saigon. How many trips has he made? Ten? Twenty?

As the South China Sea displaces bruised ground and seared grasses, he forces his hands to ease the grip on the handles and take his thumbs off the butterfly trigger. It's done, he thinks. The mission's over—his last one. The big dog in Washington was pulling the plug, leaving this broken finger of land to mend or break on its own. Another North against South, he reflects, just on the opposite side of the globe. A duke's mixture of guys from all walks of life brought together for a common purpose that didn't mean diddlysquat to them. Or was it the other way around, South against North? It didn't matter. It wasn't his war.

This one wasn't either, he thinks now. His war was being fought elsewhere . . . and without him.

He digs fingertips deep into corded shoulder muscles, listens to his heart pound in his ears, draws a breath that splinters his lungs. The wall of the helicopter becomes a shuddering crutch to keep his legs from caving.

As the carrier deck looms large, he looks across the helo. The other gunner's skin glistens with sweat; his mouth is so dry, his lips have cracked open. The man catches his eye, finds a smile. As soon as the copter settles, they slide open their doors and help the nationals disembark out the back.

Like a taxi queue, helicopters great and small form lines around waiting flattops. Huey's buzz like flies, trying to find an open slot, while the Jolly Greens lumber in for their landings. One of the deck crew runs to them, yelling in their ears to grab their machine guns and ammo bags. As soon as the helo is empty, the crew pushes it to the elevator for a ride below decks, making room for the barrage of unplanned planes from the mainland. His aircraft escapes the ignominy of being jettisoned over the side. Others are not so lucky. He listens to smaller copters groan as they splash into the sea, watches them slide beneath oil-slick waves, and feels the other gunner's slap on his back.

"That's it, man," he yells. "Damn, we must've been loony tunes, volunteering for this job. But we're headed stateside now. Home free . . ."

He forces a smile as the other man continues to talk.

"Back to the flatlands for me. Wheat fields, dairy cows, eight-foot-tall corn as far as the eye can see. And you, you're back to those hills you been bending my ear 'bout for . . . Hell, I lost track how long. I'm telling you, man, one of these days I'm gonna have a look at those Comanche hills."

"Kiamichi," he says.

"Yeah, Kiamichi." From somewhere, the man finds the energy to laugh. "Damn, still can't believe Oklahoma's got mountains." He pauses, frowning. "What's wrong, man? You was never one to run off at the mouth, but . . ." His eyes blink rapidly. "Hold on. That letter you got at mail call, was there bad news in that letter you got?"

The letter . . .

Pulling a crumpled letter from his pocket, he stares at it.

The other man hunches closer. "Somebody die, that what this is about? Somebody back home die?"

"No . . ." He unfolds the letter so he can read the return address, needing confirmation. "My wife just had a baby.

"*Baby*— You're a daddy? Hell, man, that's terrific. Damn, what a homecoming you're gonna have. First thing we do when we get off this tub is find a cold one and celebrate."

"Yeah," he says. "Celebrate . . ."

CHAPTER ONE

Sam Chitto slid across ice black as coal, struggling to keep his feet. Overnight, a February storm walloped the southeast corner of Oklahoma, leaving sheet ice on roads, frostbite on the skin, and jelled blood in the veins. Pushing through the door of the Choctaw Nation Police Department, he nodded at two women in the reception area. Shaking frozen pellets from his jacket, he proceeded to Jasmine Birdsong's desk to pick up his messages.

"You're late . . ." She hammered a staple into a packet of papers. "Again."

"Stopped to assist at a pileup." He picked up a half dozen message slips from the corner of her desk. "People around here have shit for brains when it comes to driving on slick roads." He nodded over his shoulder at the two women in the reception area. "They here to see someone?"

"Yes, indeed. *You.* Drove clear from Antlers."

"In this ice storm?" He looked up from the message slips, frowning. "Antlers is in District 7. Why me?"

"Wouldn't say. Been waitin' most of an hour. But you have a previous appointment to take care of first." She aimed a neatly plucked eyebrow toward Dan Blackfox's office. "Remember?"

Dan Blackfox, the Director of Law Enforcement, had sent word about the meeting the day before but had not

1

mentioned the reason. Chitto glanced toward his boss's office, then at the reception area again. An aluminum walker sat next to the older woman, fuzzy yellow tennis balls on the wheels. In her lap lay a manila envelope.

"Don't even think about it." Jasmine crooked her neck at the clock on the wall. "He's got a budget meeting in a half hour. Stuck his head out his door twice already, looking for you."

"Couldn't someone else help them?" Glancing toward Nate White's desk, he remembered the field officer was on assignment. He looked next to where the K-9 officer sat, a German Shepherd on the floor next to him. "How 'bout Junior. He's in this morning."

"No way, Jose. The old one there . . ." She indicated a dark lump stuffed into a stiff-backed chair. "Said no one but the Nameless One would do." She hammered another staple into a packet.

He frowned. "I've got a name."

"She said so, too. Called you Detective Sam Chitto, the Nameless One."

He shook his head, sighing. "Okay. I'll just let them know."

Introducing himself to the women, Chitto explained the previous appointment. "Officer Wharton's free—"

"We will wait," the older woman said, folding her hands. The younger woman rubbed her face, sighing.

"All right then. I shouldn't be a minute or two." Retreating to Jasmine's desk, he pointed his chin toward the cafeteria. "You, uh, you want to get them some coffee. I think they need to thaw out some."

"I don't do coffee," she said, hammering another staple. "Remember?"

∞

You want me to do what?" Chitto stared at Dan Blackfox, the Director of Law Enforcement and his boss.

2

"You heard me. I want you to help me interview replacements for Wanda."

Wanda had been the department's administrative assistant until a lifelong smoking habit and ten-year bout with bitterness caught up with her. Wanda's husband, Bert Gilly, and Chitto's father, Will Chitto, were killed while on a routine investigation in LeFlore County. Blackfox had followed procedure, turned the case over to the FBI, and the murder had ended up a decade-old-cold case.

"Not cut out for that kind of thing," Chitto said, head shaking. "I'm a field guy, not a people person."

"You have direct reports. They're people."

"*Report,*" Chitto said, downgrading his number of reports from multiple to single. "And Nine manages himself. Hell, he has to. I'm gone more than I'm here."

Nate White, aka Nine, was the field officer for District 9. Being known by a number instead of a name had become the norm since Chitto had gone to work for the Nation. While his memory of things ancient and long forgotten was renown, he had trouble with names. As a rookie, he had resorted to using the district number to ID the respective field officer. It made sense, at least to him. While people came and went, the Nation's districts remained the same.

He dropped his still damp jacket on the floor beside his chair. "Besides, I told you what I wanted in Wanda's replacement."

"More like what you *don't* want. No one that knows your family, would mother you to death, or dog your tracks. That about cover it?"

"Pretty much."

Blackfox leaned back in his chair, fingers laced behind his head "Problem is, the last item on your list is tops on mine." He narrowed his eyes. "Care to venture a guess why?"

"No . . ." Chitto paused, rolling shirtsleeves to his elbow. Being a detective, he could choose to wear plain clothes or service uniform. His duty uniforms rarely saw the light of day. "I've got a good idea."

Chitto had gotten involved in an undercover operation in the not-too-distant past, one the FBI had taken exception to, being the case was in its jurisdiction.

"Good. Glad your memory's still intact. Don't need the Exec on my back again."

Chitto glanced toward the front desk. "How about Jasmine? She's been here a while now. Knows the job and the people. Not just here in District 9 but across the Nation— and she doesn't take flak from anyone."

Jasmine Birdsong worked as a floater, filling in for open clerical positions in the various districts. To be as well known as she was, she was somewhat of an enigma. In her mid-fifties, she hailed from LeFlore County in the northern part of the Nation. To Chitto's knowledge, she had no children. Though she never volunteered the information, he suspected she was divorced, not widowed. She took her lunch alone, didn't keep pictures of grandkids on her desk, and cared nothing for hobbies like crocheting and quilting. And though she'd held onto her looks, she showed no interest in men. In short, she was an undiscovered planet circumnavigating a distant orbit.

"You got that right." Blackfox ran a hand through dark, short-trimmed hair. "Swear to God, I thought Wanda was independent, but Jasmine's got her beat four ways to Sunday. Won't even make a pot of coffee for the office in the morning. Says that's what the new cafeteria's for."

The Law Enforcement Department now occupied the vacated community center behind the tribal complex. Recently refurbished, the building had been divided into thirds, with Law Enforcement on one end, Land Management on the other, and a small cafeteria between.

"I like her, she's . . . direct." Chitto grinned. "She one of the candidates?"

"Oh, *hell* no. Said she didn't want to be tied down, rather do temp work like she's been doing. Which is fine by me." Blackfox began leafing through a stack of papers. "Interviews start next week. Monday, Wednesday, and Friday morning. Scheduled them early in case you got called out on something."

"You're so considerate," Chitto muttered. "How early?"

"Nine o'clock. I'll get you a list of the candidates HR's lined up. In the meantime, I suggest you come up with a new set of wants for Wanda's replacement. Might want to brush up on the dos and don'ts, too."

Chitto stared at him.

"The things you can't ask about."

"Oh, right. Those things."

Blackfox shook his head. "I'll have HR give you the rundown. Now get the hell outta my office. I'm late for a budget meeting."

Knowing when he'd lost the battle, Chitto grabbed his jacket and headed for his desk. It was a short walk, just long enough for him to decide it might be a good thing if he was in on the interviews. As the field lieutenant for District 9, he deserved a say in who sat in that chair.

Losing a battle didn't mean you'd lost the war.

CHAPTER TWO

Dead people leave tracks. Hair and skin. Bone. Signs of their passing. Something more than a grainy drawing in a small-town newspaper.

Chitto turned from the sketch he'd been studying, a depiction of a man's head that had been developed from a skull, to the accompanying newspaper article. What made it worthy of front-page coverage in the *Antlers American* was where the skull had been found: the coffin of a Caucasian woman murdered more than thirty years before. Based on the high cheekbones and square jawline, the artist believed the skull to be that of a man. Pending further investigation, the Pushmataha County Sheriff's Department had taken possession of the skull.

"You can't be sure this is your son, Mrs. Folsom." Laying the article aside, he looked at the woman across from him. The top buttons on her dark wool coat were now open, revealing a navy-blue dress underneath.

"It is him," Peony Folsom said.

"It's an artist's rendering." He laid the drawing next to a photo of a young man in a Navy uniform that she'd brought. "Renderings aren't always reliable." He looked across the desk again, making eye contact.

Sunshine had broken through morning clouds and now streamed through the windows, helping Chitto's back to

7

thaw. Unlike the old office, this new one was open. Roomy. The two field officers that worked out of the Durant office, Junior Wharton and Nate White, had their own desks now. His bosses, the Director and Executive Director of Law Enforcement, had offices there, too. Pulling seniority, Chitto had spoken for a desk in a back corner. He liked the abundance of windows. The privacy. No one could casually overhear a conversation, and he could keep his eye on the comings and goings outside the building. He had dropped his guard on a recent undercover case, a careless oversight that almost cost his life, and wouldn't make that mistake again.

"It is Walter." Peony Folsom's snow-white hair was tied with a faded scarf. Wrinkles deep as canyons carved her face. Dark eyes appeared hollow.

Visible signs weren't the only kind of tracks mortals left behind, Chitto thought, studying her. They left invisible ones too, traced into a person's core with indelible ink.

Exhaling loudly, he took time to read the article more closely, focusing on the report of the forensic artist, Glenda Loomis. He'd never met Loomis but knew of her reputation. She was a graduate of the University of Texas and the FBI Academy Forensic Artist Course. Her sketches had helped law enforcement bring down hundreds of criminals. He paused, reading her evaluation of the skull—*not Caucasian, possibly of Asian descent*—and studied the bone structure in the sketch again.

A man?

More than likely.

An Asian?

Possibly.

An Indian?

He glanced away, blinking. Recent research had proven that Native Americans had migrated into North America from Asia across a land bridge in the Bering Strait. Some modern-day Asians even referred to American Indians as

Mongolians. The big mystery today was not how they'd gotten to the continent but how many migrations had taken place.

"What'd the sheriff say when you reported Walter missing?" He looked between Peony and a younger woman sitting next to her. Her granddaughter, Crystal Folsom. Early to mid-thirties. No wedding band. Gray eyes, a sprinkling of freckles. Dark hair with a hint of auburn plaited in a back-swung braid. Attractive in a brooding kind of way.

Peony answered with a puffing sound. The woman called Crystal rolled her eyes toward the ceiling. Both responses said the same thing. *Nana kiyo.* Nothing.

Chitto wasn't surprised at their responses. He'd seen it plenty of times. No matter how many times he explained the convoluted legal system in the Checkerboard, that part of Oklahoma where thirty-eight Indian nations were located, people still expected the tribal police to fix things outside its jurisprudence.

"What is it you want of me?" He lifted his hands, palms up. "Call someone? Get you a name to work with?"

The last thing Chitto wanted was to become embroiled in another case involving a beheaded man—or woman, for that matter. That undercover operation he'd gotten involved in had led him across the Checkerboard, looking for the killers of three men beheaded at sacred Indian sites. The case had ended in a logjam, and he ended up in the doghouse with his boss.

FBI Agent Ramon Rodriquez had led a contingent into the office and come down hard on Dan Blackfox, asserting Chitto could've stopped the last killing from happening. When confronted, Rodriquez wouldn't reveal how he'd gotten the information. It didn't matter. Getting wind of it, Ben Wilson, the Executive Director, had dragged Blackfox into his office for an explanation. Blackfox had defended Chitto, but after everyone was through having his say, he did some confronting of his own. Chitto danced around his questions, confirming the FBI agent had nailed it on the head. "You value your job, Sam," Blackfox had said, "walk the straight and narrow here on out. Funnel any leads you get to Rodriguez."

Chitto had agreed to the condition for he'd made a commitment to find his father's killer. As a cop, he was privy to the rumor mill, and the rumor mill produced leads. Even if he couldn't get directly involved, he could pass those leads on to Rodriguez—who had recently been assigned the decade-old-cold case—and push the agent to follow through.

"Walter calls to me from the pines," Peony said. "His *shilombish* cannot rest."

Chitto sat up straight. "You think he was murdered?"

In the old way of thinking, the Choctaw believed a person possessed an inner shadow, the *shiliup,* and an outer one, the *shilombish.* After death, the inner shadow began the long journey to the west, but sometimes the outer shadow, or ghost, would not fade away until it felt everything was all right with its family, or in some instances, a violent death had been settled. As in murder.

"I *told* you, Grandma," Crystal said with a sigh. "It was just a wolf."

"Wolf?" He shook his head. "Couldn't be." No timber wolves had been spotted in Oklahoma since the middle of the last century, and red wolves had been wiped out, though some efforts were being made to reestablish them in North Carolina. "Probably a coyote, or maybe a hound on a coon's trail."

"No. My son is telling me he wants to make the journey west. You bring him home so his ghost can go to the way of shadows."

Chitto inhaled, exhaled. He had gotten a crash course in ghosts on that undercover case. Only months ago, he would've scoffed at the idea, but he'd discovered he was haunted, too. His wife, Mary, had wanted her release so she could finish her journey, only he wasn't ready to let her go. He had detained her a long time, too long before he released her.

"I don't see how I could be of help?" He picked up a stone that lay on his desk, one of many geologic finds, and rubbed it between his fingers. "I wasn't even born when he disappeared."

"The Nameless One can find Walter."

He shook his head slightly, knowing the reference was to an old Choctaw teaching, an area he worked hard to avoid. As a trained geologist, he preferred keeping both feet grounded in reality. But Walter, he reminded himself, at one time *had* been real.

From the little information he'd gleaned from Peony, her son Walter disappeared without a trace in 1980, over thirty-five years ago. In his early thirties and a veteran, he'd left the house on the outskirts of Antlers with a thermos of coffee and his old coon dog Rosebud, leaving the keys to his car, his clothes, and his wallet in his room. Neither he nor Rosebud returned. Coincidentally, a couple was found murdered the same night he disappeared, the murdered woman being the one buried with the wrong head.

"Why?" he asked. "Why did Walter leave the house?"

"To listen to the river. He went every morning. On Friday, two times." Sliding a hand between the lapels of her coat, Peony patted her chest. "He came back with soldier's heart."

Soldier's heart. Today, a newer term was used for the malaise that returning vets suffered. PTSD.

"*Grandma*," Crystal groaned. Up to then, she'd been chewing the thumbnail on her left hand, practicing restraint. The reference to soldier's heart had obviously tested her limit. "We talked about this before. He was OCD, obsessive-compulsive. For Pete's sake, he picked up garbage. People still talk about the *wacko* garbage collector." She waved a hand through the air dismissively. "He probably just wandered into the wilderness and couldn't find his way back."

"He did not get lost," Peony said, looking hard at Crystal.

Chitto studied the two women locked in a stare down. One old; one young. One brown-eyed; one gray. Both bitter.

"So, he picked up trash people threw out of their cars?" Chitto said to end the standoff.

Peony nodded. "There at the campground. Pop bottles. Beer cans. Diamonds . . ."

"Diamonds?" Chitto was aware diamonds had been found in southwest Arkansas where a kind of volcanic soil called lamproite tuff could be found. He knew of no finds in the Kiamichi, but he also knew the planet was a giant recycling machine.

"Grandma," Crystal groaned again, her preferred way of communicating, it seemed. She looked at him. "Not diamonds, just rocks he *called* diamonds."

"But he did bring back stones of some kind." Trained as a geologist, Chitto had a special interest in rocks of any kind.

"And other things," Peony answered. "He doesn't . . . didn't like how people made the ground dirty. Rotary Club does that now." She looked at Crystal. "And nobody calls them *wacko*."

Chitto rolled the piece of sandstone between his fingers, taking note of Peony's change in verb tense from present to past. After keeping him alive for thirty-odd years, the picture in the newspaper had finally convinced her that Walter was dead.

He looked at her again. "Why'd you come to me? My wife's name was Folsom, too. Mary Bernadette Folsom. You know her?"

She turned inwards, thinking. "My cousin Henry had a girl called Mary. She passed a while back."

Mary's father had been named Henry, but clearly, Peony Folsom hadn't made the connection until now. What it boiled down to, however, was clear. Walter would've been a shirttail relative of Mary's.

"*He* told me to come to you," she added.

"He . . ."

"The healer man."

He paused. "Sonny Boy Munro?"

"Yes, him."

Chitto slumped. The old pig farmer and mystic had knocked his world out of kilter on that undercover case that had gotten him in trouble. Apparently, he was back. And, he thought, probably the one spreading rumors about me being this Nameless One.

Replacing his worry stone to his desktop, he said, "I'd like to help, but other law enforcement agencies are your best bet. This newspaper article indicates the dead girl in the coffin was white. That means it's outside my jurisdiction." Returning the clipping and picture to a dog-eared manila envelope, he held it out to her. "And if you suspect foul play in your son's disappearance, the state needs to be informed. Maybe the feds."

"No. You will bring my boy home. He says you are a justice man."

Chitto inferred the "he" referenced was again Sonny Boy.

"Sorry, my hands are tied." He'd crossed the line once, pitted the Law against Justice, and found a side of himself he didn't know existed. But not again. He was walking the straight and narrow. His job depended on it.

Peony rose from the chair, leaving him holding the envelope. "Bring my boy home, Mr. Chitto." She shuffled toward the front door, scooting the yellow tennis balls on the walker across the floor.

"Wait for me at the door, Grandma," Crystal said, watching her go. "I'll catch up." She turned back to Chitto, eyes intense.

He answered the question in them before she could ask it. "No can do," he said. "Jurisdictional issues."

"There's no one else. You have to help us."

"Us?" He hesitated, frowning. "Walter was your father?"

She nodded. "Don't read too much into that. I have no feelings for him. He walked out on me when I was little. Her, too. My mom, I mean. She didn't even hang around long enough to name me." A harsh laugh atrophied to awkward silence.

He waited, watching her blink.

"Grandma raised me." She nodded at the manila envelope he held. "She tried to get someone there at the sheriff's department to believe her about that picture in the paper. When they wouldn't listen, she went to see Chuck Stovall. He was instrumental in getting that murdered girl's coffin opened, too. You know, the one the man's skull was found in."

"What did he think?"

"He seemed interested—but anything about that case interests him."

Chitto paused, blinking. "Your grandmother talk to anyone other than him?"

"I don't know, but probably. She was upset when the sheriff brushed her off. Then she was in that accident, a hit and run. Totaled her car and damaged muscles, maybe some nerves. I have to drive her around now, and my Aunt Rose stays with her when I'm working."

"Sorry to hear that." Chitto was close to his grandmother, so he could understand how she felt. "She get a plate number, description of the car?"

14

She shook her head. "Came out of nowhere. Just a big truck or SUV. Didn't see a license plate, but she didn't have time to look. The other driver was on a side road. He hit her broadside and was going fast. I figure it was someone hunting out of season. Fines are stiff if you get caught."

"What color was the vehicle?"

She frowned. "She said it looked like the trees."

"Trees?" Chitto glanced out the window at trees across the road, barren for the most part. "What kind of trees? That could help ID the color."

She shrugged again. "Pine or oak probably. Woods are thick there where it happened. Underbrush and thickets, too."

"Which could account for why she didn't see him coming," he said.

She glanced toward the front door where her grandmother sat, then back at Chitto. "I didn't show these to Grandma . . ." She pulled a small white envelope from a shoulder bag and shoved them into his hand. "I took pictures of the place where she got hit. Look at that car—what's left of it. If I ever find out who it was left her there, I'll . . ." She let the rest of her words trail off. Sighing deeply, she said, "I don't know how she survived. Thank God, a rancher friend happened by."

Glancing inside the envelope, Chitto frowned. The pictures showed a car on its top, lying at the bottom of a ravine. But the crumpled car wasn't what drew his eyes.

"You want, I could meet up with you this weekend," she said, laying a business card on his desk. "Show you around."

Holding the business card and both envelopes out to her, he said, "Sorry. My weekend's booked."

"Well, if you change your mind . . ." Ignoring the card and envelopes, she hurried to catch up with her grandmother.

Chitto leaned back in his chair, watching Crystal Folsom escort her grandmother out the door. Apparently, she had inherited Peony's stubborn streak. Depositing the card and envelopes in a bottom drawer, he picked up the first of many case reports. His desk was piled high with paperwork and he wanted to clear it out. He had not lied about having plans for the weekend. But questions eroded his concentration.

Why was a man's head in a murdered girl's coffin?

He finished off one report and picked up another.

What happened to the girl's head? The man's body?

He closed the folder, laid it in a stack, picked up another file.

Why didn't Rosebud return home?

Tossing the completed files into his outbox, Chitto walked to the cafeteria and returned with a cup of black coffee and package of corn chips. His chair squealed as he swiveled to stare out the window. The dog was a sticking point for him. He could accept a man, even one born in the Kiamichi, getting so lost he couldn't find his way out. Much of the area was unexplored wilderness. But a hound born and bred in the area? Not likely.

He picked the worry stone up again, a piece of Jack Ford sandstone found in the Kiamichi hills. For sandstone, it was hard, so hard it resisted erosion. The Winding Stair, San Bois, and Panther Mountains were made of it and they had resisted extinction for millennia. As he rotated the stone between his fingers, his thinking went to the biggest sticking point of all. The hit-and-run accident.

Returning the stone to the desktop, he pulled Crystal's white envelope out of the bottom drawer and studied the accident scene more closely. The lack of skid marks across the asphalt would indicate the driver of the vehicle that hit Peony Folsom had not braked. The way the tire tracks ended at the edge of the ravine pointed to the driver knowing just how far to push the car to ensure it went over the edge. Swiveling to look out the window, he considered the findings.

16

Was it an accident? If not, it had to be a deliberate attempt to kill an old woman. Why? Was it connected to the talking she had been doing around town, her insistence the picture in the paper was of her son? If so, Peony Folsom was still in danger.

Screw it, he thought. A man had to live with himself.

Folding a stick of Doublemint into his mouth, a substitute for nicotine, he pulled Peony Folsom's manila envelope from the drawer.

CHAPTER THREE

Overkill.

Chitto frowned as he finished reading about the murders of Leona Mann, age 21, and Billy Rob Niles, 29. The murders had been ugly. Personal. The couple had eaten supper at a local tavern on Friday, July 4, and left with a six-pack. According to a witness, the two drove away in Mann's Ford Maverick, mentioning they were going to a place outside of town. At some point, Niles was pulled from the car and shot numerous times in the head and groin area, then dragged to the side of the road. A motorist spotted his body about daybreak the next morning.

The Ford Maverick was found about a quarter mile away. Leona Mann was found in the ditch beside it, shot once in the head and wearing the same shoes and blouse she wore the previous night. Her jeans had been draped over her bare hips and thighs. According to the sheriff's report, it wasn't clear whether she'd been sexually assaulted.

Reading that the sheriff at that time found no worthwhile clues, Chitto let out a humorless laugh. Thinking back, he couldn't come up with a name to put on the nameless, and apparently clueless, sheriff. The only one he knew anything about was the current sheriff, a man named John Skrabo, who'd developed quite a reputation of his own. Not a good one. Folding the article, he reinserted it in the manila envelope and walked toward the front entrance.

"Going out to grab lunch," he said, stopping at Jasmine's desk. He laid the envelope on the corner of the desk as he slipped into his jacket. "Bring you back anything?"

"Eating here today." She pulled a brown paper bag and a large handbag from the bottom drawer. "Unlike others, I caught the weather forecast before I came to work." She looked up at him. "Cafeteria serves lunch."

Tucking the envelope under an arm, he said, "I need to look over some things."

"Um-hmm," she mumbled, eyeing the envelope. "How long you be gone?"

"Half hour at most. Those fast-food places are called fast for a reason."

A snort escaped her mouth. "You forget college is in session?"

The population of Durant was roughly 16,000, but when in session, Southeastern University added another four thousand to that number. Day or night, most of the four thousand frequented fast food places.

Chitto pinched his bottom lip, looking thoughtful. "Okay," he said. "Three-quarters of an hour."

"Um-hmm," she mumbled again. "See you in an hour and a half."

Grinning, he pointed at the clock. "Time me."

∞

Chitto drove to the closest fast-food place and groaned when he saw the length of the line. Parking his Tahoe in the lot, he raced inside. Seeing tables overflowing with the next generation to inherit the planet, he flashed his police ID at the manager. "Give me anything that's ready to go and an iced tea." Paying for the mystery bag, he filled a paper cup at the drink dispenser and returned to his unit.

20

Deciding the police parking lot would provide the best privacy, he parked under trees near the back and checked the clock on the dash. Thirty minutes to go. Plenty of time for a leisurely lunch, and in a private setting. A cold, private setting, he discovered a few minutes later. The SUV's radiator ticking away its heat, he opened the mystery bag holding his lunch and pulled out three processed chicken nuggets and two hash browns. Sighing, he popped a nugget in his mouth and removed the newspaper article from Peony Folsom's manila envelope. According to the date under the newspaper's nameplate, the article broke January 11, five weeks before. Some thirty-odd years after the double homicide happened, the forensic sketch had made it front-page news again.

Focusing on the murdered couple, he found their biographical information relatively lackluster. Leona was born and grew up in Antlers, the county seat of Pushmataha County, and had graduated high school there. Billy Rob resided in Piney, Texas, just across the state line, but was a native of Iowa. At the time of the murders, he worked for the Choctaw Electric Coop out of Hugo, Oklahoma, just south of Antlers. He stayed in a rented room when he was doing line repairs in the area.

"Why them?" Chitto mumbled around a mouthful of hash browns. Laying the article aside, he thought about the witness who reported seeing the gunshot wound in Leona's head. He wondered when her head was cut off, why it had been replaced with someone else's, and when the exchange had taken place. Given her state of undress, he also wondered why the local authorities couldn't tell if she'd been raped. Even in 1980, some kind of exam would've been done.

Or should've been, he reflected.

One question bothered him more than any other. How did Walter Folsom fit into the scheme of things? *If* he did, he thought, taking a swig of tea. It wasn't outside the realm of possibility that Walter's disappearance was coincidental. And Rosebud? According to Peony, the hound was old and crippled up. On her last legs, she couldn't have made it too far.

Noting he had fifteen minutes to go, he skimmed the article again. Because of the personal nature of the murders, newspaper reporters had pegged a jealous lover as the killer. He couldn't fault the reasoning. Knowing that was often the case in situations such as this one, he wondered if Walter Folsom and Leona Mann had been involved. If Walter had owned a gun. Murder was a damn good reason to skip town, and just as possibly, he took his faithful old dog with him.

How? a voice in his head asked.

"Right," he mumbled, finishing off the last nugget. Walter had left his car at his mother's house, and Leona's Maverick was left at the scene. Sighing, he looked for names of others listed in the article that could provide more information.

"No way," he mumbled, finding fifty people had been questioned. Briefly, he wondered what the population of Pushmataha County had been thirty-odd years ago. More surprising was none of those questioned had been named in the editorial. Not even a prime suspect.

One name did pique his interest, one Crystal Folsom had mentioned. Though not one of those interrogated, a man by the name of Chuck Stovall had become interested in the case when he held a county office some years earlier. Even after he lost that office, he had remained tenacious about finding out what happened. He'd apparently convinced Leona's younger brother that something wasn't right and that led to the exhumation and artist's drawing.

Oddly enough, Stovall now owned the tavern where the couple was last seen. Only now, it was now called Chuck's Place. When the reporter on the article asked him why he was pursuing the case, Stovall said he was convinced that Leona's ghost sometimes passed through his place. According to the paper, he'd even brought in a medium to conduct a séance once.

"Well, hell," Chitto muttered, dumping his trash in a waste can outside the front door. "Ghosts—*and* séances."

He made it back inside with seconds to spare. His reward was the surprise on Jasmine's face. His penalty was the handful of message slips she handed him.

"What do you sharpen your claws with?" he groaned, flipping through the slips. "A whetstone?"

She hid a smile behind neatly manicured nails.

∞

Shadows were long on his desk when Chitto closed up his desk. He'd gotten through most of the reports and was satisfied the rest could wait for Monday. That left the obligation for the weekend. He reached for the phone and smiled at the voice that answered.

"Hey, *Pokni*." Grandmother. "Afraid I'm going to have to postpone working on your corn patch this weekend."

He was glad his grandmother, Rhody Pitchlyn, had answered the phone instead of his mother. A tribal councilwoman, Mattie Chitto would've given him the third degree about his reason for not coming home that weekend. Demand to know what cases he was working on. Pester him as to why he hadn't remarried yet. She reminded him frequently that she still wanted grandchildren.

"There's time yet," Chitto said. "This cold snap probably froze the ground hard as a brick. When's the last day we can plant that corn?"

He glanced at the calendar, feeling bad for the delay. He reserved weekends for his family, what little remained of it. A mother and grandmother. For a fleeting second, he thought of his father. Then his wife Mary. He quickly pushed the thought into the background, knowing he had been right to let Mary's spirit free, even if it meant carving a hole in his chest the size of a boat motor. Releasing his father's spirit had been another matter, one he apparently did not have control over.

"Week, maybe two," Rhody said.

"That's good. In the meantime, I'll pick up some seed corn at the local feed store."

A pause came on the line. "The ground did not freeze."

Though Rhody Pitchlyn was not known to run off at the mouth, he read disappointment in her words. "That guy lives down the road still have that tiller?" he asked. "He does, I'll give him a call. Maybe he can burn off the garden spot this weekend, till it up next week. We can plant it after that."

"Yeh. I see him breaking up his garden last week."

"Give me his number. I'll call him right now."

"You wait," she said.

Chitto waited. Like a lot of the elderly whose backs had played out or whose hip sockets had worn down to the bone, his grandmother moved slowly. Some minutes later, he heard the sound of breathing on the line.

She read off a phone number, then said, "Mattie is gonna be real mad."

"No doubt," he said, chuckling. "But see, something's come up I need to check on." He listened to more breathing.

"You go to help our people again," she said. A comment, not a question.

"Yeah," he sighed. "But keep it to yourself." His grandmother's prescient powers never ceased to amaze him. "While I got you on the phone, what do you know about the Nameless One? You told me the story when I was little, but I can't remember all of it."

Any unanswered question was like a burr under a horse blanket for Chitto. Though not a student himself, both his grandmother and mother were well schooled in Choctaw teachings. The Removal of Indians to Indian Territory in the 1830s had robbed the people of their heritage. Then

Choctaws from Mississippi had come to the Nation in the 1950s and 1960s to teach those interested what had been lost.

"*Hatakachafa*," she said.

He waited a polite moment in case more was forthcoming, then said, "I remember this *Hatakachafa* was also called the Nameless One, but not much else."

"Many stories are told of him," she said. "He was a war chief and great hunter that killed many monsters in the forest."

"What kind of monsters?"

"A one-eyed monster. A shapeshifter who stalked hunters. An evil medicine man." She paused. "He tamed a wolf and they fought the monsters together."

"A wolf . . ." Chitto stifled an urge to laugh. Though not as rigidly set against the old stories as he once was, he still found many of them farfetched—too farfetched to be taken seriously.

"Yeh. This wolf, he taught dogs to howl when they are lonely." She paused again. "You want me to tell you the monster stories?"

"Not right now, *Pokni*. Maybe when we plant the corn."

"Okay. Mattie is driving into the garage. You want to talk to her?"

"Oh, *hell* no. Tell her I'll be up next weekend." His response was a chuckle followed by a *click*.

Chitto turned his attention to next steps. Even though a lot of years had passed, he figured some of the fifty suspects questioned would still be alive. They would know something about the case, else they wouldn't have been questioned in the first place. Looking inside the white envelope, he pulled out the business card Crystal Folsom left behind. It indicated she worked for a realtor in Antlers, one that specialized in mountain properties. It made sense. Like many small towns, the Antlers area had dried up in the last few decades, but it was making a comeback because it had a draw other towns

25

didn't. The Kiamichi Wilderness. Assuming Crystal was living with her grandmother since the accident, he opted to call her cell phone. She answered promptly.

"Where you want to meet up tomorrow? I freed up my weekend." He interpreted the quick sigh on the line being from relief.

"At Mom's Café. It's off of the beaten path, mostly locals. Turn right at Main, then left at the Clock Tower, a red brick building that sticks out like a sore thumb. Mom's is a couple blocks down. How 'bout ten? It'll take you a while to get here."

"That'll do."

"I do anything in advance?"

"Can't think of anything— No, wait." Other questions made it onto his list. "You know exactly when your father went missing? Friends he was known to associate with? If he met up with anyone else on those trips to the river?" He paused. "If he knew the couple that was murdered?"

"No, no, no . . . and no. Why?"

"Need a starting point."

"Oh." A pause. "Well, Chuck Stovall's collected a lot of things about that murder case."

"I just read about him in the newspaper article. Think he'll let me look at that collection on the sly? I'd like a list of those questioned about that murder. Some have to be alive."

"Yes, I do. I know Chuck pretty well. He'd welcome another pair of eyes. Want me to ask my grandmother those questions about my dad?"

"Discretely. I'd prefer she didn't know about my involvement just yet. Too soon to get her hopes up, and . . ."

"And?" she said, sounding tentative.

"Best if *no one* knows I'm looking into this." He listened to another pause on the line.

"Those jurisdiction issues?" she said.

"Right. One more thing," he added. "Make sure your grandmother has someone with her at all times."

A longer pause. "Why?"

Chitto's thoughts raced. Though he'd just met Crystal Folsom, he had picked up enough from her attitude and body language to suggest she could jump to conclusions, act hastily. "Just precautions," he said. "Anyone low enough to commit a hit and run can become paranoid, worry that the victim might ID him, do something stupid. Better to be safe than sorry."

"Oh."

"See you tomorrow," he said.

After hanging up, Chitto locked the remaining reports away and scooped up those he'd finished. He dropped them off with Jasmine on his way to the front door.

"I'll be out of town this weekend," he said, "and using my own vehicle. So, no radio contact and cell phone service questionable. Something comes up, call one of the field officers."

"Did I take you to raise?" She stared at him over tortoise-shell glasses that set off toffee-colored skin. "I'm a temp, remember? Quitting time comes, I'm out of here. Don't care where you are this weekend, anyone else for that matter."

"Works for me."

"Anyways, looks like you got homework." She picked up a manila envelope and handed it to him. "HR sent this over. Paperwork on the candidates for this job . . ." A wry grin made a showing. "And a list of questions you're *not* supposed to ask."

"You're kidding." Flipping open the envelope, he glanced at the list of candidates. "Hell, I don't know any of them."

"Haven't missed much."

He looked at her. "You know them?"

"Not an office I haven't worked in. Temps are pretty much ignored, so my eyes and ears have been privy to most everything of interest."

Eyes and ears, he repeated silently. Not a bad "want" for Wanda's replacement.

"So you're going off the reservation again," she said. It was more a comment than a question. "Be pretty cold around Antlers this time of the year, 'specially after this last spell."

"*Umm,*" Chitto mumbled, buying time. Dan kept tight reins on all the field people since his dad and Bert Gilly's murders, and an even tighter rein on him since the FBI came down like a ton of bricks. Did he want to confirm he was planning to work outside his jurisdiction?

"I watch a lot of movies," she said, not waiting for a reply. "My favorites are those old fifties B-movies where the Indians go off the rez."

"Yeah, you mentioned that once." Chitto felt a gut-wrenching ache in his belly. Mary had liked movies about Indians, too. Rather than the old ones, she liked those that showed contemporary Indians struggling to survive in a society that didn't make sense.

Hauling her large handbag from a drawer, Jasmine pulled out a card. "You need something, here's my cell number."

"Thanks," he said, hiking his eyebrows. "But I wouldn't want to put you out."

"Then don't overdo it." She closed the handbag with a snap.

"Why," he asked, needing his curiosity satisfied. "Why are you willing to help me out on the QT?"

She thought a minute. "You don't kowtow, don't ask for too much, like some I know." She glanced toward Daniel Blackfox's office, then back at him. "Maybe I'm just glad you're not so much trouble."

Chitto slipped her card into his pocket. He didn't know why he would need to call her, but since he was working a case unofficially, it felt good to have an ally. Or was the right word accomplice?

"My Cajun granny says you need to beware of sleeping in the moonlight," she said, watching him slip into his jacket. "Make you go moon mad."

Granddaughter of a well-known Choctaw Freedwoman, Jasmine's lineage was a mixed bag. Black. White. Cajun. One piece of her heritage had been confirmed, however. Her ancestors had been slaves of Choctaws removed to Indian Territory, and in the late 1880s, those freed slaves had been admitted to the Choctaw Nation.

He grinned. "Never took you for the superstitious type, Jasmine."

"Me? Don't have a superstitious bone in my body. My grannies, now they were another story." She looked over her glasses again. "Thought you were leaving. About time for Dan to get back from that budget meeting."

He beat it for the door but didn't get far. He was halfway across the parking lot when he heard someone call his name. Looking behind him, he saw Dan Blackfox stretching his legs to catch up.

"One more thing," Blackfox said as if several hours hadn't passed since they'd last talked. "The Exec spoke to me today about recruiting people to take SWAT training." The Choctaw Nation SWAT team was a newly trained group made up of firearms and defensive tactics instructors and certified snipers. "He thought you might be a good fit for the team if you got a little training under your belt."

"Me?" Chitto's mouth dropped open. "Why me?"

"He likes that you're a thinker. Also thought you walked like an athlete. I told him you ran track some, played ball in college. Baseball, right?"

"Yeah . . ."

"Pitcher, as I recall."

Chitto grinned. "What? They need someone to lob grenades?"

Blackfox drew a long breath, let it out slowly. "Anyone ever tell you that you're a smartass?"

"Hey, look . . ." Feeling chilled air tracing his spine, Chitto zipped his coat to the neck. "That was a long time ago, ten years or more. My interests have changed."

"Exactly my point. Book smart's a good thing, but in this business, you need to stay on your toes. Ten years can slow a man down." Blackfox paused, studying a horizon losing its glow. "He hasn't seen you at the pistol range much lately. He thinks—*we* think—you could do with a little brush-up."

"We?" Chitto laughed, hoping to defuse the situation.

"Okay, then," Blackfox said. *"I* think it would be good for you." He was not smiling.

Chitto scrutinized Blackfox's face, wondering if his boss had sensed he was going rogue again. Considering the man's concern for the safety of his people, he decided the attention fell under the preventative-care category.

"Sounds like you'd be a better candidate than me, Dan. How long's it been since you threw a knuckleball at some poor bastard's head? Twenty years? Thirty?" He wiped the corners of his mouth to conceal another grin. In his day, Blackfox had been known to throw the meanest spitball in the local league.

Blackfox sighed, shoulders slumping. "Law enforcement's changing. Weapons are more sophisticated. Officers need to be trained in hand-to-hand combat . . ." He waved a hand through the air, indicating the list went on and on.

Chitto shook his head. "I'm a lover, not a fighter."

"Lover." Blackfox's eyes remained steady. "When's the last time you showed a girl a good time?"

30

"Long time."

"When's the last time a girl showed you a good time?"

"Long time," Chitto said, observing a lot of repeating was going on.

"Well, think about it. Would put you in the good graces of the Exec."

"No, it would put *you* in the good graces of the Exec. Besides, I don't need to be in his good graces. You're in between me and him." He tested the grin again.

"You're a smartass," Blackfox mumbled, walking toward the building.

∞

The flickering light from the real-estate office next to the parking lot did little to pierce the shadows. Keying the ignition in his Tahoe, Chitto pointed it toward home, his thoughts churning. Blackfox's concern about his fitness for duty bothered him. He couldn't pinpoint the last time he'd been to the firing range, but he'd emptied his Glock recently at two fleeing vehicles that forced him off the road. He hadn't stopped either one and doubted he'd done more than ding a fender. Maybe a visit to the firing range was in order. Maybe Blackfox would see him there and tell the exec. Better yet, maybe the exec would spot him and tell Blackfox.

That's it, he thought. Just need to show my face a couple times at the firing range.

The matter resolved, he felt easier. But though his body began to relax, his mind continued to churn. He couldn't let loose of the stories he'd been told that day. Peony Folsom's about her son calling to her from the pines. His grandmother's about a wolf that taught dogs to howl when they were lonely. Neither classified as fact, but when a dead man leaves no tracks, you clutch at straws.

Especially when you're tracking a ghost.

CHAPTER FOUR

Chitto fixed an early breakfast Saturday morning, then did some quick pick-up around the two-bedroom house he occupied. He no longer worried about the bigger chores he and Mary used to do together on weekends. Laundry. Vacuuming. Taking out the trash. After releasing Mary to the Land of Shadows, he'd given in to his neighbor Hattie George's urgings to hire a housekeeper named Angelina Something-or-Other. Angelina required payment in cash, an indication she was an illegal from across the Rio Grande. That didn't bother him. Angelina was also the single mother of two children. Paying taxes on wages would eat up money needed for food, clothing, shelter. As far as he was concerned, Angelina had her priorities in order. She came every Saturday now and had proven as competent as Hattie had boasted she was.

After depositing cash on the kitchen table for Angelina, he packed a clean shirt and change of underwear in a duffle. As an afterthought, he shoved the HR files inside. If nothing of interest surfaced, he could at least look at the candidates' qualifications that evening, maybe bone up on the *verboten* questions.

At the coat rack next to the back door, he opted for his olive-green Mackinaw, long enough to hide his service pistol and keep his butt from getting frostbit, and slipped a spare magazine in the side pocket. A habit he'd picked up on the last case. Snugging a faded OU ball cap low, he locked up the house.

Walking next door to Hattie's, he knocked loudly. Hearing the bay of a hound, he made an off-the-cuff decision.

A mongrel redbone, long in the leg and square in the jaw, pushed past Hattie as she opened the door. *"Boycott,"* she scolded. "I swear, you're gonna be the death of me yet."

The dog had shown up on Hattie's back porch the previous year as a skinny pup. She'd named him after Cesar Chavez's dog that, according to the Mexican-American civil rights activist, caused him to question the right of humans to eat other sentient beings. Like Chavez, Hattie had experienced a similar awakening years before, causing her to swear off meat. The habit had not set well with her pioneer ranching family, most of which, to her delight, she had outlived.

"You really need to take this greaser off my hands, Sam." Collar and cuffs of a plaid flannel shirt stuck from under a sweater. Wool socks bulged over the sides of scuffed leather moccasins. "He's gettin' too big for me to handle. Needs a strong hand, which I ain't had in fifty years."

"Well now, that's just what I plan to do, Hattie. For the weekend anyway. Figured you could use a break." He'd been working with Boycott an hour or two when he could find the time and took him for a run most evenings. But the hound was a hunting breed and would profit from some on-the-ground training.

"Thank the Lord," she breathed. "Neighbors will appreciate it too."

He lifted his eyebrows. "What's he done now?"

A month before, Boycott had climbed the back fence and landed in the neighbor's chicken yard. No birds were killed, just traumatized to the point they stopped laying. When the neighbors threatened to sue, Hattie asked Chitto to plead her case. He tried to explain that even the best of lawyers would have a hard go defending a hound dog covered in white chicken feathers. He did, however, convince the neighbors to accept a dozen new leghorn pullets in settlement, compliments of Hattie, doubling the size of their flock.

"He dug up some chickens yesterday," she continued. "Well, the remains anyway. Neighbors butchered those old leghorns for the freezer—you know, the ones that stopped laying? Anyways, they buried the guts in their garden and Boycott climbed the fence and dug 'em up."

"Tell me he didn't eat that stuff."

She shrugged. "You think he's got some bloodhound in him?"

"Naw, he's just a growing boy," he said, grinning. "Might be a good idea to take some dog chow along."

"I'll put some in a sack," she said, "and get a pan and jug of water."

"He up on his shots and anti-tick treatment?"

Due to various reasons—warmer winters, suburbanization, increase in whitetail deer, migratory birds— ticks were on the increase. Dogs, especially hunting dogs, were often the canaries in the coalmine in identifying infested areas because they were out in the habitat. In the Kiamichi, where deer and predators ruled, it was a safe bet ticks would be present.

"Yep," she said, pausing. "Why?"

"Might be camping out."

"As cold as it is?" She continued toward the kitchen, head shaking.

"Angelina's coming in today," he said as he awaited her return. He picked up a long leash off an ottoman in the living room and clipped it to Boycott's collar. "Her pay's on the table. You let her in and lock up when she's done?"

"Don't I always?" She handed him a plastic grocery bag and a thermos. "Had some coffee left from breakfast, bottled it up, too."

"Thanks," Chitto said, eyeing the thermos. Hattie still boiled her coffee on the stove, which meant he'd be chewing grounds on the drive to Antlers.

"Not expecting any company, are you?" she asked.

"Not planned anyway. If my mother comes around, plead ignorance."

Her eyebrows lifted. "Don't say another word. That way, I can plead ignorance with a clear conscience. When you're as close to the Pearlie Gates as I am, it doesn't pay to take chances."

Laughing, he headed for his garage, the dog bouncing at his heels.

"I'm not here when you get back," she called after him, "it's 'cause I skipped town. Been thinkin' of moving down on the border. Blood's got too thin to handle cold weather. In which case, you got yourself a full-time dog."

"See you tomorrow afternoon," he said, giving her a wave.

After loading Boycott into the passenger side of his Chevy dually, Chitto stuffed his sleeping bag and duffle behind the seat. Popping open the glove box, he slipped the spare magazine for his service weapon next to packs of Marlboro Reds and Doublemint gum, duplicates of those found in his police cruiser. The reason for the chewing gum was clear: a placebo for nicotine. The reason for carrying the cigarettes was a mystery that raised the eyebrows of anyone that didn't know him well. Those that did knew he had stopped smoking cold turkey some years back, but not the reason he still carried a pack in the glove box. A private man, Chitto felt no need to explain that the cigarettes were a reminder of a promise he'd made, one he intended to keep no matter how strong the temptation. He prided himself on being a man of his word.

He paused, eying the gun cabinet where he kept his Remington 879 and Colt AR when off duty. Unlocking the cabinet, he pulled out the shotgun and placed it in the Chevy's gun rack, plus a box of shells. Another habit he had developed recently. Sometimes a pistol wasn't big enough for the job.

"Time to go undercover, Boycott," he said, backing the truck out of the garage. "Become the Nameless One and his wolf." Glancing at the floppy-eared hound, he chuckled. "Something tells me both our DNAs got screwed with somewhere along the way.

∞

The drive to Antlers was a short sixty miles and there were many ways to reach it. Chitto decided on the most direct, east on U.S. 70 then north on 271. He wanted to get into the backcountry and out of reach as quickly as he could. He would be out of his jurisdiction in more ways than one. Tribal police didn't handle felony cases involving non-Indians; those were turned over to a state investigator or the FBI. Tribal police could investigate matters dealing with Indians, but no proof existed that Walter Folsom was a missing person. Yet.

He sighed, thinking how he was encroaching on another field lieutenant's district. The Choctaw Nation was divided into twelve districts that covered ten and a half counties in southeastern Oklahoma, and each had its own investigator and field officers. Antlers was in District 7; Chitto was assigned to District 9. Though Chitto filled in for other investigators when a need arose, he had no excuse to be working in another district today. He hoped he didn't run into anyone from the Nation. Even more, he hoped to avoid local authorities, especially Pushmataha County Sheriff, John Skrabo, who was known to be a hardass.

US 70 paralleled the jagged southern edge of the hatchet-shaped state called Oklahoma. The southeast corner of that hatchet was home of the Choctaw Nation. The dirt here was a faded-yellow brown, dusty in the summer, sticky clay in the spring, and rocky year round. Creeks and spring-fed rivers roared down mountains cloaked with oak and hickory, pine and cedar. Redbuds and dogwoods daubed hillsides where the land gentled, along with pokeweed and blackberry briars. Streams lazied as the land leveled, becoming choked with leaves and ivy, mudcats and water moccasins. Insects that swarmed by day created a racket at night that would raise the dead. What didn't sting, bit. What didn't fly, crawled. It was a land to test a man's endurance and a geologist's nirvana.

Diamonds . . .

Chitto had spent many summers in this country while a geology student, and still trailered his horse there when he needed a break from civilization. At no time had he found or heard of others finding diamonds in the Kiamichi Wilderness. Besides, he thought, Walter Folsom appeared obsessed with cleaning up trash littering the land. In no way would he see rocks as trash. To bring back a rock of any kind seemed more than a coincidence.

He shook his head slightly. The coincidences surrounding Walter's disappearance and the murder of Leona Mann and Billy Rob Niles grew longer every time he revisited it.

Such as the lack of a rape test on the female victim,

The incongruity between the disfigured bodies and neatly folded jeans on the girl's pubic area,

The questioning of fifty people in a county with a population numbering in the single digits per mile,

The mix up of two skulls that wasn't caught for better than thirty years,

A missing sailor with mental problems that authorities refused to investigate,

A well-trained hunting dog that didn't return home,

An old woman deliberately being run off the road.

As the miles slipped past and he neared the cutoff for Bokchito, Chitto thought of Sonny Boy Munro. He'd told the old pig farmer to hold him a side of bacon the next time he butchered, and he needed to check on it. He also needed to have a one-on-one with the man about the stories he was spreading about him being a "justice man." Sonny Boy was the one person who could confirm *beyond reasonable doubt*, legalese lawyers used when making their closing argument to a jury, that Chitto made a decision that cost a man his life— not good information to broadcast, especially as attentive as a certain FBI agent had become.

Nearing the cutoff, he looked at Boycott. "You ever met a pig?" he asked, scratching the dog's ears. "You think chickens are fun. Just wait."

∞

Sonny Boy Monroe was mixing mash for his Yorkshire sows at the pens behind his house. He sold the offspring to various groups around Oklahoma, mainly for dances and celebrations in the fall. From beneath the hood of an oversized jacket that fit like a tent, he flashed Chitto a toothless smile. "I am still sober," he called out.

"Glad to hear it," Chitto responded. The old man had lost a battle with alcoholism recently and Chitto had gotten him into the Choctaw Nation's version of AA.

Approaching the old man, Chitto slipped the end of Boycott's leash over a fencepost, where the pup tugged at the leash and whined with excitement. "When will that bacon be ready to pick up?"

"I am waiting to hear from the packing house."

"Give me a call when it's ready."

"Sure thing." Sonny Boy ran a hand over the dog's deep red coat, cradling the dark muzzle in his hand. Whining softly, Boycott raised a paw to the old man's knee. "This dog worth his salt?" he asked.

"Not yet." Picking up a flat-back bucket, Chitto drew water from a yard spigot and began filling water tanks. "I'm heading to the high country to teach him some manners."

"No . . ." Giving the dog's head another rub, Sonny Boy returned to mixing mash. "You go to the tall country to be a Bone Picker."

"Bone Picker—"

Chitto's memory journeyed back in time to one of the old stories his grandmother had told him. Because bones survived flesh, the Choctaw of old preserved the bones of their deceased, believing their essence dwelled within. Honored people, called Bone Pickers, stripped the flesh from a body and presented the bones to the family to be placed in a burial mound.

"Yes, Bone Picker," Sonny Boy repeated firmly. "You will bring that boy's bones home so he can finish his journey . . ." He placed a hand on his chest. "And I can do a healing ceremony for him."

Chitto shook his head, sighing. "Things aren't done that way anymore, Grandfather. Besides, we don't know for sure that Folsom's dead. Even if he were, how the hell would I find bones over thirty years old—and get my hands on a skull that's locked up at the sheriff's office?"

"The Nameless One will find a way." Sonny Boy pointed his chin toward his white house with a pointed roof. "We sit in the kitchen now, drink coffee. I send up a prayer for you . . ." Pausing, he simultaneously patted his shirt pocket and looked toward Chitto's truck. "I am out of smokes."

Sighing, Chitto jogged to his truck and returned with the Marlboros. Handing the pack over, he said, "You have to stop making up these stories, Sonny Boy. I'm not this Nameless One—or a Bone Picker."

Pulling a cigarette from the pack and pocketing the rest, Sonny Boy looked at him. "I don't make up stories. They follow us, like our *hoshontika*." He indicated the shadow that Chitto cast on the ground.

"No, humans make up the stories and they tell them to people they shouldn't." Chitto took the old man by the shoulders, looking at him full face. "No more stories, Sonny Boy. You hear me?"

"Nothing wrong with my ears."

"Okay, then." He slipped Boycott's leash off the post. "I'm a cop," he said, leading the dog toward his truck. "An off-duty cop showing support for one of my wife's cousins. That's the bottom line."

"You think a person is one thing or another?" Sonny Boy called after him. "You think we choose what we are to become? You think I wanted to be a prayer man?"

"The bottom line," Chitto yelled over his shoulder. The last sound he heard before he keyed the ignition was Sonny Boy chuckling. His last sight was of smoke spiraling over the old man's head.

∞

Chitto glanced in his rearview mirror frequently, looking for vehicles that might be sticking too close, another habit he practiced when working undercover. It paid to cultivate cautious habits if you valued your life.

Turning north on US 271, he poured a cup of Hattie's coffee and turned the radio to KDOE, an Antler's station, hoping to catch a local news report. He listened to an update on the Bearcats, the high school team; a sale that day at the Red Barn Mini-Mall; the specials at Pruitt's Grocery Store; the Sunday sermon topic at the Cowboy Church; and the latest count at the deer processing plant.

Boycott nosed his arm, breaking his attention.

"Yeah," he said, rubbing the hound's head. "I think we've got a bead on things."

Turning off the radio, he rolled down both windows. He tossed cold coffee out his side, watched the dog gulp air through the other, and smiled with satisfaction. His decision to bring Boycott along had been a stroke of genius. The dog gave him a reason for being in another lawman's jurisdiction. This weekend, he was just a man taking a young hunting dog to the hills for training.

CHAPTER FIVE

Chitto dropped his speed a notch as he spotted Standpipe Hill, the outcrop that overlooked the town of Antlers. Situated in the Kiamichi River valley, the town straddled two watersheds that drained into the Kiamichi River. Creeks too numerous to count drained off the Jack Fork and San Bois Mountains to the north, the Kiamichi and Seven Sisters Mountains to the east.

Did Walter go to the big river every day, he wondered, studying the distant hills. Or one of the creeks? He hoped it was the river. He had neither the time nor inclination to crawl through the tick-infested thickets that lined the creeks.

A sign on the right of way caught his attention: Welcome to Antlers – Deer Capital of the World. He laughed quietly, recalling the call letters for the radio station and the mascot for the high school. Local names reflected the town's claim to fame: hunting and fishing. But he knew it wasn't always that way.

As a trained geologist, he knew the terrain of the Nation like the back of his hand and, because of that, something of the history. Once, Antlers had been known for something far different from hunting. Fueled by the lumber industry, it had become a railroad town in the 1800s when the Frisco Railroad ran a line from Fort Smith, Arkansas to Paris, Texas, paralleling the Kiamichi River. From what he could remember, Antlers was selected for a station because of a freshwater spring, and the name came from a large antler rack nailed to a tree to mark the spot. He'd visited the old Frisco depot once, now designated a historic place. He supposed it was historic, but its claim to fame was darkened by its architectural design. To meet the requirements of segregation, separate waiting rooms had been built for whites and blacks. In an effort to be true to the past, both rooms had been preserved.

But much of the area's past had faded into obscurity. Even before the railroad's coming, indigenous people had occupied this land. Following the Removal, when Choctaws were forced to leave their homes in Mississippi, this area was known as Jack's Fork County of the Choctaw Nation. As evidenced from arrowheads found in the region, there had been prehistoric activity there, too. Most of the prehistoric sites sat atop hills. He could understand that choice; it wasn't dissimilar to European peoples who built on tall places that would be easier to defend. Rights of occupation and defensive maneuvers didn't always keep a people safe, however.

He eyed a motel on the highway, thinking it might be a good place to hole up on a cold night. It was your typical single story motel with doors facing onto the highway. Then a smaller sign caught his eye: No Pets Allowed. A problem he hadn't considered. He scratched Boycott's head and kept driving. There was always the sleeping bag behind the seat. If need be, they would bed down at one of the campgrounds in the area.

"Think we'd go mad in the moonlight?" he said to the dog, recalling Jasmine's superstitious grandmother. "Think that's what happened to Walter and old Rosebud?"

The dog squirmed close to him, giving him an insistent nudge. Simultaneously, a putrid odor filled the truck's cab, a warning sign that chicken parts were about to be raised from the dead again.

"Okay, boy," he said. "Let's find you some grass to fertilize."

Chitto turned his attention to the street names. Having boned up on the area the night before, he knew where the Police Department and Sheriff's office were located and planned to avoid both. His research had turned up other things, as well, such as Sheriff John Skrabo being a veteran law officer with over thirty years in the business. There was a good chance the man would be familiar with the murder case, in all likelihood even worked it. Unfortunately, Skrabo was the last person he wanted to talk to.

U.S. 271 became C Street inside the city limits and within minutes, Chitto encountered Main Street. He slowed to a stop at the intersection of C and Main, also known as US 271 and OK 3. It was a wide street, like many in strip towns where a highway served as the major thoroughfare. The storefronts were mostly one story and the majority made of red brick. Given the time of year and recent weather, a skin of dirt crusted the roadways.

Being Saturday, the town was bustling, as much as a town with a population numbering a few thousand can bustle. Pickup trucks came and went in both lanes, dogs riding inside the cab or the backend and long guns showing through rear windows. The drivers' dress followed a pattern, too. White men wearing Stetsons or ball caps, plaid jackets, and boots. Latinos wearing Stetsons or ball caps, plaid jackets, and boots. Indians wearing Stetsons or ball caps, plaid jackets, and boots.

"In like Flynn," he said, stroking Boycott's head.

The Clock Tower building became visible down the street, and the clock seemed to be functioning perfectly. Checking against his watch, Chitto confirmed he was a few

45

minutes early. Just enough time to take care of Boycott's digestive problem.

Turning the corner, he drove another couple of blocks and pulled into a dirt parking lot next to a single-story frame building with Mom's Café painted on the window. He parked beneath a clump of willows at the back of the lot, snapped Boycott to his leash, and led him to a weedy, overgrown spot. Boycott wasted no time in doing his duty. In supervisory capacity, Chitto paid little attention to another truck that pulled in.

"City ordinance prohibits letting a dog crap on public premises," someone said.

Chitto turned to look into dark glasses on a blunt-featured man. A brown felt Stetson with a partridge feather in the headband was cocked to one side, revealing reddish-brown hair streaked with gray, a sprinkling of freckles and age spots, and dull gray eyes. A Pushmataha County Sheriff insignia was evident on the sleeve of a bomber-style jacket, the buttons on the khaki-colored shirt underneath stretched to the breaking point. Probably as tall as he was once, the man had settled to a shade under six feet.

"*City* ordinance," Chitto repeated, emphasis on city. Noticing the hackles on Boycott's spine bristle, he pulled the dog into a sit position.

"City's in the county," the man said.

Translation: Jurisdictional lines didn't mean dick.

"Guess it is at that." Chitto eyed the overgrown spot. "Looks like others didn't know about the ordinance either."

The man gave his head a slight shake. "You're pushin' your luck, boy."

Chitto paused, considering his options, then said, "Got a plastic bag in the truck. I'll pick it up."

"Damn right you will."

Slamming the door on a beet-red pickup with Sheriff painted on the tailgate, the man ambled toward the street, his sidewinder walk indicating he planned to make sure Chitto followed through.

With Boycott stowed inside the Chevy again, Chitto retrieved the bag of dog chow and water dish that Hattie had bagged up. Depositing the contents in the floorboard, he hurriedly scooped up the damning evidence Boycott had left behind. As he tossed the bag in the rear of the pickup, he saw the county lawman watching from the street. Lifting a hand in a mock salute, Chitto watched until he disappeared behind a building.

Cracking open windows in the pickup, Chitto filled the water bowl from the jug that Hattie provided and set it on the floorboard. Locking the truck, he walked to the entrance of Mom's, hoping the man in the fancy Stetson was headed elsewhere. Given his age, he'd bet a two-dollar bill he'd just made the acquaintance of Sheriff John Skrabo.

In front of the cafe, he paused to look over a flyspecked menu taped to the window. It was short and sweet. One egg with bacon or sausage. Two eggs with bacon or sausage. Three eggs with bacon or sausage. A short stack with maple syrup and bacon or sausage. Sausage gravy and biscuits was the special of the day, every day. Chitto liked the simplicity of the menu. Menus divided into entrees and sides, skillets and omelets, low fat and lactose-free turned eating into a chore.

Listening to his stomach growl, he pushed through the front door and looked for Crystal Folsom. She was nowhere to be seen. The man in the fancy Stetson and bomber jacket, however, was. Skrabo sat squarely facing the front door, mopping up sausage gravy and biscuits and wiping his mouth on a greasy paper napkin.

His appetite gone, Chitto looked for a booth at the back. The inside of the café turned out to be as simple as its menu. His choice of seating included a table with metal chairs in the front half or a table with wood chairs in the back half. He took aim at the furthermost table and sat down facing the front door, back to the wall.

Conversation lagged as regular customers looked over the strange duck that had landed in their pond. Country-western hits coming out of a boombox in the kitchen filled the vacuum. Drumming fingers on the table, Chitto turned his attention to the clientele, a mix of genders but slanted toward male and indigenous. A stout woman wearing a nametag that said Mom worked tables: delivering food, clearing dishes, filling cups and glasses. She and a fry cook with the physique of a wrestler and chef's hat on his head appeared to be the café's total staff. Both boss and employee showed the dark traits common to the café's clientele. Hair and eyes dark, skin warm in tone, cheekbones high. Sheriff John Skrabo being the exception.

Working her way to the back table, Mom pulled a cheat sheet from an apron pocket and said, "What'll it be, hon?"

"Coffee, black."

"One coffee, high and dry," she said, jotting down the order. She looked at him. "That it?"

"For now. I'm waiting for someone."

When Mom headed for the kitchen, he resumed the drum roll on the table: watching the front door for Crystal, hoping to see the sheriff leave before she arrived, listening to Patty Loveless singing, *Someone's gonna do you, baby, like you done me . . .*

As the chatter at nearby tables resumed, he turned an attentive ear. Talk of newcomers moving into the area dominated the conversations, mostly Californians buying up the wilderness. Consensus? The clientele didn't like their country being Californicated. His thinking went to Crystal, wondering how they felt about one of their own selling them out.

Chitto relaxed as Skrabo got up from his chair, then tensed as the lawman headed his direction. As he walked,

Skrabo smoothed kid-leather gloves onto his hands, finger by finger. Once on, the gloves looked part of his hand. Though his physique spoke to too many heavy meals and the red face to alcohol abuse, he beat the coffee to the table.

"Took care of the dog business like I said I would," Chitto volunteered, noting Mom's Café had become silent as a morgue. He glanced at a clock on the wall shaped like a black-and-white cat. According to the dial in that cat's belly, Crystal was ten minutes late.

"Saw that." Standing spraddle-legged, the sheriff stared down at him. "Couldn't help but notice that shotgun behind the seat. Suppose you've got a permit for it."

"Yes, sir. Never can tell what you'll encounter in the woods. Rattlers. Wild pigs. Bear. Thought it'd be a good idea to bring it, 'specially since I'm training that pup out there to track."

Skrabo's eyes narrowed to slits. "Suppose you've got a concealed carry permit, too."

Chitto's mind raced. Skrabo's eyesight was better than he'd hoped. If forced to show his gun permit, he could kiss subterfuge goodbye. Then again, lying could get him searched.

"Sure do." Chitto waited, hoping the sheriff wouldn't press the issue.

Skrabo folded his arms across his chest.

Sighing, Chitto handed over his tribal police ID and watched the sheriff's eyebrows knot up.

"You're with the Nation—"

"*Dammit*—" A breathless Crystal Folsom hurried up, faded jeans hugging slim hips, padded jacket hugging a flannel shirt, scuffed hiking boots hugging her feet, and a look on her face that said she knew Chitto had been made. "Don't you have better things to do than hassle people, John?"

Stretching tall, she locked eyes with the sheriff. "What is with you? Just can't let a day go by without making one of the Folsom's lives miserable? Sam here's my cousin."

Chitto held his silence, deciding then was not the time to debate the finer points of being Crystal's cousin, especially as Mary was two years gone.

"Cousin," Skrabo mumbled. "How come I never seen him around." He handed Chitto's ID back to him.

"'Cause he works for a living." Crystal turned to Chitto. "Ready to go look at that property I told you 'bout, Sam?"

"Let's take my truck," Chitto said, glad Crystal was quick on her feet. He looked at the sheriff. "Thought I'd kill two birds with one stone. Look for a weekend hunting cabin and . . ." He held Skrabo's eyes. "Work my dog."

The skin on Skrabo's face darkened by degrees, the blood flowing upstream from his neck. Again, Mom's Café took on the atmosphere of a funeral parlor.

"You, uh, you still want this, hon?" Mom stood to one side, a steaming mug of coffee in her hand. Her eyes moved around the triad, looking for an optimistic sign that said her place wasn't going to require massive reconstruction. The fry cook was more of a pessimist. He stood behind her with a ten-inch butcher knife in his hand.

"You bet." He reached for his wallet. "Maybe you could make it to go."

Crystal waved him off. "Make it *two* to go, Mom. And it's on me."

"High like usual?" Mom asked.

"Right, cream only. And I need a receipt since I'm on the clock."

Crystal faced the sheriff again, back stiff as a two-by-four. "I'd love to stay and chat, John, but some of us have to work for a living." She paused, giving him a humorless smile. "You should try it sometime."

"Don't push me, missy." Slipping dark glasses over his eyes, Skrabo marched out the front door.

"Well, now," Chitto said as he and Crystal retrieved their coffee and exited the cafe. "That went well."

He opened the passenger side door and dumped the water bowl on the ground. "In the back, Boycott."

"Yeah, I know." Crystal set the coffee into holders in the console after the dog jumped into the backseat. "Not too cool, but old John gives me the willies, has long as I can remember. Even when I was little, he made me feel . . . prickly."

"Prickly," he repeated, thinking the description fit into the same category as vehicles the color of trees. Vague.

"You know, like when you get prickly heat in the summer. Skin crawls like a nest of spiders hatched under your skin."

"Oh, *that* feeling," he said, the hint of a grin showing.

She pointed to the left as he stopped at the corner. "Go that way."

He turned left on Main. "I get the feeling everyone kisses old John's ass. How do you get away talking to him the way you just did?"

"Did I come on too strong?" She turned to stare through the windshield, looking pensive. "I guess I did. It's just that since Grandma got hurt, it's getting harder to . . . You know, keep the lid on."

"Tell you what might be cool right now," he said, nodding at the rearview mirror. "Try laying off old John for a while. Gonna be hard for me to keep a low profile, you keep pissing him off."

Her eyes sparked as she spotted the sheriff's truck in the side mirror. "I can fix that," she said.

Chitto listened to Crystal talk to someone on her cell, keeping an eye on his rear. He drove slow, giving her time to put into play whatever plan she had in mind.

"Yeah, I'm good. Auntie Rose," she said into the phone. "Bob still there? Good, put him on." Glancing at Chitto, she said. "Grandma's niece is staying with her today" and turned her attention to the phone again. "Hey, Bob. Suppose you and Andy could create a diversion? You know, one bad enough old John would be called to the scene?"

She listened. She smiled. She said, "That should work." She hit the disconnect button.

"So?"

"Follow the curve," she said as he reached the split where US 271 turned north. "And take your time."

Chitto took note of another motel as he made the turn north, observing it lacked a sign that said No Pets Allowed. The two-story motel backed onto vacant land. A room at the rear would allow him privacy and a place to walk Boycott when the need arose. Things were looking up.

"Wanna tell me what to expect?" he said, glancing in the mirror again. The sheriff's pickup followed about a quarter mile behind. Clearly, Skrabo felt no need to be subtle.

"Old John's about to get a call about a drunk and disorderly at a joint west of town, outside the city limits. *His* jurisdiction." She grinned. "A certain dumpster might even get lit up."

A couple of miles later, Chitto saw the beet-red pickup make a tight U and a flashing light appear on top of the cab. Glancing to the west, he saw a plume of black smoke drifting skyward. "Damn," he said. "Pays to have friends in high places."

She grinned. "More like cousins with low morals."

He laughed, glad that Mary's clan had multiplied and produced cunning offspring. "Handy, too. What do Andy and Bob do when they're not creating diversions?"

"Work as guides, fishing and hunting mostly. Sometimes trail rides."

"Nice work if you can get it. Must know the country well."

"They do—*we* do." Leaning back in the seat, she undid her jacket. "That's how we spent our time growing up, crawling around those hills out there." She stared at the blue-green mountains rimming the east side of the valley. "That's the one benefit to this crappy real-estate job. It gets me out of that one-horse town and into the wilderness."

"We headed up there?" He nodded toward the high country.

"No, Grandma's place. It's a few miles up the road. That's where she last saw my dad walking away. Made sense you'd want to start there." She glanced at him. "Can't take you right up to the house, don't want her to see us. She, uh, she keeps hoping my dad will miraculously reappear." She looked out the side window, shaking her head. "I mean, *seriously?*"

"Well," he murmured, "you know what Pope said. 'Hope springs eternal in the human breast.'"

"Who?" A deep wrinkle creased her forehead.

"Alexander Pope. Eighteenth-century poet."

"Poet?" She stared at him.

"Never mind," he said. "Close is good, especially if it's near where that couple was found murdered."

"Let's take a look." She pulled a map out of a shoulder bag. "Oh—" She looked at him again. "And we're meeting up with Chuck Stovall as soon as we're done. At his place. He got his file out of his safe deposit box and bringing it to the café."

"That would be the old tavern."

"Yeah . . . Was that mentioned in the newspaper article?"

He nodded.

"Chuck thinks it's haunted."

"That was mentioned, too." He glanced her way. "Glad you set up the meet with Stovall. Got a lot on my plate. This weekend's probably all I can give you."

"Probably," she said.

"Probably," he repeated.

She took up staring out the window again. "Lot of years have gone by," she said a couple of miles later. "Think you can figure this mess out in a weekend?"

"Do my best," he said, his tone not expressing much optimism.

She sat a half minute, staring at the centerline striping the narrow two-lane asphalt and rubbing Boycott's head, which he'd stuck between the front seats. "There's got to be a connection, don't you think? Between those murders and my dad going missing, I mean."

Chitto translated the trepidation in her voice. She was wondering what effect piecing together Walter's story would have her grandmother. The truth didn't always set a person free.

"It does if any of this is going to make sense," he murmured.

CHAPTER SIX

Peony Folsom lived in a story-and-a-half house tucked back on a wooded hillside a mile off Highway 271. Pulling binoculars from his light pack, Chitto studied the place. Though thick as hair on a dog's back, the trees had not fully leafed out, giving him a good view. Last year's leaves, now rich brown mulch that cushioned his step, smelled of mold and decay.

"The car belong to your aunt?" he asked, pointing his chin toward a blue Chevy sedan. She nodded.

Random additions made over the years gave the house a slipshod look. A lean-to addition at the back probably added to the size of the kitchen or housed a laundry room. Similar additions on the sides provided additional bedrooms as the family grew. A propane tank identified the fuel source, a pump indicated the house used well water, and a dark-green hump on the downhill side gave witness to a septic tank. Though in need of a whitewash, the house was neat, well kept. Curtains at the windows downstairs had been opened to allow light inside. The window upstairs was dark, curtains closed. Unbroken ground in a fenced-off area indicated a garden plot, long unused. An older model car was parked next to a detached garage. Body rusting. Tires flat.

"Given this cold snap," Chitto said, putting binoculars away, "when you figure to plant corn? I figure a couple weeks."

"Corn?" Crystal lifted an eyebrow.

"Corn patch would make the place look lived in." He retrieved Boycott, who was tethered to a tree stob. "That old car your dad's?"

A sigh. "That rusting hunk of junk's right where he left it." She shook her head. "Grandma clings to things."

He nodded. "So, this is the old trail your dad walked every day?" He peered down a rough path, much of which was barely visible. Chalky blue sky and mountains merged with cool grays in tree limbs and trunks, a tangle of underbrush. The air was sharp with the smell of pine and colder than a meat locker. A plus when it came to tick worries. A negative if you'd dressed too light. He snapped his jacket to the neck.

"Right." Crystal pulled on gloves. "According to what Grandma said, she figures he connected up with the old railroad bed after a bit. Trains used to run through here, but the rails and crossties have been pulled. Some trace of the roadbed's still there, though."

"The Frisco line. It paralleled the Kiamichi through this part of the country."

"Could be," she said, tugging at her jacket zipper. "Some of the older folks would know that kind of thing. Chuck, too. He's the self-appointed historian for these parts."

She looked toward her grandmother's house. "Tried to get something about my dad out of Grandma, but she wouldn't say much. Sounds like he didn't have any friends, none that came visiting anyway. Didn't go anywhere except . . ." She rolled her eyes. "Those daily walks to the river to drink coffee. Grandma said he'd start out walking that way . . ." She pointed to the trail. "And return on the country road."

She indicated the narrow, two-lane highway they'd driven in on. "A loop of sorts."

"He didn't work?"

"No, at least not there at the end. Seems he couldn't hold down a regular job. Didn't like being around people, worked as a handyman in between picking up garbage." She paused, breathing deep. "Those lousy coffee breaks at the river were the most important thing in his life."

Chitto waited a minute, letting the bitterness ebb. "He go the same time every day?"

"So she says. Left after breakfast, was back by dinner."

"Two, three hours then."

She blinked a couple of times. "Sounds right. Except Friday, he'd go twice on Friday."

"What time he go that second time on Friday?"

She pulled at an earlobe. "She didn't mention a time, just said he'd leave after supper."

Chitto rubbed the back of his neck, thinking about habits. By and large, country people ate on a schedule you could set your clock by. Breakfast between five-thirty and six, dinner at high noon, supper around six, later during harvest.

"That's the one that interests me," he said. "Sounds like it was an appointment." He looked at her. "Who would he be meeting up with?"

"Look . . ." She pinned hands to hips, eyes to Chitto. "You'd get more out of Grandma than me. She seems reluctant to talk to me about him—or *her*. Always has been."

He inferred the "her" was Crystal's truant mother. "Well, let's see how it goes with Stovall."

She sighed, the picture of impatience.

He turned again to look down the trail, overgrown from lack of use.

Crystal glared at him. "Care to share what're you thinking?"

"You always this angry?" he said, frowning at her. "If not, I'd appreciate it, you'd tell me what I just said to piss you off."

She tossed her head, long braid flipping. "It's not what you say, it's what you *don't* say. If this weekend's all you've got to give Grandma, you're sure as hell taking your time."

"Okay, then," he said, feeling his gut wrench. "I was thinking your dad was a lonely man." Was he really working on his third year without Mary?

"Or just plain nuts," she snapped.

"Anything's possible," he said, shrugging. "But a lot can slip through the cracks if people think you're nuts."

She shook her head, resignation in her eyes. "Okay, now what?"

He looked down the ragged trail again. "Oh, thought I'd take off down that way and when I find the river, wander along the edge till I find him."

"What the hell kind of cop are you?" she said, shoulders drooping.

"Get your coffee," he said, grinning. "Let's go pick up some garbage."

∞

It took between thirty and thirty-five minutes of hard walking for Chitto and Crystal to reach the campground. Discovering the old service road that once connected section houses made the walk easier. The skeleton of an old trestle served as a portal to the river's edge.

"I gotta say," she said, pausing to catch her breath, "you walk faster than you talk. How far you figure we've come? Mile and a half, maybe two?"

"Maybe. Twenty-minute mile's the average."

Chitto figured Walter wouldn't have wasted too much time in getting to his coffee place. Addictions could come in all flavors. Process addictions included an obsession with sex, compulsive spending, germs, orderliness. Substance addictions dealt with what kind you ingested, shot up, inhaled. Hell, he still craved a smoke at ten, two, and four, like clockwork. Now, it was chewing gum.

And coffee . . .

Letting Boycott off leash, he sat on a boulder near the stream's edge: sipping cold coffee, staring at water fringed with rime crackled as shattered glass, and listening to the sound of wind whining through the pines. He wondered if the mournful song could be interpreted as a wolf's howl.

Crystal sat on an adjacent boulder, her jacket pulled to her chin. "He won't run off?" she asked, looking toward Boycott.

He glanced at the dog, currently exploring old slag piles and depressions on the pockmarked hillside. Evidence of wildlife lay on the ground. Deer. Raccoon. Rabbit. "Plenty here to keep him occupied, and he'll come when I whistle. Tell me about this place."

Looking around, she shrugged. "Nothing special, just another campground. Lots of them scattered around here."

"No history to this one?"

She took a minute. "When I was in high school, the kids came here to make out. Still do, I guess." She shrugged again. "And drink. Kids come here to drink, too."

He nodded. "Probably been that way since the place was constructed. Not too far from town. Private. Pretty." He looked around. "Or could be. Seems like those garbage cans are going to waste." He smiled at her. "Rotary Club's not doing its job."

Managing a grin, she said, "Maybe I'll report them." She went back to staring at him.

"What size thermos your dad carry his coffee in?" he asked a couple minutes later.

"*Thermos?*" She rolled her eyes. "I was supposed to ask my grandma that?"

He shook his head slightly, sighing. "Took me about ten minutes to finish off a large, cold cup. I figure your dad brought a thermos that held three, four cups, maybe picked up trash in between. To get back home in time for lunch, he'd spend about an hour or two here. Head back around eleven thirty."

"Okay . . ." She nodded slowly. "I get it. You're walking in his shoes."

"And his dog was so old, she couldn't have made it too far," he added.

She looked around the campground, seeing the place with new eyes. "So he really was here. Oh, jeez . . ." She hesitated, eyes wide. "You think this is where that couple came that night? You think the killer was here, too?" She rose slowly, rubbing the back of her neck. "Crap," she said, laughing nervously. "For a minute, I had the feeling the killer was watching us."

"Let's not get ahead of ourselves." Walking to a trash barrel, he tossed his cup inside. "Murderers are known to revisit the scene of the crime, but after all this time, I doubt he'd still be inclined. Then too, a lot of years have passed. He might not even be alive."

Hearing Boycott growl, Chitto watched the dog walk stiff-legged down the lane that connected the campground to the county road. Looking around, he saw nothing out of the ordinary, just trees casting noonday shadows, leaving a dark blanket under the canopy. As Boycott continued a muffled growling, he took a second look. Narrowing his eyes, he half expected to see a deer or a bear, as raccoons and opossums preferred the darkness of night. Then, a shadow caught his eye, moving independently of the trees' shadows.

He knelt beside Boycott, who was also following the movement. Feeling Chitto's hand on his shoulder, the dog swept his tail and nosed him, then turned back to the movement. Whatever it was disappeared, but minutes later, the sound of an engine grumbled to life and slowly died away. Standing, Chitto found a clear spot in the trees and watched a rooster tail of dust rising from the highway.

Chitto walked back toward Crystal, listening. A high wind whistled through the pines. Rime ice breaking up on the riverbank pinged like wind chimes. Squirrels jumping through tree branches chattered noisily. A few months ago, a similar commotion from crows preceded an attack from a shapeshifter that left him with a cracked skull. He'd hunted as a boy, as kids did in Oklahoma. Squirrels. Rabbits. Deer on occasion. As an adult, his interests had turned more cerebral, but his grandmother often told him he came from a long line of hunters. Warriors. Here recently, those instincts had been tested and he'd come up short. One thing he did know. Squirrels raised cane when humans and predators were around.

"You think someone was watching us?" she whispered.

He ran a hand across the Glock at his back. "Think I'll walk around a bit. Can come, if you want."

"I want," she said, walking up close.

"Bring that map that shows where that couple was found."

They spent another thirty minutes, surveying the campground area and orienting themselves. They found more old railroad paraphernalia: a rusted switch, old storage box, lock long busted, a few spikes. And plenty of garbage: empty beer bottles, pop cans, greasy food wrappers, Styrofoam containers containing mummified French fries, used condoms.

Tail wagging, Boycott bounded to Chitto's side, something hanging from his mouth.

"What've you got there?" He pulled a dark object from between the dog's jaws.

"What is it?" Crystal asked, bending lower to see.

"Old piece of rawhide, probably leftover from railroad days." He tossed the strip into the brush. "In dog language, a chew toy." Boycott raced away, nose to the ground, and returned with the chew.

"As long as it's not people leather," she said, shivering.

Eyebrows raised, Chitto extracted the strip of leather from Boycott's jaws and examined it. "Nope, too thick. Probably cowhide."

"Would you get serious?" She shook her head. "You're giving me the heebie-jeebies."

"I wonder . . ." Chitto put the dog in a stay position. Winding up his throwing arm, he sailed the strip of leather up the brushy hillside. Looking at the dog, he said "Find" and watched the dog race away.

"What the hell are you doing?" she asked, eyes wide.

"I told Skrabo I was here to train my dog." He rubbed away a grin with a thumb and forefinger. "Now you can tell him with a straight face that's what I did."

"Like I care?" she snapped.

As Crystal returned to scowling, Chitto squatted on his heels and raked his hands over the ground.

"Now I suppose you're looking for diamonds," she said, her tone mocking.

"Maybe." He nodded toward the far hills. "Those mountains have been eroding for millions of years. They've been fractured and broken many times over, probably washed inside out with hot water from underground springs." He looked up at her. "Never know what you find, you look close enough."

"Gravel," she said, scooping up a handful. "That's what I see. The county hauls it in from the quarry on the other side of town. Put new down just this last fall on all the country roads."

"That's good, means the roads are passable." He stood, watching Boycott weave his way down the hillside. A minute later, the dog sat in front of him, the piece of leather hanging from his mouth. "I'll be damned," he said, kneeling beside the dog. "You do have a nose on you, pup."

Crystal threw her head back, groaning.

Getting to his feet, he gestured toward her grandmother's place. "Let's head back. It'll take us a good thirty minutes to get there and . . . what? Another thirty to get to Stovall's?"

"About that," she said, dusting her hands against her jeans. "We going back on the county road?"

"No. Along the old tracks. Something tells me anything of interest would be there."

She paused, looking toward the county road. "So I've been thinking . . ."

Chitto waited, watching her eyes blink.

"That guy that was killed . . ."

"Billy Robb Niles," he said.

"Yeah. He was found just down that way on the county road, shot to hell." She paused, to reposition herself, angling her body slightly. "The girl . . ." She paused, looking at Chitto.

"Leona Mann," he said.

"Leona," she repeated softly. "Billy Robb and Leona . . ." She brushed a hand across her face. Two long-dead people had just taken on life again. More than that, they had walked into *her* life, along with her father.

"Well, anyway," she said, clearing her throat. "Leona was found a little further off, and it makes sense that this is where they came after they left the tavern. And my dad was probably here, too. Which means, he and Leona were friends."

Chitto frowned. "He and Leona?"

"Well, *yeah*. That guy Niles wasn't from here, and climbing highline poles when he was."

He grunted softly. "That makes sense."

"But see, it *doesn't* make sense." She glanced toward the county road again. "What the hell happened, Sam? I mean, how'd they get from here to there? Who drove the car down the road after Billy Robb was killed and . . . and who raped and killed Leona? And if my dad did suffer from PTSD, was he . . ." She paused, swallowing hard.

"A ticking bomb?" he said, finishing her thought.

She nodded, then frowned. "But if he was involved, how'd his skull get into Leona's casket?"

"Don't let this get surreal," he said. "If that skull is your dad's, then in all likelihood he wasn't involved in the killing. Let's go see what Stovall has. Maybe he can make sense of things." As much as someone who holds séances with ghosts can be thought of as sensible, he thought.

"Oh, God, I hope so," she said, looking hopeful.

"Important thing to remember is the murderer's human."

"Which means?" she asked.

"Which means he's human," he said.

And prone to blind spots, added the voice in his head.

CHAPTER SEVEN

It was lunchtime at Chuck's Place, a rambling cedar-sided building just beyond the city limits, putting it in under county jurisdiction. John Skrabo country. Chitto left Boycott in the truck, chewing on the strip of leather he'd found at the campground, and he and Crystal walked to the entrance. The parking lot was packed, as was the dining area, a large room paneled in gleaming pine floor to ceiling. From hidden speakers, a fiddle melody was just audible over the babble of voices and clink of dishes.

"Oh, no," Crystal whispered, turning her back on the crowd.

"What is it?" Chitto let his eyes travel around the room.

"Bud King's here. He was the sheriff before Skrabo. Sitting alone, front table by the window."

Chitto turned slightly, so he wasn't looking directly at the man. King bore the same life scars as most men in their seventies and eighties: thin skin laced with blue veins, liver spots big as silver dollars, a frame so wasted it looked skeletal. But it was the frosted blue marble in the left eyeball that turned Chitto's blood cold.

"What happened to his eye?" Chitto had seen opaque eyes before, on animals as well as humans, typically caused by injury or ulcers.

She glanced toward the table, fidgeting. "Burn, I think. Chemical burn of some kind. Can't see it from here, but his skin's scarred, too. Scary-looking bastard, isn't he?"

"Doesn't give me a warm, fuzzy feeling."

Abruptly, the old man waved to them.

Chitto looked at her. "He waving at us?"

"'Fraid so," she sighed. She weaved her way through tables toward King, Chitto following behind.

"How's my girl?" King took one of her hands and began stroking it. "Still as pretty as ever, I see."

"How are you, Bud?" She pulled her hand away, the smile on her face looking as bona fide as a three-dollar bill.

"Join me," he said, nudging an empty chair toward her. "Tell me who this young buck is you're with."

She quickly introduced Chitto as her cousin. "Wish we could, but I need to show Sam some slicks on places for sale in the area. He's looking for a . . . getaway."

The former sheriff's one working eye fixed on Chitto's two good ones. "Get away from what?"

Chitto huffed a laugh. "Civilization, I guess."

"Uh huh . . ." The old sheriff gave Chitto a visual pat down, lingering where Chitto's jacket concealed his service pistol.

"Come on." Crystal linked her arm through Chitto's, pulling him away from the table. "Later, Bud," she said over her shoulder.

They found a table at the back of the café and waited for one of several harried-looking servers to bring menus. Noting the stuffed head of a ten-point buck on one wall and a black bear on another, Chitto anticipated the local fare would lean toward feral. When the menus showed up, he was surprised to see barbecued chicken as the lunch special and choice of sides that included coleslaw, baked beans, fried okra, and potato salad. Given he had forgone sausage gravy and biscuits at Mom's that morning, he was hungry. They ordered the chicken and house wine of the South, iced tea so sweet it made your teeth ache, and waited for Chuck Stovall to show up. Both let out a sigh when Bud King left, walking with the gait of someone who was still in charge.

"He the sheriff when the double homicide happened?" Chitto asked. "And who refused to investigate your dad's disappearance?"

"Yes, but he still keeps his fingers on things. He and John Skrabo are like this." She pressed two fingers together.

"Think he'll let Skrabo know we're here?"

She shrugged.

They'd finished off a tall glass of tea when a stocky man in a plaid flannel shirt and running shoes brought their order. A sugar high had Chitto's feet tapping a jig under the table and his ears buzzing. He needed stick-to-the-ribs food to mellow out jangled nerves.

"Hey, Chuck," Crystal said, helping the restaurateur unload plates. She introduced Chitto in the process.

"Figured as much." Stovall pointed his chin toward a door in the corner and talked in a low tone. "Got my stuff in the office. Soon as it slows down, I'll show it to you." He looked around, eyes flitting from table to table. "Some people in these parts are gettin' tired of me sticking my nose in this business, so wait for me to give you the nod."

Chitto had been checking the tables, too. Though the clientele leaned more toward white than red, cattlemen from the preponderance of Stetsons, steel-toe wellingtons, and split-cowhide vests, John Skrabo was not among them.

Filling their glasses again, Stovall disappeared among the tables, chewing the fat with locals, yelling for busboys to clear tables, and refilling tea glasses to the brim.

Diners who finished their meal dropped by to chat it up with Crystal and meet the new man in her life. Crystal, it seemed, was a popular girl. They showed genuine surprise when she introduced Sam as a cousin in town looking for real estate. The story was repeated so many times, Chitto actually began to think of himself as a legitimate relative. It was a feeling he liked. Being part of Mary's clan brought her closer. The problem was, he was getting a lot more attention than he needed.

"Existing cabin," one stiff-backed man walking with the aid of a cane said. "Or raw land?"

Crystal shook her head slightly. "Don't worry, Riley. He's not looking to buy land."

The rancher shuffled away, sucking on a molar.

"I get the feeling locals aren't real fond of what you do for a living." Chitto knew the indigenous view on the matter. The Choctaws considered themselves children of the forest, making the wilderness sacred. He figured the ranchers were more interested in summer grazing rights on mountain pastures.

She sat up straight, jawbones clinching. "It's not like there's a lot to choose from, and I have responsibilities that keep me from leaving. Though God knows, I'd like to." Staring out the window, she shook her head. "But I'll be damned if I follow in either my mother or father's footsteps."

Chitto looked out the window, too, taking in the lay of the land behind the old tavern. Frowning, he said, "Is that slag?"

She shot him a look that said, Is that a serious question or another bullshit comment?

"Slag's crushed rock that's put under railroad tracks. Frisco run behind this place?"

"Oh," she said, looking out the window. "I think so. Why? Is that important?"

"Just an observation."

The place had almost emptied when they got the nod from Stovall. Chitto made a stop at the men's room en route. He'd lost track of the glasses of iced tea he'd consumed. Time was another matter. They'd been there almost two hours. The weekend was going fast, and he only had this weekend to give.

Probably, said the voice in his head.

∞

"Maybe you could do some summarizing," Chitto said, noting the fat, accordion-pleated file on Stovall's desk. Inside the flap, he could see manila folders with neatly printed tabs. "I'm cramped for time, and I assume Crystal's told you, should anyone ask, I'm here to look at real estate."

The office was small with walls in need of paint and unadorned. An assortment of file cabinets lined the wall behind the desk, both cabinets and desk looking to be government issue recycles. Clearly, the lacquered pine and stuffed animals in the dining room were to impress the clientele, not the pragmatic owner. Chitto took this as a good sign. But then, he was looking for anything to balance out ghosts and séances.

"She did," Stovall said, rubbing a hand across his mouth. "I gotta say, I'm a little nervous letting these outta my hands." He indicated the accordion folder. "There's a lotta work in there."

"I'll guard them with my life," Chitto said and wished immediately that he'd hadn't been so liberal with his promises.

"Well, here it is in a nutshell." Stovall leaned back in his chair. "That whole murder investigation was a cover-up. Too much to prove otherwise. What's got me bumfuzzled now . . ." He paused, looking at Crystal. "Is how Walter Folsom was involved. Man, finding his skull in Leona's casket really threw me for a loop."

"No positive proof the skull belongs to him," Chitto said. The comment generated a grunt from Crystal, which he ignored. "Let's just stick with the murder of Robb and Mann for now. Why do you think it was a cover-up?"

"Okay, here's the lowdown." Stovall leaned forward, elbows planted on the desktop and fingers clenched. "That case was botched from the get-go. Mixed reports from people who saw the body on just where Leona was shot. Back of the head, in the face, in the chest . . . No autopsy on either body, so there's conflicting stories on what caliber gun was used. Family wanted Leona buried in a pink-flowered dress and when the coffin was exhumed, the dress was found stuffed inside the coffin, like it was put there in a hurry." He shook his head. "I ask you, is that any way to send someone off to their hereafter? Buried in the same bloody clothes she was murdered in?"

"Who would've been responsible for that?"

"Why, George Forsyth, the mortician that handled the burial. It was a closed coffin, which is understandable if she was shot in the head. But pretty damn unorthodox handling of the body, you ask me. Especially since the skull buried with her wasn't even hers."

"That mortician still alive?"

"Yeah, but he's old and suffers dementia. Rumor is it's progressed to Alzheimer's." He shook his head. "Unreliable."

"Sounds like he's still around. Where could I find him?"

"Nursing home on the north side of town."

"Go on. What else doesn't stack up?"

Stovall laughed. "Strangest thing is the case files disappearing right when Bud King retired. Speculation is he took them with him."

Chitto's jaws went slack. "The case files on the murder?"

Stovall nodded.

"So how'd you gather so much info?" He indicated the file on Stovall's desk.

"Well, see, I was a county commissioner for a couple of terms. That's when I got interested in the murder. I read what files I could find, made notes, even copies of some things."

He paused. "I know Bud taking the files sounds unorthodox, but keep in mind that this is a small rural area and the good old boys were in charge. Hell, still are. Bud King was not to be fooled with or you paid, and John Skrabo's just as ornery."

"Worse," Crystal said, shivering.

Chitto smiled, figuring she was experiencing a case of the prickles.

"That's when I started talking to Leona's family about exhuming the body," Stovall went on. "Finally talked Leona's little brother into signing the papers. Paid for the examination myself and went for the best there was because I wanted the findings to be reliable—and believable. When it became questionable that the skull belonged to Leona, I had that forensic artist, Glenda Loomis, do that drawing." He looked at Crystal. "That's when Crystal's grandmother paid me a call."

Chitto nodded. "Figured she might. What'd you tell her?"

"Told her what I thought. Comparing that picture of Walter she brought with the artist's rendering of the skull, I'd say they were one and the same."

Chitto sat back, thinking. "You send Walter's picture to Loomis, that artist?"

Hesitation. "No. Should I have?"

"Wouldn't have hurt." Chitto paused, second-guessing his own logic. "What about Billy Robb Niles? Could the skull belong to him? Maybe it's a simple matter of mixing up body parts. That mortician doesn't sound like he had a lot on the ball. Wouldn't be the first time something strange took place in a funeral home."

"No dice. Niles's family took his remains back home for burial, wouldn't hear of having the body raised. Wanted him to rest in peace. But that wasn't the main problem. See, Niles was really messed up, both his head and his . . ." Stovall hesitated, glancing at Crystal.

"I'm not a child, Chuck," she snapped. "I know the guy's nuts were shot to hell."

As Stovall's neck reddened, Chitto made a poor effort at hiding a grin.

"Well," Stovall said. "Point is, witness who found Niles said he wasn't only shot in the head and . . . elsewhere, but looked like someone had laid the boots to him. Bashed him pretty good."

"And the skull found in the coffin?"

"No bullet hole, no crushed bones. Don't know how the guy the skull belonged to died, but . . ." Again, he hesitated, looking at Crystal. She stared at the floor, face a stone mask.

"So, other than being separated from the body, the head found in the coffin had no visible injuries," Chitto summarized.

"Right."

"Clean cut? Was the neck severed cleanly?"

Stovall thought a minute. "That I don't know."

"Glenda Loomis would've noticed that kind of thing. Bones tell a story."

"Her phone number's in here." Stovall began rummaging through the accordion file.

"I've got a question," Crystal said, looking at Stovall. *"When* did Leona's head get cut off? I mean, it sounds like the bodies were intact when they were hauled to the mortuary."

"Well now," Stovall said. "I figure that took place at the mortuary."

"Wouldn't that take a doctor? At a minimum, someone with medical training?"

"Morticians need some training to do their work but . . ." Stovall shook his head. "Trouble is, I just can't feature old

George having the stomach for it—or a reason to do so. I mean, what would've been the motivation?"

Maybe he went mad in the moonlight, the voice in Chitto's head taunted.

"Who transported the bodies?" Chitto asked. "Medical examiners do autopsies. I figure old George doubled as the ME, so he had to be present when the bodies were taken in."

"George wasn't a medical examiner . . ." Stovall paused to hand Glenda Loomis' business card to Chitto. "He was the coroner all right, but he wasn't called to the scene."

Chitto frowned considering this bit of news. Medical examiners were physicians, in most cases trained to be forensic pathologists, and appointed to their positions. Coroners were elected to the position and often had no or little medical training.

"Well then, since neither a medical examiner nor coroner was called, had to be one of the deputies hauled them in." Chitto pointed his chin at the files. "Information on the deputy at the scene in there?"

"It is, but a deputy didn't do it," Stovall said. "Bud King hauled 'em in himself."

"The sheriff? He didn't delegate it?"

"He and his deputy and another guy loaded the bodies into the back of his truck. Bud covered them up with a tarp and drove 'em in."

"You read that in one of the files?"

"No, sir. That came from old Edgar G., the one who found the bodies. Last name was Guthrie, but folks called him Edgar G. He drove to a nearby house and had the woman there call the sheriff, then went back and waited. He was told to go home once they started the loading, but he drove a little ways down the road and watched."

"And he didn't see more than the two bodies?"

"Just the two."

"And Mann's head was still attached?"

"He didn't say it wasn't, and I figure something like that would've got his attention."

Chitto nodded. "He see the sheriff make a detour down the track to the campground near there?"

A pause. "No, but he didn't hang around once the bodies went into the truck." Stovall looked at Chitto, blinking. "Why'd you ask about that campground?"

"Just curious. Edgar G. still around?"

"Oh, no. Died not long after the murders." Stovall turned thoughtful. "Near as I can remember, from natural causes."

Chitto frowned again. "If he died soon after the killing, how would you know what he saw?"

"Wrote it down in a letter to his brother." Stovall pointed to the accordion file. "Copy of it right there in the file."

"Let me guess." Crystal smiled wryly. "John Skrabo was the deputy, wasn't he?"

"Matter of fact, no. Another deputy assisted."

Chitto leaned forward. "He still work for the sheriff's office?"

"Not anymore. Shot to death while on duty."

"How convenient," Crystal said, shoulders slumping.

Chitto made another mental note, then frowned. "Hold on. You said another man helped the sheriff and deputy load the bodies?"

"*Jeez . . .*" Crystal looked at Chitto, eyes wide. "You think it was my dad?"

He considered the possibility, then turned to Stovall. "Edgar see a dog while he was watching?"

"Didn't mention one. Besides, it couldn't have been Walter. Edgar G. said the guy worked for the railroad. Didn't know his name, but he'd seen him in town from time to time. Trainmen worked odd shifts, so many days on, so many days off, and laid over on each end."

Chitto's eyebrows hiked. "That trainman still alive?"

"Don't know." Stovall paused, looking at the accordion file. "That's the one name that's not in there."

"And this trainman just happened to be driving down the road."

"So it seems. I figure he was working or just got off work. According to Edgar's letter, the guy was a mess. Clothes dirty and stained with grease and oil. A service road ran down by the river. Passenger service was stopped years before, but freight was still running back then. Always figured he was checking track, heard the commotion, and came out to check." Stovall paused. "You think it was something else?"

Chitto took a minute. "No, that's a fair assumption. Name would've been helpful."

"Just another one of those things that got botched." Stovall watched Chitto rub a hand across the back of his neck. "What're you thinking?"

"Wondering why he'd stick around to help load the bodies and the man who discovered them was sent away?"

Stovall blinked several times. "Don't know that either. But Edgar G. wasn't a spring chicken and most railroaders are pretty stout. Coincidence, I figure."

Chitto wondered if it was that simple. "Many of those trainmen stick around after the line shut down?"

Stovall exhaled slowly. "Another question I don't know the answer to, but I'd bet not many. Those that stuck it out would've had to find work around here, and with the lumber business pulling out along with the railroad, pickings would've been slim. I figure most of 'em moved on down the line so they could stay with railroading. Those that did stay are probably dead by now." He glanced at his watch. "Look, I gotta get things going for the dinner hour."

"Okay," Chitto said. "I've got a handle on things and those files will fill in any gaps. The list of people questioned in the file?"

"Sure is. Crystal said you wanted to see that, so I made an extra copy and put it at the front." He sucked spit out of his cheek. "'Fraid it's a short list."

"Figured it would be. Too bad that old sheriff took the files. I guess you asked him about them."

"Oh, yeah." Stovall snorted loudly. "Gotch-eyed old fool lives to make life hell for anyone he can."

Chitto picked up the accordion-pleated folder. "You, uh, you got a black plastic bag? Something to conceal this in."

"Got all kinds." Stovall rose from his chair, pointing Chitto and Crystal toward the dining room.

"Maybe two or three extra then," Chitto said, "if you can spare them."

Given the dispositions of the sheriffs in the county, it paid dog owners to be prepared.

CHAPTER EIGHT

Except for employee vehicles along the back, the parking lot at Chuck's Place was empty. The perfect time and place to look at the list of suspects. Stovall had taken the time to mark those who'd been questioned that had died, which included most of the list. Another dozen was shown as no longer living in the area. Others were designated *Wits too far gone.* Three highlighted with a yellow marker indicated those considered still fit and able. Looking over the list, Chitto got the feeling the county's citizens had shorter-than-average life spans.

"You know these three?" He handed the list to Crystal.

"My whole life," she said, looking at the names. "Can't believe any of them would've made the short list." She tapped a finger on one of the names. "You already met Riley Campbell. He's the old rancher you talked to inside."

"The one who wanted to know if I was buying up raw land?"

"Right. I mean, he's older than dirt and can hardly get around. Grandma went to school with him. Came back from the war in bad shape."

"Which one?"

"Which . . . *Oh*, Korean, I think."

Early nineteen-fifties, he thought, sorting through the various wars in his memory. That would make Campbell around eighty now. Thirty years ago, however, he would've been in his fifties. Fit and able.

"Suffered a spinal injury over there. That's why he wears a back support and uses a cane." She glanced at the next name on the list. "And Harry Bradshaw's just as bad off. He calls it asthma. Might've started that way. Given he's a chain smoker, I figure it's COPD by now. He's hauled an oxygen bottle around long as I can remember."

He nodded, figuring the problem wouldn't have required a portable oxygen bottle thirty years before. "And Quince Winters?"

She looked away, blinking. "There's something about him I never could put my finger on, but I'd bet my bottom dollar he wasn't involved." She smiled to herself. "He's one of the few people in this county that I like."

"Maybe we better visit him first," he said, grinning.

"You forget this is Saturday? These guys won't head back home till late and they all live outside town. Quince's place is *way* out in the sticks." She shrugged and said, "What now?"

He snapped Boycott to his leash. "Another walk."

"So, what do you think?" she asked some minutes later.

He sighed. "I think I'm coming back next weekend."

"Thank you baby Jesus," she sighed, casting eyes skyward.

"I'll look over those files tonight, talk to those who were suspects tomorrow. Sounds like finding them will take some time."

"I'll go with you, that'll speed things up."

He glanced her way. "Thought you had to make a living. Weekends probably the best time to show those rich Californians around."

"Yeah, but Grandma needs answers." She rubbed a spot between her eyes. "There's just so many unanswered questions . . ."

Right, he thought. Grandma wasn't the only one who needed answers.

"Besides, there's no time to waste," she said, glancing at him. "These guys are old, counting minutes, not days."

"Given this county's history," he said, "I'm wondering how they lived this long."

Chitto let Boycott off leash where the old tracks once ran. Following the dog down the railroad bed, he noted the way it veered away from the river. Here was where the Frisco and Kiamichi River parted company. The river made a wide bend around Antlers because of Promontory Ridge, then changed its flow from south to east. Recalling maps of the area, he knew the Frisco line had run straight south into Texas, but his interest lay the other direction. He turned, facing north, following the service road alongside the roadbed as far as he could see.

"What's with this damned old train track?" Crystal's hands were back on her hips, the spark back in her eyes. "We're trying to keep my grandmother alive, not explore old railroads—remember?"

"Look," he sighed. "I know your grandmother's at risk. What I don't know is why? But I do know it had something to do with your father, so what we need to figure out is what happened to him?"

"Oh." She adopted an apologetic look and mumbled, "Does that mean we're going for another walk?" She looked down the old service road.

"Not a walk exactly," he said. "But there is someone I'd like to go see."

"Who?"

"Someone who no longer spends Saturdays in town." Whistling for Boycott, he jogged with the dog back to the truck.

Crystal was on his heels. Swearing.

∞

"George get a lot of visitors?" Chitto eyed the clipboard the receptionist at the nursing home handed him. A guest register. To refuse to sign it would draw attention, perhaps suspicion. Picking up a pen off the counter, he signed in as Alexander Pope and shoved the ledger toward Crystal, tapping his signature as he did so.

She looked at the signature, rolled her eyes, and signed Harriet Forsyth under it.

"Mr. Forsyth doesn't get *any* visitors," the white-haired receptionist said, "unless you count those from the church. They volunteer to sit with those who've lost touch with things, just so they don't feel so lonely. But he won't have anything to do with them." She turned, looking across a large room that doubled as a dining room and social area. "Said he'd rather be alone. Sits in the corner there by the windows, staring at the mountains. I swear, don't think that man's said a dozen words a year since I've worked here. And that's been twenty-some years."

"It always been that way? With visitors, I mean."

"Pretty much. Didn't have a big family to begin with, and the young ones moved away when the old ones died off. Seems to be the way it is anymore." She made a *tsk-tsk* sound, then thought some more. "Some of the people he worked with used to drop by. You know, the ones at the funeral home, the county offices, the sheriff's department . . ."

"John Skrabo?" Crystal said, eyes wide.

"Oh, no. The *old* sheriff. Then after Mr. Forsyth's memory got real bad, the sheriff stopped coming, too. Men don't have the patience to sit the way women do." She repeated the *tsk-tsk* sound. "Such a loss. Mr. Forsyth was just the nicest undertaker we ever had, could preach a better sermon than an ordained minister, too. And the bodies—oh, the bodies. Just wonderful, especially the women. I swear, he must've studied cosmetology somewhere. Dressed them

80

himself, too. Why, they were prettier in death than they were in life. Always wanted him to do me, but . . ."

Leaving the receptionist envisaging her final remains, Chitto led the way through a maze of tables where visitors were having coffee and cookies with family and friends. The clinking of cups harmonizing with the chatter gave the impression it was a Sunday afternoon church social. The stringent smell of disinfectant provided a dose of reality. He slowed, feeling Crystal nudge his shoulder.

"*Jeez*," she whispered, looking over her shoulder at the receptionist. "What did you make of that?"

He glanced down at her. "Sounds like Forsyth enjoyed his job."

"Not him—*her*. Was she for real?" Though the room was overly warm, she shivered. "I didn't know whether to laugh or run screaming from the building. I'll tell you one thing—George Forsyth will never lay a hand on me or Grandma."

He laughed softly. "Don't think you need to worry about that."

"What do you expect to get from old George? Sounds like he's had Alzheimer disease for years."

Pausing for a nurse's aide pushing a wheelchair, he said, "Alzheimer's is an unusual affliction. Affects recent memories first, while recollections of things that happened in the past are more resistant."

"You're hoping thirty-year-old memories are still there?"

"Something like that." Stopping a few feet away from the elderly man, he looked at Crystal. "Why'd you choose that name? Harriet Forsyth?"

"What? I was supposed to sign in as Virginia Wolff?" She paused, shrugging. "It was, uh, it was the first name that popped into my head."

"Harriet real or fictitious?"

"Real, for a short time anyway. She was George's granddaughter. I went to school with her and . . . Well, Harriet was nice to me—you know, the girl whose parents ditched her?" She glanced up at him. "She, uh, she died of tick fever in the fourth grade. Anyone died of something like a bug bite made an impression on country kids."

No matter how short the life, he thought, everyone had a story to tell. "And you figured no one would remember her?"

"Doubtful. Besides, my face would've been familiar to that receptionist, so it made sense to use a name she'd recognize. You know, like a distant relative. Harriet's about as distant as you can get. If anyone does bother to check, they'd be hard put to locate her."

"I don't know," he said grinning. "You look more like a Virginia Wolff to me."

"*Thanks,*" she snorted. "Just because I live on the frickin' moon doesn't mean I don't read. I know Wolff had gender issues." She looked at him quickly. "I don't, in case you're wondering."

Chitto laughed softly, thinking it had crossed his mind. Noticing she was still looking at him, he said, "What?"

"I was just wondering if you were married."

"Widowed." He glanced at her. "You?"

"Thought about it once." She glanced toward the slumped figure staring out the window. "Hey look, I need to check in with Grandma, see if she needs anything from town. This is shopping day for us, too. She'll be expecting me home by supper, and I, uh, I really don't care to be around that man over there."

"I understand." Turning thoughtful again, he said, "I need to hole up somewhere and go through Stovall's files. That motel there on the curve pet-friendly?"

She nodded. "Hunters and fisherman put up there because it's on the road to the wilderness. Some of them bring dogs. Pick me up outside." She walked away, cell phone in hand, scanning the room for a quiet spot.

Chitto approached the thin, balding man, wondering how to break through thirty-five years of cobwebs. He sat down near Forsyth, who was staring through rain-streaked windows at blue hazed mountains.

"How you doing, George?"

Chitto listened to the clink of pottery, watched a flock of birds queue up on a utility line, glanced at his watch. As minutes ticked off and Forsyth remained mum, he decided a frontal attack was needed.

"What'd you do with Leona Mann's head, George?" He swiveled his chair to better see the man's face.

Forsyth turned slowly, frowning. "You with that church?"

"No sir."

The frown deepened. "I know you?"

"We never met before today."

"What'd'ya want?"

Chitto leaned forward, talking low. "I want to know what happened to Leona Mann. You remember Leona, that girl that was murdered? You prepared her body for burial. A closed casket because she was shot in the head . . . and beheaded."

Eyes sunken into a face shriveled as a dried apple, Forsyth resumed staring out the window.

Shock treatment not working, Chitto leaned back in his chair, wondering where to go next. Feeling the need for a nicotine fix, he pulled a stick of Doublemint from his pocket and folded it into his mouth. The motion did not go unobserved. Over the years, Chitto had learned that people who worked with dead bodies knew how to mask the smell of death. Vick's or toothpaste under the nose. Saline nose spray. Chewing gum. Not breaking the silence, he held the pack out to the old man.

Forsyth reached for the pack, then shook his head. "Sticks to my dentures."

Alzheimer's, my ass, Chitto thought. Forsyth's been hiding out in a fake mist all these years. The old faker's physical health might be gone and his mental health weakening, but he was still aware enough to know he was a target in someone's sights.

He pulled his chair closer. "Why didn't you put Leona in that pretty dress, George?"

Silence.

"Her mother really wanted her buried in that dress."

The old man rubbed a hand freckled with age spots across a face equally as spotted.

"Her daddy, too."

Forsyth's breathing grew shallow.

"That wasn't your style, George. That pretty pink dress would've been a lot nicer than the bloody clothes you left her in."

"Wasn't me . . ."

"What?" Chitto leaned closer, Forsyth's voice so weak, it was barely audible. "So it was Bud stuffed her dress in the casket?"

"No."

"No?" He paused, blinking. "Well, if it wasn't you and it wasn't Bud, who the hell was it?"

Forsyth struggled to his feet, legs trembling. "Nurse," he mumbled. "Nurse . . ."

Watching Forsyth's trousers darken with urine, Chitto bellowed, *"Nurse."*

A nurse's aide hurried toward them, pushing a wheelchair.

"I'm sorry, George," he whispered, helping the old man into the chair.

"I didn't cut off Leona's head," Forsyth whispered in his ear. "After he was done . . ." He sucked air in and let it out. "Such a pretty girl. Just couldn't let anyone see her like that."

Chitto froze for a second, then quickly pulled a business card from his wallet. Considering the circumstances, he crossed through his office phone number and wrote in his cell number.

"Call me at this number when you can, George. We need to talk." He inserted the card in Forsyth's pocket, patting it to emphasize where it was, then turned him over to the waiting aide.

Well, hell, he thought, listening to the wheelchair's wheels rotate across the tile floor. We've got a live one.

CHAPTER NINE

Pulling into an almost empty parking lot at the motel, Chitto thought he'd have his pick of rooms. It didn't work out that way. The motel on Highway 271 did cater to hunters, but though antlerless deer season had ended in December and turkey didn't begin until April, few rooms were available. Out-of-towners looking for a real-estate bargain had reserved the rest. Taking the last ground-floor room at the back, Chitto hauled his duffle and shotgun inside, along with Boycott's food and Chuck Stovall's accordion-pleated file.

The file the first order of business, he set it on the king-size bed and stripped down to his undershirt, jeans, and stocking feet. Stovall had a right to be protective of the file. It was a hot potato. Its contents told the story of two cold-case murders, maybe three, and clues on how to solve them. Chitto's goal was to finish looking at the contents that night and return it to Stovall the next morning.

I have the key in my hand, he thought, flipping open the cover. Just need to find the lock.

After an hour, he paused to assess his progress. Stovall had summarized things well. A flawed investigation, from beginning to end. The sheer number of suspects muddied the water. Not calling in a medical examiner on a murder case was unorthodox. Not involving the FBI on a double homicide, out-and-out subversive. The sudden deaths of the two witnesses, too coincidental. The omission of a third witness's name, too convenient. The disappearance of the case files, a deliberate obstruction of justice.

Initial impression? A pattern was emerging. Strong-arm tactics made sure there were no leads to pursue. Dismemberment of the bodies spoke to a sociopathic personality. Deliberately ignoring jurisdictional protocol spoke to someone with the mentality of a Genghis Khan.

I am the flail of God, he thought, recalling one of Khan's rules. *Had you not created great sins, God would not have sent a punishment like me upon you.*

What, he wondered, had two people done that was so heinous it marked them for death?

Back stiff and aching, he rose, slipped into his jacket, and put Boycott on his leash. Locking the room, he walked the dog toward the grassy field behind the motel. The moon was flirtatious, showing its face sporadically from behind wind-driven clouds. Hit-and-miss rows of pines, visible along a distant fence line, cast shadows that wriggled like snakes in the grass. A high keening from the pines, sounding like a lone wolf in search of its pack, caused the skin on the back of his neck to crawl.

Might as well paint a bull's eye on my back, he thought, remembering the number of guns with scopes he'd seen around town.

"Boycott, *heel.*" Hustling back to the motel, he made a stop at the soft drink dispenser before returning to his room.

Pulling up the folder again, he began looking for a spark he could fan to flames. An hour later, he put the last file back into the folder and looked over his notes. Nicknamed the Hottie of Antlers, Leona Mann had a reputation for loving and leaving the boys. Those she had dumped would probably include half the male occupants of the county. Billy Robb Niles began working as a lineman in the area four or five years before and, contrary to men his age with a healthy libido, apparently liked the remoteness of the work. He and Leona dated a couple of years before they were killed, the last year seriously according to family and friends. The only other thing of interest dealt with two unnamed railroaders: the one who assisted the sheriff with the body and another who helped break up a fight at the old tavern between Niles and another man. Neither of the two railroaders' names was known. As for Walter Folsom, there was no mention.

Chitto jotted down a few questions on a yellow legal pad. Was there a dumped boyfriend who'd held a grudge? Why had a farm boy from Iowa retreated to the backwoods of Oklahoma? What was Walter Folsom's connection to the pair? Was there something or someone at the scene of the crime that could've connected the dots?

Assessment? Someone needed to speak from the grave.

Pitching the legal pad aside, Chitto pulled out a business card from his wallet and punched a number into his cell phone. Remembering it was a Saturday night, he hoped to reach a live person instead of answering machine. He was relieved to hear the voice on the other end growl, "If this is a telemarketer, I'm gonna report you to the FCC."

"It's Chitto, Jasmine. Need to take you up on your offer to check on a couple of things."

"Let me get a pencil." A minute later, she said, "Shoot, Luke, or give up the gun."

Chitto grinned. She was watching old western movies. Quickly, he read off the names of Edgar Guthrie and Deputy Willard Price.

"What'd they do?" she asked.

"Died prematurely. See if you can find out when and how."

"Death certificates would have all that. Call you tomorrow."

"Hold up, Jasmine. See what you can find on Crystal Folsom's mother, too."

"Crystal . . . She was the younger of those two women that came in."

"That's right."

A pause came on the line, then, "I need her mama's name, Sam."

"Oh. Well, see, I don't know that."

"Crystal's birth certificate's probably the best way to go then."

"Yeah," he said, impressed with the way Jasmine's mind worked.

"Mama die prematurely, too?"

Sighing deeply, he said, "She did for someone."

Another pause. "You sleeping in the moonlight?"

He laughed. "Don't worry. I've got a roof over my head."

"Call you tomorrow."

Chitto heard a *click* in his ear that said the conversation over.

Listening to his stomach growl, Chitto picked up the house phone and called the desk. A couple of minutes later, he was ordering a pepperoni-sausage pizza from a local cafe. Picking up the TV remote, he flipped through channels and settled on a reality show set in the Alaska wilderness. In a half hour, he could settle in for the evening. Having gathered as much as he could from Stovall's files, he felt both tired and satisfied. And he had a witness. George Forsyth would tell all on a witness stand, and he was safely tucked away in the nursing home. Most importantly, he'd stayed below John Skrabo's radar.

Thirty minutes to kill proved long enough for Chitto to grow nervous about the accordion file he'd sworn to protect. Returning it to its black plastic bag only made it more obvious. He wondered if his truck would provide a better or worse place to conceal it and decided on worse. He needed a safe deposit box. Turning in a slow circle, his eyes came to rest on a return-air vent. His pocketknife serving as a screwdriver, he soon had a safe at the ready. As added precaution, he placed Peony Folsom's manila folder inside the vent and replaced the outer cover. That left only the envelope from Human Resources that contained files on the three candidates he needed to bone up on. Pulling them out, he proceeded to spill his soft drink on the top file.

"Damn," he mumbled, wiping off the cola with a towel he grabbed in the bathroom. Throwing the files on the foot of the bed, he noticed the stain on the top folder looked like an animal. A howling wolf.

"Damn," he mumbled again. He was so hungry, he was getting delusional. Laying down on the bed to wait for the pizza, he thought about the visit with George Forsyth and the man's last words: "After he was done . . ."

Who was the *he* referenced? What was it he had been done with?

Final assessment? There could be only one reason George Forsyth was still in hiding. The murderer was still out there. And hunting.

∞

Chitto pulled out of a deep sleep, listening to what sounded like bones being ground up in a garbage disposal. Stomach juices, he decided, wondering if a spicy, late night pizza was taking its toll, if a reality show portraying bloody carcasses being skinned and quartered had warped his senses. As the sound grew louder, he recognized it as a dog doing some serious growling. Throwing back the sheet, he reached for his Glock and set his feet on the floor.

The door to the motel room was the patio type, hung with vertical blinds to provide privacy. Moonlight coming through the slats created stripes across the carpet that looked like bars on a cell. In the castoff light, he could see Boycott's rump sticking from between the slats. He walked quietly toward the door.

Parting the blinds, he looked into the darkness. In tandem, he heard a sharp sound, followed with hissing, and watched the front of his truck begin to list.

"What the . . ." As Chitto threw open the door, Boycott rushed past him, knocking him to the ground. Struggling to his feet, he watched a lone figure rounding the corner of the building. Another dark figure, running low to the ground, was right behind. Boycott.

"Stop," he yelled at the person rounding the corner. Aiming his pistol overhead, he let loose three rounds.

Room lights flooded the parking area. People in gowns and pajamas rushed outside. From somewhere, a dog yelped. Swearing under his breath, he whistled for Boycott.

The dog returned from around the side of the building, limping. At the same time, he heard a car engine start up. Looking toward Highway 271, he watched to see if the car went north, the only direction he had a view of. It didn't. As he knelt to examine Boycott, a white-haired man came around the corner of the building, shotgun in hand. Chitto recognized him as the manager.

"I heard shootin'—who's doin' the shootin'," the man yelled.

Those in gowns and pajamas pointed at Chitto. The manager rushed toward him, shotgun leveled.

"I'm a cop," he said, reaching for his ID. Too late, he realized he was wearing a tee shirt and briefs.

"Hands over your head," the man ordered. "I called it in a'ready. Sheriff's on his way."

At that moment, a beet-red pickup rounded the building and screeched to a stop.

"Well, hell . . ." Chitto mumbled and simultaneously heard a voice in his ear.

The best laid schemes o' mice an' men, Robert Burns whispered.

∞

92

"I'm not going in like this," Chitto said. He stood in his underwear outside his motel room, his right hand holding a tight grip on Boycott's collar, his left serving as a fig leaf in front of his genitals. Squatting at Chitto's side, Boycott sounded like he was gargling rocks.

The set of John Skrabo's face competed with the coldness of the night. The sheriff stiff-armed a large revolver, aiming it at Chitto's chest. The night manager and other motel guests stood in a semicircle, watching.

"You'll go in buck naked, I say so," Skrabo said, tucking Chitto's Glock into the back of his belt.

"I like the sounds of that," a woman in a floral-print kimono said. She adjusted her position to better see Chitto's hindquarters.

"Shuddup, Rene." A man in a Bass Pro Shop cap and striped pajamas turned to Skrabo. "What're you arresting him for? Looks to me like he's the victim here."

"Indecent exposure to begin with . . ."

"Oh, honey," the woman named Rene crooned. "You've gotta get out more."

" . . . and discharging a firearm in a public place."

Rene's husband lifted shaggy eyebrows. "Hell, I'd a shot at the moon, too, somebody deliberately ruined one of my tires."

"Nobody did anything," Skrabo snapped. "Plenty of places he could've picked up a nail. Railroaders and loggers left plenty behind."

"And his dog?" a plump woman in a fleece robe countered. "We heard that dog yelp, didn't we Hal?"

"Yup," Hal said. He was dressed in thermal underwear and a fishing vest, crappie and bass lures hanging off it like Christmas ornaments. Walking to Chitto's truck, he ran a hand over the tire.

"Likely a stone bruise," Skrabo said, giving a quick glance to Boycott. "This guy's been training that dog up country. That's prob'ly where he picked up the nail."

"Wasn't a nail," Hal said. "Puncture in the sidewall."

Striped Pajamas was pacing now. "Look at his tire, man. It's clear as the nose on your face that someone punched it with an ice pick." He stopped pacing to point a finger in Skrabo's face. "It's also clear you're bound and determined to haul his ass to jail. Least you can do is let the man get dressed."

"I vote for buck naked," Woman in Kimono said.

"Shuddup, Rene." Striped Pajamas began pacing again. "If this is the way you do things in this country, we'll just get dressed and leave, too—permanently."

"Us, too," Fleece Robe chimed in. Hooking an arm through Thermal Underwear's, she said, "Right, Hal?"

"Yup," he said.

Skrabo's lips tightened. "Get dressed," he snapped, waving his revolver toward Chitto.

Hurrying inside, Chitto called Crystal and explained the situation.

He's hauling you to jail?" Even with bad cell phone reception, her disbelief rang clear. "For what?"

"Discharging a firearm in a public place for beginners, indecent exposure for another." Phone tucked to his ear, he stepped into his jeans and pulled on a shirt. From the door, he could see Skrabo attempting to disburse the crowd in the parking lot.

Crystal said, "Indecent exposure?"

"I'll explain later. Right now, just listen." He told Crystal to call the cousins to take care of his flat tire and remove the objects hidden in his motel room's return-air vent. "Have them hold on to them for me. Right now, you just need to get your butt down to the county jail."

Seeing Skrabo walk toward his doorway, Chitto hung up and put Boycott in a down position in front of the return-air vent. Leaning his shotgun against the bed, he sat down and began lacing up his boots. As the sheriff pushed through the doorway, gun still in his hands, Boycott resumed his gurgling growl.

"I don't think that dog likes you much," Chitto said. "Wonder why that is?"

"That dog's a menace." Skrabo took a step toward Boycott.

"Don't bother my dog, John." In a heartbeat, Chitto had the shotgun leveled.

Skrabo stopped, eyes blinking. Any man in this country knew that doing harm to a man's dog was a line you didn't cross.

"Look, no need to get kinetic, man," Chitto said, recalling Dan Blackfox's ultimatum about the straight and narrow. "I handed over my service piece and I'm going in peacefully. My dog can stay here until I get back to pick him up." He pointed his chin toward the cell phone on the bed. "My people know what's going on. I called them while you were placating those outsiders." Leaning the shotgun against the bed again, he raised his hands, palms up. "No harm, no foul."

Skrabo glanced toward the gun, his eyes indicating he was evaluating his choices. In the midst of his assessment, he noticed the envelope holding personnel files on the foot of Chitto's bed.

"What the—" Holstering his gun, he scooped up the files. "You get these from Stovall?"

Damn, Chitto thought. He thinks he's got his hooks on Chuck's files . . .

Chitto's mind went into overdrive. "Those are confidential," he said. "You've no right to confiscate them."

"I'll confiscate anything I want . . ." Skrabo hesitated, eyes blinking. Pulling Chitto's gun from his belt, he handed it over. "I'm gonna do you the biggest favor of your life, boy. But I want you outta my county and don't wanna see your face in it again. Understood?"

"Understood. Believe me, those files aren't worth dying for. Soon as I get my truck running, I'm gone."

Giving a nod, Skrabo was out the door.

Grinning, Chitto locked the door and called Crystal's number. "Where are you?

"Almost to town."

"Good," he said. "Forget county lockup. Pick me up at the motel and put it in high gear."

∞

"Wish I could've been there to see those rich dudes put old John in his place." Crystal sat on the side of the bed, watching as Chitto pulled files from the air vent. "He's nobody's fool. Incidents like that could squelch growth in this country, and that would mean less money in the county coffers."

"I don't think that was it." Chitto thought of the patterns he'd been observing. Pushmataha County sheriffs didn't want other jurisdictions—federal, state, city, or Indian—sticking their nose in their business. "I think it had more to do with not wanting the Choctaw Nation on his back."

"You called your office? Thought you didn't want anyone knowing you were here."

"I don't," he said, grinning. "It was a bluff."

She laughed, then turned sober. "What now? You, uh, you heading back to Durant?"

Stuffing Peony's folder into the black plastic bag with Chuck Stovall's file, he slung it and his duffle over his shoulder. "Think the coffee on at Stovall's place?" he asked.

"So you're not running out on me?"

"Hell, no. Things are just getting interesting. First, we need to swap rides with the cousins." His shotgun in his free hand, he looked around before stepping outside. "C'mon. Coast is clear."

She hurried after him. "Where we going?"

"Undercover."

She grinned. Outside, she introduced him to two dark-haired, dark-eyed cousins named Andy and Bob who'd been busy putting the spare tire on his truck.

"Make it fast, boys," he said. "I've got a feeling the sheriff will be back this way real quick."

"This spare's pretty slick," the cousin called Andy said.

"I know," Chitto said. "I just had these others put on a couple months ago. Kept the best of the old ones as a spare. It'll have to do for now."

Together, they came to an agreement on a place the other side of the county line to meet later for a vehicle exchange. Chitto breathed a sigh of relief watching his and Crystal's vehicles disappear down a rutted track that led toward the pine-covered fencerow.

"You drive." He loaded Boycott and his belongings into the cousins' battered blue Ford SUV. "Take a back way to Stovall's place. I want to be long gone before Skrabo starts looking for me."

CHAPTER TEN

After returning the accordion-pleated file to Chuck Stovall, Chitto and Crystal left for the backcountry to interview former suspects in the Mann-Niles murder. While at the café, Crystal called ahead to make sure Riley Campbell and Harry Bradshaw were available for a house call. Since Quince Winters didn't have a phone, they'd have to take a chance on catching him at home.

Campbell and Bradshaw were eager for a visit. Since the article in the newspaper had broken, complete with a picture of the reconstructed skull found in Leona's coffin, interest in the case had peaked again. Locals had not forgotten the two were once among those questioned, and once a suspect, always a suspect. Especially when the murderer was still at large.

The Campbell spread was huge and cowhands plentiful and cautious. Those on horseback carried rifles in saddle scabbards. Those in pickups hauled them in a gun rack behind the seat. They found Riley Campbell at one of the barns supervising a son called Junior, who was aiding a cow in labor. The water sac, a collapsed yellow sphere, lay on the ground near the cow's tail.

"That's not good." Chitto crouched next to the cow, looking at two small feet protruding from the birth canal, pointed up. A breech birth. "Vet on the way?"

"Tried reaching him." Riley Campbell stood to one side, leaning on his cane. "He's not at his place and cell phone wasn't working. Happens a lot out here."

"How long's she been down?"

"Couple hours. Junior could use a hand getting her into the headgate. She's tuckered out. You up to lending a hand?"

"You bet." Chitto stripped his jacket off and handed it to Crystal. He was surprised to see her peeling out of her own.

"I'll pull from the head," she said, wrapping her arms around the cow's neck. "Junior, you pull on her tail. And Sam, when she gets her feet under her, lift for all your worth."

Chitto shouldered up close to the cow's body as Junior Campbell applied leverage to the rear.

"Up we go, girl," Chitto said, helping the cow get her feet on the ground. Slowly, the cow struggled upright. Junior Campbell quickly restrained her in a head gate and proceeded to a spigot, where he washed down both arms with antiseptic soap. "Need to reposition those feet," he said over his shoulder. "Could use some help keeping her straight."

Chitto and Crystal pushed hard against the cow's hips as the young rancher wrapped a calving chain around the calf's two tiny hooves. Before long, the calf slipped out.

"Enough to make you believe in God, idn't it?" Riley Campbell wiped mucous from the calves nose with a towel. "Nothing more beautiful than a newborn baby." Turning the calf over to its mother, he nodded his head toward the ranch house. "I'm in a celebratory mood. Wash up and join me."

On the way to the house, Chitto looked at Crystal.

"What?" she said, brushing dirt and manure off her jeans.

"You're a tough lady, and that's a compliment."

"Oh," she said, the hint of a smile showing.

Campbell ushered them into the house with a grin as crooked as his back. "Heard you got busted last night," he said to Chitto.

Chitto returned the grin. "Got off with a warning. Old John's not much of a poker player. Fell for a bluff."

"Well, I'm a damn good poker player. Knew that real-estate story was a pile of crap from the get-go. That cousin bit, too."

"What gave me away?"

"You have the look of a lawman."

"How's that?"

"Beady eyes."

Chitto laughed. "Just for the record, I'm off duty."

"And he really is a cousin," Crystal said, removing her coat at the front door. "Sorta."

They settled into overstuffed leather chairs before a fireplace that took up one end of the front room. A tray of hand-thrown coffee mugs sat on a large mahogany coffee table, along with a bottle of Jesse James bourbon whiskey and a Colt .45 single action. From the sheen on the gun, Chitto figured it was cleaned daily and kept loaded.

Campbell excused himself to get refreshments and returned carrying a coffee pot still perking in one hand, his cane in the other.

"Wife put this to brewing before she left," he said, filling three mugs. "Should be just about thick enough. Didn't have a spare hand to carry the milk carton, so you'll drink it black."

They took the mugs he offered, without complaint.

"What do you remember about the murders?" Chitto asked, taking a sip of boiled coffee that would rival Hattie George's.

"Only what I read in the papers." Campbell eased into a power-lift recliner. "Never could figure out why I was a suspect. Didn't really know either one of them kids. Hell,

101

fella was a stranger, don't know as I ever set eyes on him. And the girl . . ." He paused, eyes softening. "Well, she *was* a pretty little thing, hard to overlook. But good Lord, she could've been my daughter." He stuck a finger in Chitto's face. "Swear to God, even if I could've and she was willing, I wouldn't have." He shook his head, teeth clamped. "Burned the hell outta me, Bud King would even suggest such a thing. Hell, I fought for my country, and what was King doin'? Hiding behind a tin star."

Chitto took note of the healthy dose of bourbon the old rancher poured into his cup. "When's the last time you remember seeing Leona?" he asked.

Campbell thought a minute. "Had to be at the drugstore where she worked. Picked up a prescription every Saturday. Still do. I suffer from an old war injury, you see." He glanced out the window, absorbing a sky blue as a robin's egg and mountains purple as a plum, then looked at Chitto again. "I'm not your man."

"I don't doubt it. You see any other men hanging out at the drugstore those times you were there? As pretty as she was, I bet Leona could've had her pick of the county."

Campbell chuckled. "That she did, but I didn't take notice of those things. Had my hands full running a cattle ranch and healing, as best I could. 'Fraid I can't help you out."

"Figured as much, just wanted to hear it from you." Chitto pulled a business card from his wallet and wrote in his cell number. "Call me if you're struck with any sudden insights."

Pocketing the card, Campbell pushed the button on the power-lift recliner. Shaking Chitto's hand at the front door, he said, "To my thinking, being a suspect entitles an innocent man. Appreciate it if you'd let me know the name of the sorry bastard that killed those kids, you find out."

"One way or the other, I'll get word to you." Noting scraggy eyebrows raised in skepticism, he said, "I'm known to be a man of my word, Riley."

∞

Harry Bradshaw's ranch was a half hour drive from Campbell's. The man's home place was somewhat less modest than his neighbor's, but his cautionary nature on an equal par. Walking ranch hands carried guns on their hips, those riding, carbines. As for Bradshaw, he kept a sawed-off shotgun leaning next to the front door. Working to make a living in an unforgiving land seemed to level a man's perspective. Those considered worthy were let live. Those considered provisional better not trespass.

"We, uh, we smell like the barnyard," Crystal said at the front door. She briefed him on the difficult birth at Riley Campbell's place.

"Calf make it?"

"It did."

"Mama okay?"

"She's good, too."

"Well, then, it's a good day, idn't it?" He pointed to rows of bushes bordering the ranch house. "My wife Millie was a city girl, if you can call Broken Bow a city. After we married, she planted lilacs clear around the house 'cause some fool told her it would cover the smell of cow manure." He paused, grinning around a pipe stem. "Those purple flowers do smell good in the spring. Problem is, cow shit's a year-round problem."

"How does she deal with it when the lilacs aren't blooming?" Chitto asked.

Bradshaw made a *phish* sound. "Doesn't even notice it now. Over time, a thing grows on you." He pointed at two chairs, settled himself in a third. "Rest a spell, ask those questions you had of me."

"Anything you've got would help."

103

"Was hoping you had something to share with me." Bradshaw adjusted the tube that ran from his nose to an oxygen bottle on wheels. "That whole business was a joke, just not the kind that's funny. Man who'd do that kinda thing had to be crazy. Give my right arm to know who the bastard was . . ." He shook his head, letting his words fade.

They sat in front of a pellet-burning stove glowing red hot, a pot of cinnamon-flavored apple cider steaming on top, compliments of Millie. Bradshaw explained that she was in the kitchen fixing Sunday dinner.

"How did you know Leona?" Chitto asked, sampling the cider.

"Didn't. Might've bumped into her somewhere, but I have no memories of the girl. Millie knew her mother from church functions. She's big into that." He gave Chitto a level-eyed look. "Never understood trying to put a roof over the Almighty."

Chitto nodded, pausing over another sip of cider. "And Billy Robb Niles?"

"Same song, second verse. Never laid eyes on the man. Stockyards and the sale barn were the only places I went when I set foot off the ranch. Except Saturdays when I was driving Millie 'round town. The kids picked her up for church on Sundays." He looked at Crystal. "Women didn't do much driving back then. Nowadays, it's the other way around."

Crystal nodded. "Grandma didn't learn to drive until my father went into the Navy. No choice, I guess."

"Saw your dad now and then. Picking up trash there on the road. Offered to give him a ride once when it was colder than a witch's tit, but he declined. Said he was following doctor's orders."

"Doctor's orders?" Chitto leaned forward, noticing Crystal edge up, too.

104

"That's what he said." Bradshaw made another adjustment to his oxygen tube. "Polite a man as you'd ever meet, soft-spoken, too. But to be seein' a doctor, he had to be in some kind of pain. Hell, that's the only time I suffer myself to go to a sawbones."

"Ever see him with someone else? Man? Woman?"

Bradshaw scratched a place under his ear. "Only thing I ever saw him with was that hound. I remember because it was gray in the muzzle and stiff in the legs. Kind've identified with it."

"You folks ready for dinner?"

Chitto turned toward a doorway where a short, gray-haired woman in faded jeans, long-sleeve flannel shirt, and ruffled apron stood. Millie Bradshaw. Chitto glanced at his watch. Twelve o'clock high. He glanced at Crystal.

She turned to Millie "Thanks, but we have another stop to make."

"Might can fill you in on some things I heard at the church." A dimpled smile appeared.

"Hell, I could eat." Chitto motioned Crystal toward the dining room.

"You, uh, you mentioned church talk?" Chitto spoke between spoonfuls. Millie set a fine table and kept the food coming. "You hear anything about Leona?"

"Preacher talks against gossiping," she said, cheeks dimpling. "He's a big city boy, doesn't understand out here we call it catching up." Gathering dinner plates, she nodded toward the kitchen door. "Just let me get dessert goin'."

She returned with a carton of ice cream and pan of cobbler. Spooning dessert into bowls, she said, "Leona dumped some guy before she started dating that new man that came to town."

Chitto looked at her quickly. "What was the name of the man she dumped?"

"Didn't call his name, but Leona told her mother he worked for the railroad. He had any sense, he would've figured out Leona wasn't serious about him."

"Why you say that?" Crystal said, finishing off her bowl of cobbler and ice cream.

"Because she never brought him to church. Around here, especially back then, that was a woman's way of introducing her intended."

Chitto leaned forward, elbows resting on the table. "Are you saying she brought Billy Robb Niles to church?"

"Sure did. I was there the day he was saved—and the day he was baptized. We believe in full emersion, you know. Washes away all your sins. He seemed at peace after he was baptized, like he'd laid down a heavy burden." She looked at him. "That's the way it is when you let go earthly encumbrances."

Chitto's thinking went back to the night he let Mary's spirit go. "That's what I hear," he said, folding his napkin.

Dragging his oxygen bottle behind, Bradshaw escorted them to the door. For the third time that day, Chitto corrected the phone number on one of his business cards. For the third time that day, it went into a shirt pocket. Deposits he hoped would bring returns.

"A man deserves to have his name cleared while he's alive to hear it told." Bradshaw talked around the pipe stem in his mouth. "You find out who killed those people, I'd appreciate knowing."

"One way or the other, I'll get word to you."

No matter whether alive or dead, an innocent man needed his name cleared.

∞

"So, what do you think?" Crystal asked. The car fishtailed down a narrow road leading into the Kiamichi foothills.

106

Chitto reached for the grab handle above the door. "I think the county overlooked putting gravel on this stretch of road."

"Seems the money runs out right here every year." She glanced at him. "We didn't get any answers about my dad, just more questions."

"No, but the bit about Niles and Mann was interesting. Just have to figure out what it means in the scheme of things."

She slipped and slid another mile, knuckles white on the steering wheel. "In case you haven't noticed, we're running out of people. If Quince can't tell us something, Grandma's your last best hope. Sooner or later, you're gonna have to talk to her."

"You've got a point. How'd you get to know this guy?"

"Quince? Everybody knows him. He's been around forever. You know, the local kook."

"Kook," he repeated. "Kind've like your dad?"

Her jaws popped open, then snapped shut. "Anyone ever punched you just for the hell of it?"

He grinned. "Seriously, how'd you get to know him?"

"I don't know, he was just there." She paused, eyebrows knitting together. "He was always nice to me, knew my name even before I knew who he was." She smiled to herself. "He'd devour the old magazines. You know, the ones that were outdated?"

"Sounds like he was out of touch with things, but not by choice."

She shrugged. "I started bringing him new magazines every week. *Times* and *Newsweek*, he liked those best. This job makes it easy to drop off things when I'm up his way." She hesitated, glancing at him. "Sometimes I pretended he was my dad. Stupid, huh?"

Chitto's cell phone prevented him from answering. Glancing at the display, he said, "I need to get this."

She nodded, putting her concentration on the road.

Holding the phone close to his ear, he said, "What've you got, Scout?"

"Scout?" Jasmine said. "Oh. Someone with you?"

"Yes, indeed."

"All right then, here it is in a nutshell. Both those men died within a week of each other. The old one named Guthrie was found at home. Aneurism's listed as cause of death. Dropped dead on the spot, according to the obit. The cop was found behind the wheel of his car, shot in the head. Tire marks on the highway indicated whoever it was got away clean."

"So," he sighed. "Another FBI cold-case file."

"Just cold. From what I can tell, no other agency was called in."

Patterns, whispered the voice in his head.

"Happen in the county's jurisdiction?" The sound of paper rustling filled the pause on the line.

"Push County Sheriff handled the investigation."

"Medical examiner mentioned?"

"Man named Forsyth." A pause. "Glenda Folsom's shown as the mother on Crystal's birth certificate. Walter Folsom as the father. Funny thing is, the hospital noted the baby's name as Baby Girl. The name was written in later."

"Find an address on her?"

"Found nothing at all."

Chitto's forehead wrinkled. "What do you mean, nothing?"

"As in not hide nor hair. Unless she changed her name or went into a witness protection program, Gloria Folsom dropped off the face of the earth. Got a picture of her, the one on her driver's license. I enlarged it so you could see it better. Want me to fax it to you?"

Chitto paused. "No, lock everything up in your desk and keep it for me. I'm heading back this afternoon."

A *click* in his ear indicated the scout was headed back to her teepee.

"What was that all about?" Crystal asked.

"Just filling in some gaps." He glanced at his watch. "How far to Winters' place?"

"See that smoke up there?"

He looked to where a white spiral coiling skyward indicated a fire was burning in another living room.

"One more thing . . ." She gave him a quick glance. "For his own good, it's best to leave Boycott in the car. Quince lives a . . . subsistence lifestyle."

"A survivalist," he said, doing a quick translation.

"Or a doomsday freak."

∞

Crystal pulled into a dirt track leading up a heavily wooded hillside and stopped at a gate.

Chitto reached for the door handle. "I'll see if it's locked."

"*No.*" She grabbed his arm. "You don't know where to step. Trust me, he knows we're here."

Hearing the whine of an engine, Chitto saw an ATV heading their way, three dogs racing alongside. Taking Boycott by the collar, he hooked him onto his leash and lashed it to one of backseat grab handles. "Stay," he ordered, forcing the excited dog into a sitting position.

"That's Lolo, Liz, and Sophia," she said, nodding at three speckled hounds.

"You even know the dogs' names?"

"Never change. One dies, he replaces it with another and gives it the same name." She looked at him. "I told you he was a kook."

A lean, grizzled man stopped in front of them. Camouflage clothes top to bottom. Dark eyes glinting like black marbles beneath a frayed cap with earflaps. A 30.06 Springfield propped up in the floorboard.

109

Crystal rolled her window down partway. "This is a cousin, Quince," she called out. "He's helping me find out what happened to Leona Mann and Billy Robb Niles. Did you see the paper?"

A short pause. "Don't know anything more than I did then."

Chitto rolled his window down a crack. Immediately, the dog pack was at it, trying to get at Boycott in the back seat. "Slightest thing could make a difference," he called over the yelping pack. "Be the tipping point."

Winters rubbed his mouth.

Chitto rolled his window down a little further. "Might even eliminate some unnecessary worries, help a man sleep easier at night."

Winters let the thought resonate a minute, then climbed off his ATV. "Follow me," he said. "Don't drive where I don't. Don't step where I don't."

Chitto got a better look at Winters as the man closed and locked the gate behind them. Muscles stringy as jerky. Skin tanned brown as dirt. Eyes, sky blue and probing. "He always lived this way?" he asked Crystal.

"I wouldn't remember, of course, but the short answer is no. Rumor has it he used to be a hell-raiser."

"Pretty wild then." More a comment than a question.

"So I'm told. Seems all those railroaders liked to whoop it up, drink and party hearty."

"He was a railroader?" He glanced at the man on the ATV again. "He at the old tavern that night Billy Robb and Leona were there?"

She turned slowly, watching Winters climb back on the ATV, and murmured, "I don't know . . ."

Chitto felt his back muscles tense.

∞

Smoke curled out the chimney of the small log cabin in the clearing. Wild raspberry brambles grew thick under the windows. A Ford Super Duty was parked out front, mud up to its hubcaps. A long stack of firewood fenced off one side of the clearing, an outhouse occupied another, and a pole shed outfitted with traps and snares sat on the last side. Chitto recognized the pelts of black bear, badger, and cougar tacked to its walls. Doghouses and tie-downs filled spaces in between.

Chitto got an uncomfortable feeling as he looked around the grounds, envisioning booby-trap devices he'd heard about but never seen—Punji stake pits, snare traps—and wished Frank Tubbe had come along for the ride. He suspected the Chickasaw tribal policeman would be an expert when it came to anti-intruder devices.

He looked at Crystal. "Where'd Quince serve?"

"Serve?"

"He do time in Nam?"

She hunched her shoulders. "Never talked about it."

"Your dad would be about the same age. Where'd he do his duty?"

She opened her car door and slid to the ground. "He was in the Navy, remember? I had to guess, I'd say on a boat."

He gave his head a shake. "Lots of ocean out there, Crystal." She slammed the door in his face.

Though Chitto found the outside of the cabin intriguing, the inside made his jaws drop. He expected to find an arsenal and stockpile of goods, not bookcases stuffed to overflowing. Scanning book spines, he felt tense muscles relax. Fiction. Non-fiction. Classics. Philosophy.

Picking up a well-thumbed copy of *Don Quixote*, he felt Winters' eyes on him. "Some say Cervantes was saying the belief in something is worth more than the thing itself," he said.

"Um-hmm," Winters responded, looking thoughtful. "Others say it was living in a reality of our own making is better than a life of despair. How you like your coffee?"

"Hot." Rubbing his hands together, Chitto noticed ice rimmed the cabin's windows.

"Same for me," Crystal said, who was warming her hands at a potbelly stove.

They settled onto benches at a hand-hewn pine table, steaming mugs in front of them. "What's on your mind," Winters asked.

Crystal recited their reasons for visiting former suspects in the Niles-Mann murder. "But we're really looking for something about my dad. Grandma thinks that artist drawing in the paper is him."

Winters rubbed fingers lightly across his forehead, his eyes trained on the floor.

"You know Walter?" Chitto asked, unsure how to interpret the non-verbal response.

Winters shook his head. "Saw him now and then."

Getting nowhere, Chitto decided to make the leap. "I hear you worked for the railroad, Quince."

Winters made eye contact. Speaking slowly, he said, "Was a brakeman. Some people called us switchman. Same difference." He paused, added, "That's when I'd see Folsom, while I was riding the back car."

"You saw my dad?" Crystal's eyebrows shot up. "You never mentioned that."

He shrugged. "Didn't see the point."

"You see him there at that campground by the river?" Chitto asked.

"There, and on the hillsides from time to time."

"What was he doing?"

"Damned if I know. Not much of a view from a caboose window. Sometimes, I'd sit on the back stoop. That's when I'd spot him and that dog up in the rocks."

"Up in the rocks . . ." Chitto's eyebrows knotted. "Ever hear of anyone finding precious stones out this way?"

Winters thought a minute. "Some gold found over near Lost Mountain, but I heard nothing about gemstones." He let out a short laugh. "And if I ever did chance on something like that, I wouldn't advertise it. Hell, it'd be another California gold rush." He glanced at Crystal. "No offense, girl. I know you're just doing your job."

She brushed a hand through the air. "Believe me. It didn't put clothes on my back and food on the table, I wouldn't be doing it."

"So," Chitto pressed, "why'd you give up the railroad job? I hear the pay's pretty good."

Winters took a sip of coffee. "No future in it for a man who wanted to stay put. Head office shut down passenger service, freight trains followed suit, timber companies gave up logging this part of the country, then . . ."

Chitto waited, giving the man time to transport himself back in time thirty-plus years. Nothing forthcoming, he asked, "What do you remember about the night at the tavern? I figure you were there when the skirmish broke out." Hearing Crystal's sharp intake of air, Chitto signaled her to keep silent.

Again, Winters took his time answering. "Not as much as I wish. I was three sheets to the wind that night." He shook his head slightly. "I remember Niles stirring it up with another guy, shoving and swearing mostly. Then the guy and his girl took off and I went back to drinking. Woke up under the table the next morning, smelling like pigswill. Next thing I know, I'm a suspect in a double killing." He laughed softly. "Shit, I couldn't walk two feet without falling on my face. How the hell was I supposed to kill someone?"

Smokescreen, whispered the voice in Chitto's head.

"That man who stirred it up with Niles stay in the area or move on down the road?"

Winters looked at him, eyes slitted. "Stayed put," he said.

Chitto pulled a list of those questioned from his hip pocket. "It would help if you could point him out. I'm working on eliminating suspects."

Fitting reading glasses on his nose, Winters looked over the list and shoved it back at him. "Not there," he said, folding up his glasses. "Then, didn't expect it would be. There's people in this county believes in taking care of their own."

Chitto reinserted the list into his pocket. "Who was it that was taking care of his own?"

Another long pause. "The guy's uncle."

Uncle, Chitto repeated. Contemplating the county's primary occupations, he said, "So, this nephew was a rancher's kid?"

"No . . ." Winters let another long minute pass. "Trainman."

"Trainman?" Chitto locked eyes with Winters. "You remember his name?"

A harsh laugh. "Like I'm apt to forget that son of a bitch."

"Who?" Crystal said, eyes round and unblinking. "Do I know him?"

Winters looked at her, head shaking. "Saying the devil's name can invoke his presence. For your sake as well as mine, I won't chance it." He turned to Chitto, mouth a hard line. "I will tell you he was the sorriest excuse for a trainman I ever met and the worst kind of whoring bastard God ever made." He swiveled his head, looking at Crystal again. "Sorry for the foul language, girl."

As she shrugged off his concern, a cell phone in her pocket beeped. "The boss tracked me down," she said, looking at the digital readout. "Need to check a client file in my bag." She stopped at the front door, looking at Winters. "Those dogs leave me alone?"

"Give me a minute." Preceding her outside, Winters hooked the dogs to their tie downs. "You're safe now," he called out.

Chitto stood on the porch, noting the way Winters' observed Crystal as she walked to the car.

Spotting him, Winters sidled up next to him. "Didn't hear you come outside, Chitto. Around here, it's a good idea to let your presence be known."

"I'll remember that." Chitto nodded toward Crystal. "What's the story there?"

"Direct bastard, aren't you?" Winters grinned, then looked toward the car again. "She reminds me of her mother. Glenda's dad worked on our ranch, so I grew up with her."

Noting the flush crawling up Winters' neck, Chitto deduced the man had felt more than friendship for Glenda Folsom. "Too bad Crystal didn't get to know her." He turned suddenly, listening to the yipping of coyotes on a nearby hillside. "Peony says she hears a wolf call now and then."

"That so?" Winters looked toward the hillside, too. "No wolves around here. Hunter will sometime use its call to signal others in the party where he is."

Chitto nodded slowly. "That makes sense." He looked at Winters again. "Before I take off, Quince, maybe you can clear something up for me. Is it my imagination or do people in these parts die more often than the average?"

"Depends on your definition of imagination," Winters said. "If you're saying that's the way you perceive it . . ."

"I am."

"Some say perception is reality." Winters held out his hand. "You watch your back, Lieutenant."

"Will do." Chitto paused, releasing Winters' hand slowly. "Language is a strange thing. Can mean something to one person, something totally different to another. Need you to clarify a couple things."

"You've made your point. Speak your mind."

"What would've gotten Walter's attention there at the campground?"

"That's got me wondering, too." Winters stared at a sunset the color of a ripe pumpkin. "You mentioned gemstones. When the tracks were built, the railroad tore jake outta those hills to get dirt for that elevated roadbed. All that brush was to be removed, place would look like landmines exploded everywhere. Maybe he found a good pocket."

"Think you can pinpoint the hillside you saw him on?"

Winters glanced away, blinking. "Would be a long shot, but let me think on it. Anything comes to mind, I'll get word to you."

"Here's how to reach me." Chitto corrected the phone number on a business card and handed it to him. "One more thing." He cleared his throat, then rubbed the back of his neck. "What, uh, what's the worst kind of whoring bastard God ever made?"

Winters laughed softly. "Don't get out much, do you, kid?" He leaned in close, holding Chitto's eyes. "The kind that raids another man's henhouse. But that's only half the question you need to be asking."

"What do you mean?"

Winters paused to stare at the darkening sky. "You read parables? Bible's full of them."

"Not as a rule."

"Might be time you did. Start with the one about Nathan and David." Winters started walking toward his ATV. Over his shoulder, he said, "I'll follow you down, lock the gate behind you."

"You're frowning," Crystal said when Chitto climbed into the car. "What'd he tell you?"

"You wouldn't believe me if I told you."

"Nothing that comes out of your mouth would surprise me. Now spill it, I've got a right to know."

"Okay, if you insist." He gave her a sideways look. "He told me to read the Bible."

"You jerk." She stomped on the gas pedal, charging down a rutted road the consistency and color of freshly mixed cement. "Can't you for once be serious?"

∞

Chitto was glad to get back to his truck. Crystal's cousins had found a gas station just across the Choctaw County line and had the hole in the flat tire plugged.

"Good as new," said one of the cousins. Squatting next to the truck, he ran a hand over the tire.

"But you might look at a new tire here pretty quick," said the other.

To Crystal's offer to buy him a new tire, Chitto said he was sure the plugged tire would hold. Accepting his word and a business card with his cell number on it, she muttered a final admonition.

"I'm telling Grandma you were here and that you're coming back next week. No more motels. You'll stay with us."

"It's best if we're not seen together. But I do need to spend some quality time with your grandmother. We'll work it out."

Now, as he turned west onto Highway 271, he punched a number into his cell phone.

"I told you not to overdo it, Sam," the voice on the other end grumbled.

He grinned. Already, Jasmine had memorized his number on Call Waiting.

"This one's urgent. Need you get copies of those HR files."

Hesitation. "What happened to the ones I gave you?"

"Lost 'em."

"Child, you need a keeper." A loud sigh came from the line. "All right. Seeing your first interview's at nine tomorrow morning, I'll do what I can. Though Lord knows, I don't know what I'm gonna tell that woman in Human Resources. I swear, her face would crack, she was to smile."

"Tell her the dog ate my homework," he said.

A pause. A sigh. A *click.*

CHAPTER ELEVEN

Melting ice permeated cracks and fissures in the asphalt, leaving the Choctaw Nation parking lot dark as lead shot and smelling of oil and brake fluid. Though not as cold as the week before, Chitto's breath still misted when he exhaled. The air bitter and the light thin, he turned up the collar on his jacket. Pushing through the front door, he glanced toward the reception area where a lone woman sat, then proceeded to Jasmine Birdsong's desk.

"You're late," she said.

"Busy weekend."

The short sixty-mile drive back to Durant the night before turned into a long nightmare. The plugged tire had not held, meaning he had to jack up the truck and put the spare back on. It wasn't anything he hadn't done before, but the narrow highway shoulder and the wide-bodied truck—heavy-duty tires and four wheels on the rear axle—made the job hazardous. And since he valued his life, he had taken extra precautions. Late when he finished up, he'd called Hattie George to say he'd return Boycott the next morning.

As the miles rolled under his wheels, his thoughts flitted from one person to another. George Forsyth, a witness that could prove misconduct in the handling of the double homicide. Glenda Folsom, a new mother that abruptly abandoned a newborn baby. Billy Robb Niles, a utility lineman that had lain down some kind of heavy burden after a soul-saving baptism. Walter Folsom, a returning veteran apparently under doctor's orders.

He made it back to town in time to catch a drugstore open, where he replaced the pack of Marlboro Reds he'd given to Sonny Boy Monroe and bought a six-pack of Doublemint gum. On the final leg to his house, he drove through a fast food drive- thru and picked up two cheeseburgers with double orders of fries, temptation enough for Boycott to desert his newfound chew toy. Temporarily.

A hot shower relaxed stiff, tired muscles, but sleep would not come. Boycott rediscovered the leather chew sometime in the night and worried it noisily. Peony's manila lay on his nightstand, glowing in the moonlight as if lit from within. The edict from Sonny Boy about being Walter Folsom's Bone Picker needled his subconscious, a sore reminder of an unreasonable duty to perform. Old stories tugged at his memory. Ancient ones about bodies left on rough platforms to rot until the flesh could be stripped from bone. Mythical ones about a faceless warrior and a wolf prowling the hills hunting monsters. A story called a parable, a teaching story meant to aid him in with another mystery, yet to be revealed. Throughout the troubled night, a poem resurfaced like a refrain.

The woods are lovely, dark and deep, but I have promises to keep . . .

Now, he glanced toward the woman in a reception area. Steel gray hair done in a tight perm. Hands unconsciously smoothing her skirt. Eyes glued to him. "She the candidate I'm supposed to interview?" He glanced at the clock on the wall. "She's not due for another thirty minutes."

"Some people believe in arriving early." Raised eyebrows signaled Jasmine was in a judgmental frame of mind.

He took a breath and forged ahead. "You get a copy of those files?"

She handed him three folders, the word Confidential stamped on the front in red ink.

He opened the top folder. "So, she's Norma Jean Burns?"

"Yes, indeed."

Chitto scanned the folder, then flipped quickly through the others. "Wait . . . Where's the list of questions I'm not supposed to ask?"

Jasmine's shoulder's drooped. "You didn't say anything about that Don't Ask list."

"I just assumed . . ."

"I'm a literal person, Sam."

"Okay, then. Give me the down and dirty."

She glanced around the office, eyes slitted. "I feel the need for coffee. Walk with me to the cafeteria."

Jasmine walked slow, talked fast. "All these gals have the skills for the job. They can type, not as accurate as some others, but they get by. They can also talk on the phone all right, some to a fault."

"What's that mean—"

"Just listen. They can keep up with the filing, just need to give them time to find where they put it if you need it back."

Chitto rubbed a spot on the back of his neck. "And Norma Jean falls in that category?"

"What did I just say? *All* of these gals have the basic skills."

"What am I supposed to ask then?"

She sighed. "Job-related questions." She stopped in front of a commercial-grade coffeemaker, stacks of Styrofoam cups beside it, cartons of creamer and sweetener to one side.

"You just said they all have—"

"What is it you *want* to know, Sam?" She filled a nine-ounce cup, lightened it with hazelnut creamer, and stared at him.

"Well, things like does she know my family. My mother, in particular. Does she belong to groups that could . . . influence her?"

"Groups," she repeated, eyebrows knitting together.

"You know, the kind that can distort a person's judgment."

Her eyes widened. "You mean, like the KKK?"

A grin surfaced. "I was thinking of the Choctaw Historical Society."

"Oh. Well then . . ." She waited as he filled a twelve-ounce cup, then started back toward the office. "You ask questions *around* those you want to ask. Ask her to tell you about her work history. If she ever worked in District 13, you can bet she knows Mattie Chitto."

He gave her a sideways glance. "How well do *you* know my mother?"

"Not well. I avoid her kind." She looked at him, shrugging. "Politicians."

He paused, giving thanks that Fate had allowed Jasmine and his paths to cross, then asked, "So how do I find out about groups they might be associated with?"

She tapped the folders that now lay on his desk. "It's all right there. Ask what volunteer work she's done that would prove helpful on the job. HR gathers that kind of stuff to see if you're . . ." She snuffled a laugh. "Well-rounded."

"Okay, I got it. What about the Don't Ask questions?"

"Just stay from anything personal. Like, how old is she? Is she married? Does she have kids? Has she ever been arrested? What's her religion? Is English her first language? Does she have any . . . bad habits?"

Noting the pause, he rubbed his bottom lip. "Give me an example of bad habits."

She stared at the ceiling a minute. "Oh, like dumping her liquor bottles in her neighbor's trashcan to hide the fact she's an alky. Like using drops in bloodshot eyes. Like blaming the tremblies on low blood sugar."

"Uh-huh . . . Think I got a handle on it." He glanced at his watch. "Time to get this show on the road. Show her in."

Poor Norma Jean, he thought. What was the chance she'd sit down with someone holding an inside straight?

Fate was a fickle bitch.

∞

The Norma Jean Burns' interview had been short. She did have bloodshot eyes, her hands did tremble, and she was a star-struck fan of his mother. Putting an end to her nervous chatter, Chitto escorted her to Dan Blackfox's office. Returning to his desk, he picked up the phone.

"Hey, Mama. Grandma up?"

"Where were you yesterday? I expected you for Sunday dinner."

"Didn't Grandma tell you I wouldn't be there?"

"She said you couldn't plant her garden."

"Well, if I couldn't be there to plant her garden, I couldn't be there for Sunday dinner, could I?" He paused, listening to silence, sensing hurt feelings in the quiet interval. "Hey, look. I'm sorry I couldn't make it. Something came up."

"What?"

He drew a long breath, exhaled slowly. His mother was tribal councilwoman for District 13 but had expanded her job to include keeping a close eye on the goings-on in District 9, his stomping ground. "A favor for one of Mary's cousins," he said, refusing to stoop to a bald-faced lie.

A pause. "I'll put your granny on the phone."

He listened to the shuffling sounds of a phone being handed off., then said, "Hey, *Pokni*. Look, afraid I need to postpone working on your garden this next weekend. That, uh, that other business is taking longer than I thought it would."

"*Hatakachafa* business," she said.

"Right, but with the cold weather holding, I figure we can wait another week or so. Have the guy down the road rake it after he plows. That'll save me some time. You got the corn for planting?"

A long pause. "You said you would get it at the feed store."

"Oh, yeah. Well, I'll pick some up."

"Sweet corn, not field corn. You bring the fish, too."

"Fish." He rubbed his neck. "Why, uh, why do I need to bring fish?"

"To feed the corn."

Damn. His grandmother wanted to plant corn the old way, in a mound with a dead fish buried at the bottom. Natural fertilizer.

Cell phone still at his ear, he took time for a drink of coffee, "I don't have time to go fishing, *Pokni.* My job, this *Hatakachafa* business . . ."

A protracted pause, then, "Okay."

He felt his neck muscles relax. "Touch base with you next week?"

"Yeh." *Click.*

"Dodged a bullet that time," he said, hanging up the phone.

Problem is, the internal voice said, *you're standing in front of a Gatling gun.*

∞

"Want to get a bite to eat, talk about the candidate?" Dan Blackfox stood in front of Chitto's desk, an HR folder hanging from his hand.

Chitto paused, silently prioritizing needs. "Well see, I ruined a tire this weekend. Need to check on a new one at lunch."

Blackfox frowned. "How'd you ruin a tire?"

"Puncture." Over Blackfox's shoulder, he spotted Jasmine walking toward his desk with message slips in her hands.

"You try patching it?"

"Beyond patching."

"Must've been one big nail."

He nodded.

"Too bad." Blackfox eyed the HR folder on Chitto's desk. "So what'd you think?"

Chitto interpreted the question to mean, what did he think of Norma Jean Burns. "Well, her credentials looked okay."

"I thought so, too." Opening the file, Blackfox flipped rapidly through it, eyes a sponge. "Affable type. Friendly. Real eager to please."

"She was at that, but it's a little early to make a decision. Two more to go."

"Right, right." Blackfox squinted as if Chitto was a microbe and he was viewing him under a microscope. "You didn't ask anything that's gonna come back to haunt me, did you?"

"Nope."

Blackfox's eyes skimmed Chitto's desk, taking in the various piles of folders. "Any problems that need elevating?"

"Nope."

"And you're keeping your nose clean ." Another microscopic look.

"Yes sir," said with emphasis.

Catching sight of Jasmine in his peripheral vision, Blackfox turned to face her. "Those for me?" He nodded at the message slips in her hand.

"Him." She handed Chitto the slips.

"All right, then." Blackfox walked away, the HR file slapping against his thigh like a metronome.

"You're a lousy poker player," Jasmine said. "Give me some of those files. I'll weed through them, handle what I can."

"Lousy poker player? Should've seen the bluff I pulled off this weekend." Grinning, he handed her a stack of files and watched as she returned to her desk.

Opening his bottom drawer, he pulled out an old manila envelope. Fishing out a business card, he left a message for Glenda Loomis, the artist who did the drawing that appeared the *Antlers American*. She returned the call a half hour later.

Quickly, he explained how he'd gotten her phone number and proceeded to the question that was top of mind. How was the skull in Leona Mann's casket removed from the body?

"Was it a medical procedure, you wanna ask me," Loomis said, her Texas drawl soft and buttery.

"That's exactly what I'd like to know."

"It wasn't." A long sigh filled the space. "I swear, I've wondered a hundred times if I should've said something, but . . . Well, it wasn't an official case."

"Understood. So, what's your assessment?" Listening to the silence on the line, he envisioned a head shaking in disbelief. "What'd the bones tell you, Glenda?" he murmured.

"That a madman was on the loose," she whispered. "Bones splintered and crushed like someone was lopping off a chicken's head with a hatchet. Lord help, I just hope the poor man was dead when it happened."

Chitto sat for a while after the call to Loomis, staring at the photo of Walter Folsom. His concentration was so intense, he didn't pick up on another presence.

"We need to go get another cup of coffee?" Jasmine laid the folders she'd worked through on his desk, the skin between her eyes wrinkled as a prune.

"No. I, uh, I think I've had enough stimulation for one day." He turned Folsom's picture face down so he didn't have to look at it.

She sank into the chair in front of his desk, waiting.

He shook his head. "Doesn't seem right, does it?"

"What?"

"That the war doesn't end after a warrior returns home."

She picked up the picture and looked at it. "What happened to this boy, Sam?"

He relayed what Loomis told him. "What do I tell his mother?" he said after a pause. "All those years she wasted hoping . . ."

"Nothing," she said, mouth as straight as a blade. "You tell her nothing. A mama deserves better. She doesn't need to hear ugly things were done to her baby. She just needs to know things will be put right."

He lifted both hands, palms up. "See, that's just it. I can't give her that. Anyone that knew anything useful is dead, or unreliable, or . . ." He paused, thinking of Quince Winters. "Talks in riddles.

She picked up the manila envelope. "This what old Mrs. Folsom brought in?"

"Yeah?"

"I'll get it back to you before you leave today." Tucking the envelope under her arm, she rose from the chair. "Wells run deep. Something tells me this one hasn't run dry yet."

CHAPTER TWELVE

Chitto stopped at an automotive supply store on the lunch hour and ordered a new tire, then moved on to the feed store where he picked up a pound of corn for planting. Sweet corn, not field. With the delay last weekend, he wasn't exactly in his grandmother's good graces. If he brought the wrong kind, she wouldn't hesitate to remove his scalp-lock and burn it on top of the root cellar. Parking in front of the Choctaw Tribal Police building, he wished he'd saved the chore for later. He'd forgotten about the photo shoot scheduled that day. He had no choice now but wait for it to end.

The SWAT instructors stood in front of the building in full gear. The Choctaw Nation didn't restrict hiring to people of Indian blood, and the squad reflected that philosophy. Ten serious-faced men of all descriptions stood before the camera in camo uniforms and Kevlar vests, high-power rifles pointed at the ground. Dead center of the group was the Executive Director of Law Enforcement, Ben Wilson, who'd organized the group when Homeland Security raised concerns that terrorists were at work in the country. To his right stood Junior Wharton, the K-9 officer. A former football player, Wharton was a beefy man with thick neck and sloped shoulders.

Chitto stared at the lineup, thinking he'd stood for similar team photos when he played ball, but never wearing camo. In a wooded setting, the men would disappear like shadows. He frowned as something rattled in his memory. Something about a heavily wooded intersection. Just then, the photographer finished snapping pictures and the team broke rank. Getting out of his car, he moved quickly through the milling men, wanting to get inside and out of sight.

"*Chitto* . . ." Wilson cut him off at the door. "Dan said you were considering coming in for some training."

A pause. "He did, huh?"

"Said you were concerned about getting rusty." Wilson spoke in his usual direct, no-nonsense tone. "Especially given that recent incident a few months back."

"He said *I* said that?"

Wilson nodded toward the other men. "How about this weekend? I'll line up one of the men to work with you."

Chitto cleared his throat. "No can do. I'll be out of town."

"Then the next weekend."

Chitto exhaled slowly. "See, I'm helping my grandma plant her garden that weekend." He held up the bag. "Corn."

"Corn." Wilson stared at him.

"She's old, not many years left." He squirmed, feeling like he'd been called to the high-school principal's office. "But I'll check my calendar, see what's open."

"You do that." Doing an about face, Wilson returned to the group.

That went well, said the voice in Chitto's head.

"Shuddup," he growled, walking inside the building.

"What?" Jasmine's eyes went round as silver dollars. "I didn't say anything yet."

"Not you. I was talking to . . . Never mind." Sinking onto the corner of her desk, he set the sack down.

"What's that?"

"Corn. My grandma wants a Tom Fuller patch this year."
Tom Fuller was a corruption of *tafula*, the Choctaw word for
corn.

"Um-hmm. You keeping an eye on the moon?"

He looked at her.

"Shouldn't plant corn when the moon's waning."

He continued looking at her.

She sighed. "If the left side of the moon's dark, then the
light part is growing. That's called a waxing moon. If the
right side of the moon is dark, then the light part is shrinking.
That's a waning moon."

"I knew that."

She lifted an eyebrow. "Here . . ." She handed Peony
Folsom's envelope to him. "I made me a set for later."

He interpreted "later" to mean after she'd put in her
regular hours.

"Don't worry," she added. "I'll guard it with my life."

"No," he said quickly, recalling a similar commitment
he'd made to Chuck Stovall and the ensuing encounter with
John Skrabo. "You are *never* to put yourself in a threatening
situation."

She frowned, eyes blinking. "Someone threaten you this
weekend?"

He pulled at an ear, sighed, and said, "More or less."

"Stand up." Walking around her desk, she stood next to
him. "Now, do what I do." She stumped her right foot and
turned around three times, then looked at him. "Well?"

"And why am I supposed to do that?"

"To keep bad luck away."

Insight was slow in coming. "Which one of your
superstitious grandmothers you learn that from?"

"Cajun." She cocked her head, forehead wrinkling. "Or
maybe it was my African grandpa. He was a prophet, could
see and foretell things when he was in the fiery trivets.
Swears he could influence things before they happened."

"Fiery trivets . . ."

"When the spirit was in him."

"I'll take my chances," he said, grinning.

She sat down again. "You've got a lot of book smarts, Sam, but you're life dumb. Better to avoid a problem then wait till it has a knife at our throat. Here's your messages."

Officially dismissed, Chitto tucked the corn and manila envelope under his arm and walked to his desk.

∞

Chitto made it home that night about seven o'clock. He'd spent the bulk of the day handling calls that took him on the road. A drunk and disorderly. A quarrel between a husband and wife that ended up a slugfest. A standoff between a repo man and an angry young buck who swore he'd made the last payment on a Dodge pickup. Bottom line? He hadn't had time to think about Walter Folsom, but the circumstances of his mysterious disappearance surfaced quickly.

He spread the contents of Peony Folsom's envelope across the kitchen table he'd converted to a workplace on the last undercover case. The map titled *Tribal Jurisdictions in Oklahoma* was still taped to the wall, multicolored stick-on notes showing where murders had taken place across the Checkerboard. The Murder Map. All doubts gone now, he knew he was now looking at adding three more. These three undeserving of their fate.

Selecting a pad of green sticky notes, he pinned up one for Walter Folsom, Billy Robb Niles, and Leona Mann, clustering them north of Antlers. Looking inside the envelope again, he pulled out the picture of Walter Folsom dressed in his Navy uniform. Another picture that fell out with it caused him to frown. The round-faced woman in the photo was shown from the chest up, facing forward. A police lineup or driver's license photo? he wondered. Then things fell in place.

Glenda Folsom.

Jasmine mentioned she'd discovered a picture of Walter Folsom's wife. While she was making a copy of Peony's information for herself, she'd inserted Glenda's picture into the envelope. Looking further, he found a printout of the woman's driver's license. Height, 5'3". Weight, 130 pounds. Color of hair: brown. Color of eyes: brown. Address: Antlers, Oklahoma.

Taping both pictures up next to the map, he turned his attention to supper. Retrieving a can of beef stew and box of saltines from the pantry, he felt the couple's eyes following him. As he set the crackers on the table, he paused to stare into the two sets of dark eyes.

Reproachful, he wondered, or insistent?

Sighing, he peeled off another green stick-on note to represent Glenda Folsom and stuck it in the Pending area on the side of the map. A matter to be resolved later.

Putting a fresh pot of coffee on to brew, he dug a small stewpan out of the bottom drawer on the stove and set it on a burner. Hearing a loud knock, he moved the pan off the flame and walked to the door. His first sight was of an animal, its head misshapen, reared up on its hind legs. Startled, he took a step backward. A second later, he recognized Boycott, the old strip of leather hanging from his jowls.

"*Get down.*" Hattie George pulled at Boycott's collar. "I swear, you're not too big to feed to that tomcat in the alley."

Heart doing a drum roll, Chitto opened the storm door to let her in. "A little late for you to be out, isn't it?"

"Well sir, my stomach told me it was time for supper and that's when I remembered your mama came by with Sunday leftovers to get to you. She left her key at home, you see." She handed him a large plastic container. "Boycott fought me all the way over, wanting some."

He pried the lid off the container and identified the contents as glazed ham, sweet potatoes, and a zip-lock bag of cornmeal muffins. "Damn sight better than what I had planned." He set the container on the counter. "Care to join me?"

She snorted. "Nothing with fur or feathers passes over these gums. Besides, got a load of wash in the dryer, don't want it to wrinkle." She walked toward the back door, then paused. "Oh, where'd Boycott get that old dog collar?"

"Dog collar?" Eyeing the strip of leather in the dog's mouth, his heart sped up. "Why you think it was a dog collar?"

"Had holes punched in it. Could've been part of a man's belt, I suppose, but given its length and heft, I'm inclined to think it was for a good size dog." She pulled Boycott closer, exposing his collar. "See, 'bout the same length as this one."

He examined the leather strip. "Looks more like a strap to me, probably for securing gear. Boycott picked it up near an old railroad track. Want me to get rid of it?"

"*Goodness, no.* Keeps him busy. Carries it around with him like it was gold plated." She paused again, catching sight of the picture on the wall. "Well, now. That sailor saw a lot of duty, didn't he?"

He looked at the picture of Walter Folsom. "Why you say that?"

"All those ribbons on his chest." She pushed the door open. "C'mon, Boycott."

He watched from the doorway to make sure Hattie made it back to her house, then returned to the kitchen. Replacing the canned soup and box of crackers in the pantry, he fixed a plate of ham and potatoes and slid it in the microwave.

Taking Walter Folsom's picture off the wall, he held a magnifying glass to it, studying bits of ribbons on the man's chest. The scraps of fabric told him nothing, but his science and law background told him the smallest of things could lead to big discoveries.

His eyes went to the map on the wall again, targeting the town of Ada in the Chickasaw Nation. The small pieces of cloth might be written in a language all their own, but he knew someone who spoke their language.

∞

Chitto searched through his bookshelves, looking for one book in particular. It wasn't one of his or Mary's; for a fact, he didn't know where it came from or why he'd hung on to it. Perhaps because he considered books of any kind too priceless to discard, either one he'd read a dozen times or never at all. Finding the Gideon Bible in the corner of a bottom shelf, surrounded by books about mythology and philosophy, he pondered the placement. At some point, he'd obviously found it logical and now wondered why. Perhaps, because mythology dealt with things that never happened but always were, philosophy with the pursuit of truth. The Bible could fit in either category. Or neither, he admitted grudgingly. One thing he did know. He didn't have a clue where to begin to find the story of Nathan and David.

Placing the red-jacketed book on the end table, he made a small fire in the fireplace, pulled his cell phone from his pocket, and settled into an easy chair.

"Hey, Jasmine. Am I calling too late?"

"Still a few minutes before bedtime. What do you need?"

"Want you to tell me a story."

"You're a little old for bedtime stories."

"Way too old, but I need one tonight. Something tells me your grandfather told Bible stories when you were a girl."

A pause. "He did. And?"

"You know the one about Nathan and David?"

"Nathan and David?"

"You don't know it?"

"Of course, I know it," she snapped. "Old Nathan was a prophet and one day he paid David a visit." The sound of breathing came on the line. "You *have* heard of David?"

"Of course. He was a wise ruler . . ."

"Supposedly."

" . . . with lots of wives."

"That part's true. Well, anyway, Nathan told David this story about two men, one rich, one poor. The rich man had lots of flocks and herds while the poor man only had one ewe lamb that he loved like a child of his own."

"Sort've a pet," he said.

"Like a child of his own," she repeated with emphasis "Then one day this traveler arrived at the rich man's house. Since the rich man didn't want to kill any of his own animals to feed the traveler, he took the poor man's lamb and slaughtered it."

"Right. It was a custom in those days to feed travelers."

"Still is in some places."

"And he could do that, just take another man's property."

A short laugh came from the phone. "What planet you live on, Sam?"

He waited another half minute, then said, "That's it?"

"That's it."

He rubbed his mouth. "Care to tell me what it means?"

"Different things to different people." The sigh that came over the line resonated with frustration. "See, David had to figure out why Nathan told him *that* particular story. That's the way parables work." A lengthy pause ensued. "Why'd you want to hear it?"

"Not sure yet. What, uh, what'd David figure out?"

"Depends on who you ask, but I figure it had to do with something he did that old Nathan didn't take kindly to. One thing leads to another, you know."

"Yeah," he mumbled. "A causal chain."

136

"Bedtime, Sam." *Click.*

CHAPTER THIRTEEN

The lunch hour, Tuesday. The office, empty. Chitto pulled up a number he'd programmed in his cell phone and pressed Dial. Four rings later, a voice on the other end said, "What goin' on, Chitto?"

He smiled. Frank Tubbe still had his number programmed into his phone. "How you doin', little brother? Interpersonal skills improving?"

A laugh came over the line. "How do you know Chata wasn't the youngest brother?"

It had become an ongoing argument between Chitto and Tubbe. According to the old migration story, Chata and Chiksa were brothers. After the two had a falling out, Chiksa and his followers splintered off from the Choctaw, becoming the Chickasaw.

"Hey, we were the ones that gave up part of our land here in the Nation to you Chickasaws. That shows maturity. Big brother taking care of little brother."

"Gave it up, my foot. We had to go to the great white father in Washington to make that happen." Tubbe laughed again, then said, "You're not one for shooting the breeze, so cut to the chase. Why are you interrupting my lunch?"

"Could use another set of eyes on something. Fax machine handy?"

Rattling off a number, Tubbe said, "I'm headin' there now."

Phone pressed to his ear, Chitto walked to the fax machine in his office, listening to scuffling noises and the sound of voices in the background.

Tubbe said, "What're you sending me?"

"Picture." He fed Walter Folsom's photo into the machine. "Let me know when you get it."

A minute passed. "Okay, it's coming through." Another minute went by. "What am I looking at?"

"That's what I want you to tell me. Look at the ribbons on his chest."

The scuffling noises returned and the sound of voices receded. "This picture looks old. What're you doing with it?"

Chitto sighed. He'd hoped to get the information he needed without an explanation. He should've known better. "I'm sorta helping out a friend.

"Sorta."

"Sorta," he repeated, knowing Tubbe had figured out it was an off-duty investigation. Sighing again, he briefed Tubbe on the old double homicide. The man's head that surfaced in the woman's coffin. The artist rendering in the paper. "Sailor's mother swears it's her son who went missing at the same time. I'm backtracking, thinking those ribbons might lead to something."

A moment of static. "You could've found all that on the Net. Why'd you call me?"

"Thought this would be faster, and . . ." Chitto paused. "As I recall, you spent some time up in Colorado after you got out of the service."

A prolonged silence, then, "So?"

"This woman said her son went to the river every day to drink coffee. Never took anything except a thermos and old dog. Didn't come back one day. Dog either."

Static on the line, accompanied by verbal silence.

"Yeah," Chitto said, deciding to fill the gap "The guy mentioned once that he was following doctor's orders."

More static and silence.

Chitto continued. "Appears the head was chopped off. Not pretty. Sheriff there in Push County confiscated the skull as evidence. Who the hell knows where the body is." He paused. "Anything come to mind?"

The sound of Tubbe clearing his throat filtered across the line. "Well, couldn't be connected with that last case we worked on. Happened too long ago."

"Right. Thing is, this woman's been waiting over thirty years for her son to come back. Says he calls to her at night, from the hills because—"

"His spirit can't rest," Tubbe said, completing the thought.

"Correct. Anyway, when the woman tried talking to the local sheriff, she was run off the road. Hit and run, banged up pretty bad." He paused once more. "It was deliberate. Attempted murder."

A long sigh punctuated with intermittent static followed, then, "What're you not telling me, Sam?"

"She, uh, she wants me to bring her son back home. The head . . . and the body."

Tubbe laughed. "After more than thirty years, won't be anything left except gristle and bone."

"Exactly. I'm supposed to carry the bones back to her, so he can be buried with his people."

A pause. "Like in the old migration story?"

"Something like that."

Tubbe made a noncommittal grunt but Chitto knew he was recalling the migration story when the Choctaw and Chickasaw were one people. In the beginning, a sacred leaning pole guided Chata and Chiksa on their long journey from their beginning place in the west to a new home. Every morning, the brothers let the white staff fall where it would and followed the direction it pointed. The staff led them to what is now Mississippi. No one who died on that journey was left behind. Bone Pickers stripped the flesh from the bones, presented them to the family, and the families carried them to the new place where they were deposited in mounds.

"What's this guy's name?" Tubbe asked, the sound of paper rustling in the background.

"Folsom. Walter Folsom."

"I'll get back to you."

∞

About mid-afternoon, Chitto laid several completed case files in Jasmine's in-basket and slipped an arm into the sleeve of his duty jacket. "Those can be filed," he said. "Need to follow up on a couple things this afternoon." He slipped into the other sleeve.

"Um-hmm," she mumbled, eyes glued to her computer monitor.

He turned toward the door. "Might not make it back to the office. Cell's on, you need to reach me."

"Figure it out yet?" she said.

He deduced she was referring to a certain parable. "Working on it." He paused, looking around to see if anyone was near enough to overhear them. "You come up with anything new on your end?"

"Working on it," she said as he walked away.

Doing a one-eighty, he returned to her desk. "One more thing. Got that second interview tomorrow morning at nine. Woman by the name of . . ." He hesitated, head cocked.

"Denise Longjohn," she said, eyes still locked on the monitor.

"Right. Any . . . bad habits I need to be aware of?"

"Not I know of."

Nodding, he walked toward the door again.

"Follows rules to the letter," she said to his back.

Another one-eighty. "Elaborate," he said.

She met his eyes. "Counts every paper clip, metes out file folders like they were gold plated, runs unscheduled safety checks on computer cables to make sure no safety rules are being violated."

"Sounds attentive."

Wanda, the former department assistant, had been attentive, following Blackfox's orders to the letter about knowing the whereabouts of everyone at all times. That attentiveness had almost been Chitto's downfall.

"Try anal." She looked at him over plastic-rimmed glasses. "Has eyes in the back of her head and an acute sense of hearing."

He breathed in, out. "Those types typically like to rub shoulders with the higher-ups."

"Um-hmm," she mumbled, turning back to her monitor.

"See you tomorrow," he said.

"If the good Lord's willing and the creek don't rise."

∞

Chitto drove to the tire shop on the outskirts of Durant after he left the office. He let out a soft whistle as he wrote out a check for the tire he'd ordered, thinking the favor he was doing for Mary's cousins was not only disrupting his sleep but also leaving sizeable holes in his bank account.

New tire stowed in the back of his patrol unit, he continued on his mission. Pulling into the parking lot at Southeastern University, he locked his car and jogged toward the History Department, dodging students changing classes.

Dr. Roy Reeves sat in an office lined with bookshelves and file cabinets stuffed to the gills. He wore a threadbare wool blazer, cotton shirt unbuttoned at the neck, Dockers, and running shoes. Head of the History Department, he had an M.A. in Religion in American Life and completed a Ph.D. in History at Norman, where he and Chitto shared some classes.

"Anything new on your dad's murder?" He gestured Chitto toward a chair across from his desk.

"Couple leads that went nowhere." Cozying up next to a heat vent, Chitto unzipped his jacket.

Reeves leaned back in his chair, arms clasped behind his head. The action stirred up dust motes, creating a minuscule snowstorm. "I remember the day you got the word. Sure you do, too."

"Like it was yesterday," Chitto said. "Speaking of which, I went upcountry last weekend to help out a family member that experienced a similar loss. In the process, it was recommended I look at the parable of Nathan and David. The story itself seems straightforward enough. A greedy rich man steals a poor man's only sheep and kills it to feed a traveler. But it's rare something's as simple as it seems. Illuminate me."

Reeves shook his head, laughing softly. "Good old Nathan and David again." He rocked his chair slightly, hands loosely clasped in his lap, thumbs twirling. "Remember that philosophy class where we looked at the premise man was defined as a rational animal? And the debate you and I had on the difference between being a rational being and a thinking being?"

"Yeah . . ." Chitto's eyelids fluttered as he leafed backward to another life. "How man might be a thinking animal but most of what he does is neither logical nor rational."

"And that Euripides was probably closer to the truth when he described Man as filled with conflicted desires."

Chitto nodded. "Especially when it came to women."

"Freud believed something similar," Reeves said. "That what really motivated men was the libido. Essentially, sexual desire."

"I see. So the beloved ewe was a woman and the rich man killed her." Chitto shook his head, frowning.

"Something's not tracking. You're saying David was the rich man and he killed the wife of this poor man. If he was sexually attracted to her, why would he kill her?"

"Didn't say he killed her." Reeves clasped his hands behind his head again. "Need to keep in mind that a parable's meant to teach a lesson."

Chitto paused, thinking. "You're saying parables may not be historically correct."

"Right. Most people interpret the story being about Bathsheba," Reeves said, "who was married to a soldier in David's army that just happened to be away at war. Keep in mind that David had many wives, which could be construed as flocks and herds. This soldier only had the one. A single ewe, you could say, that David took a shine to."

"Away at war . . ." He hesitated. "And David got her knocked up while this soldier was gone?"

"Bingo."

Chitto's heartbeat thudded in his temples. Had Crystal been conceived while Walter Folsom was in the service? If so, who was her birth father? Would that explain why Glenda Folsom disappeared right after Crystal was born?

He frowned again. "Wait, David married Bathsheba, didn't he? That means he didn't kill her."

"Married her and she bore him a child. You're confusing parable and history again."

"So what was the point of the parable?" Chitto said, voice edged with impatience.

"To force David to make a judgment on what the rich man had done. See, old Nathan asks David what he thought should be done with the rich man in the story, and David says the man should be put to death. That's when Nathan told David that he was that man. I had to make an educated guess, old Nathan told him that story to wake him up to the severity of what *he'd* done."

145

"His irrational act . . ." Chitto frowned again. "Something's still not stacking. Someone had to die, else Nathan wouldn't have mentioned the ewe being slaughtered."

"Well, here's the rest of the story. David couldn't marry Bathsheba if she was married, so he arranged to have the soldier killed on the battlefield." Reeves made the sign of a knife slicing his throat.

"The soldier was the one who was slaughtered . . ."

Chitto felt more confused than ever. Walter Folsom had returned home from the service and lived several years. But in thinking about Glenda Loomis' description of the bones, he decided slaughtered was an accurate description. His mind's eye migrating to the sticky tab in the Pending area of his map, he wondered if Glenda Folsom had suffered the same fate.

"You're saying the soldier wasn't mentioned in the parable, but he was the only one who actually died."

"At that time, yes. That child of David and Bathsheba died later though, as a punishment from God, some say."

"The child conceived in adultery?"

"Right." Reeves watched as Chitto turned to stare out the window, his face a patchwork of shadow and ambiguity. "What's not adding up, Sam?"

"Too much," he said, facing Reeves. "One more question. This traveler's never identified. I take it his role in the parable was circumstantial."

"In this parable, perhaps. But if someone wanted you to look at this particular one in conjunction with that family member you're helping, maybe he plays more of a role. Everything's situational."

Nodding, Chitto said, "A particular set of circumstances existing in a particular place or at a particular time . . ."

"Exactly." Abruptly, Reeves rocked his chair forward. "Didn't you say you went upcountry to help this family member."

"That's right."

"Well, hell, Sam. Maybe you're the traveler. Think someone's planning to kill somebody's precious ewe to satisfy your hunger?"

Feeling a sudden chill, Chitto turned up the collar on his jacket.

∞

That evening, Chitto changed out tires on his truck, replacing the spare with the new one. After stowing the spare in its rightful place, he studied the big pickup. He needed a different ride for the trip back to Antlers. Something less conspicuous. Something John Skrabo wouldn't spot.

Wiping his hands on a rag, he walked to the garage door and looked toward Hattie's driveway. He wondered if she'd let him borrow her little Ford 150, if she could handle the big Chevy if she needed to get somewhere.

Not a good idea, he decided.

Stomach taking precedent over problems still days away, he closed the garage door and walked to the kitchen where leftovers waited. Warming a plate, he walked to the living room, replaying his conversation with Roy Reeves and thinking about particular sets of circumstances existing in a particular place or at a particular time.

Finishing his dinner, he spent the rest of the evening in front of a quiet fire applying the Nathan parable to the piece of history he was currently living in. Then to the piece that Walter Folsom had occupied. No matter how he played it, everything came back to one question. Why had Quince Winters wanted him to look at that particular parable? That led him to the future. No matter which way he scryed the crystal ball, he got the same response.

The child conceived in adultery was in danger.

CHAPTER FOURTEEN

Chitto pushed through the front door to the Choctaw Police Department at eight o'clock sharp on Wednesday morning and looked immediately toward the reception area. Seeing no one there, he proceeded to Jasmine's desk.

"You're on time," she said, eyes wide.

"Wanted to beat Attentive One in."

"Afraid she'd tell on you if you were late?" A flicker of a smile played at the corners of her mouth. "You're a little nervous about this one, aren't you?"

"Me? *Naw.*"

She raised her eyebrows.

"I just want to get it over with," he said, shrugging "You've worked with her. Any suggestions?"

"Might start early," she said, nodding toward the front door. "Looks like Attentive One decided to scope things out in advance."

Turning, Chitto saw a thin woman with short-cut hair in a gray wool suit, the handle of an aluminum attaché case clutched in her left hand. She stood like a robot, eyes slowly ratcheting around the office. Noticing her eyes come to a halt, he looked to see what had captured her attention. Sergeant Junior Wharton sat reared back in his chair, feet the size of footlockers resting on his desk, popping crackerjacks. His reward after an all-night stakeout. A black German

Shepherd named Jake sat beside him, ears alert and eyes locked on the strange woman at the door.

"Maybe I better," he said. "Jake looks like he's waiting for someone to give the attack command."

"By the way," she said. "Candidate number three rescheduled to Thursday afternoon, one o'clock."

"Why?" he said, pulling up short. She gave him the I'm-just-a-temp shrug, from which he deduced the woman in HR had struck again. "Wait a minute . . ." He pulled out his pocket calendar. "I've got something on Thursday."

"Yes, you do." She flipped a page in her daytimer. "Four's coming down that morning to testify in a case involving dog baiting and wants you there. Case was scheduled for Friday morning initially, then got changed to Thursday. One Leon Messina . . ." She removed her glasses and looked at him. "He from LeFlore County?"

"Right. Leon's father's dead. His grandfather, Victor Messina, raised the boy." He paused, thinking. "That's one hearing I don't want to miss."

Four had connected Leon Messina to a dog-fighting ring in LeFlore County and called Chitto to assist with the interview. It was during that interview that Messina let it slip he knew how Will Chitto and Bert Gilly were killed.

"Looks like it'll work," he said, penning the new interview time on his calendar. "Hearing at ten, Candidate Number Three at one o'clock." Pulling a long breath, he said, "Here goes nothing."

Walking to the waiting woman with the metal briefcase, he introduced himself to Candidate Number Two.

"Denise Longjohn," she said, extending a limp hand. "Don't mind me. I'll wait here until our appointed time."

He made a gesture, indicating she should walk with him. At his desk, he pointed with his chin to a visitor chair, dropped his well-worn nylon briefcase on the desk, and peeled out of his coat.

She looked at her watch. "It's not time . . ."

"You're here. I'm here." He gave her a sideways glance. "You got a problem with that." Wadding up the jacket, he tossed it in the corner.

"No, not at all." She sank into the chair, her eyes taking in the collection of worry stones strewn across the desktop, the tangle of cables creeping from under his computer, the crumpled jacket in the corner. Setting the attaché case on her lap, she clicked it open and pulled out a steno notebook and mechanical pencil.

"What's that for?" he asked.

"I take notes." She scribbled something on her pad.

Chitto prided himself at being able to read upside down. What he tried to read right then looked like hen scratches on a double column notepad.

Denise Longjohn looked at him. "I take dictation. A hundred-twenty words a minute."

"People can actually talk that fast?"

She clicked the lead in her pencil.

He made a guttural sound. Pulling the HR folder from his desk drawer, he laid it unopened before her. "Other than what's in here, what qualifies you for this job?"

Denise Long john's eyes took flight. "Well, uh, I suppose that says it all."

"Good enough for me," he said. "I'll show you to Dan Blackfox's office."

∞

It was about ten thirty when Chitto's cell phone rang. He'd spent the morning working on case files and documenting new incidents. The public had the impression that police work was exciting, the stuff TV shows were made of, but in truth, it was mostly paperwork. The ringing of his cell phone promised a break from the tedium. Glancing at the caller's number, he grinned, knowing the promise had become a full-blown reality.

Holding the phone to his ear, he said, "What's up, little brother?"

"'Bout an hour," Tubbe said. "That café there on 70."

"I know the one," he said and hung up the phone.

As he was pulling Peony Folsom's manila envelope from his bottom drawer, Chitto spied Dan Blackfox escorting Denise Longjohn from his office. No sooner had the woman disappeared out the front door than Blackfox appeared in front of his desk.

"Didn't talk to this last candidate very long," Blackfox said.

Chitto made a noncommittal grunt. "What'd you think of her?"

Blackfox sat down across from him. "Capable woman. Well organized. Even gave me a list of things she thought would improve our efficiency. Kind've made me feel like I wasn't on top of my game." He paused to chew on his bottom lip, then glanced toward Chitto's wadded up jacket in the corner. "You think we present a professional image, that I'm too easy on people?"

Chitto smiled. "You're on top of your game, Dan. This isn't the state pen and you don't have Warden in front of your name."

Snickering, Blackfox stood to leave. Glancing at the manila envelope in Chitto's hand, he paused. "That a case you're working on?"

"Family stuff." He slipped the envelope into his briefcase.

"All right, then," Blackfox said, slapping Denise Long john's file against his thigh. "One more interview to go, then we make a decision. You get the word the last candidate changed her appointment to Thursday afternoon?"

Nodding, Chitto shook the wrinkles out of his jacket and slipped it on.

"Why you in such an all-fired hurry?" Blackfox asked.

"Call just came in. Need to follow up on it."

"Must be of a critical nature."

He gave his head a quick shake. "Guy's just hard to catch up with. When opportunity knocks . . ." He let his words hang.

Blackfox looked at him.

Chitto waited. Though he complained about him occasionally, he held nothing but the highest esteem for his boss. Dan Blackfox had gotten his position as Director of Law Enforcement the right way: working his way up through the ranks. He'd even held Chitto's job before being promoted. He knew the ins and outs of police business, worked hard to maintain cross-jurisdictional partnerships, trusted his people to do their jobs, and looked out for their welfare. Plus, he'd been blessed, or damned, depending on the viewpoint, with the ability to read people like a book. He knew when someone was being straight up or dumping a load of horse hockey on him.

"Uh-huh." Blackfox nodded slowly. "Stop by when you get back, catch me up on what you're working on. You know how I feel about being blindsided."

A sigh. "Believe me, Dan. I'm trying real hard to make sure that doesn't happen."

∞

The Saltlick Cafe on the north side of U.S. 70 was known for old-fashioned cheeseburgers at old-fashioned prices. Chitto parked next to a green GMC 4x4 pickup, the bed topped with a camper shell. Khaki-colored mud splashed along its sides had dried to flakes, the left rear fender was dented, and the back bumper listed to one side. In a grove of trees, it would disappear into the shadows.

Camouflage . . . Chitto's thoughts became a row of dominoes falling into place. Someone in Pushmataha County owned a vehicle painted in camo colors.

Opening the door, he turned his attention from the GMC to the man leaning against its front fender, his dark duty jacket bearing the emblem of the Chickasaw Lighthorse Police. Sergeant Frank Tubbe.

"How are you, Frank?" He gripped Tubbe's hand, grinning.

"Borderline perfection," Tubbe responded, flashing his lop-sided grin.

That he was, Chitto thought. A hair above six foot, muscular shoulders, thin hips. Square jawline, cleft in the chin. Dark hair worn in a short, military cut, accented with a jagged scar zigzagging front to back. Tubbe was what his wife Mary would've called a sexy hunk, the kind that played bad-boy leading men.

Chitto had met Tubbe at CLEET training a decade before, required for all law enforcement trainees, but the Chickasaw had dropped out of sight after that, resurfacing on the undercover case a few months ago. On duty, Tubbe was sharp-witted and quick to act. Off duty, he was quick to laugh and easy to like. But Chitto could never shake the feeling that what lay on the outside was veneer and that he didn't want to find out what lay underneath.

He paused to read the sticker on the GMC's bumper. *Illegitimi non-carborundum.* Translation: Don't let the bastards grind you down.

"You getting erudite on me?" he asked. Tubbe wasn't known for his interpersonal skills. He figured the sticker was his subtle way of rebelling against the establishment. As subtle as Tubbe could get.

"Little trick I picked up from you, professor. Use words no one understands and you can get away with all kinds of shit."

Chitto laughed. "Where'd you get this hunk of junk?" Looking inside the truck, he noticed a Chickasaw police binder on the bench seat. "You working undercover?"

"Hunk of junk?" Tubbe looked offended. "Don't insult Jimmy. He's gotten me down a lot of rough roads."

"This is yours?" He raised his eyebrows.

"My patrol unit's in the shop."

Taking a closer look at the GMC, Chitto noted it was outfitted with all-terrain tires. New ones with deep treads. "Ever loan Jimmy out?"

Tubbe's grin faded. "Are you shittin' me?"

"Let me buy you a burger, little brother," Chitto said, slapping him on the back.

∞

Out of habit, Chitto and Tubbe migrated toward a quiet booth in the back with a window that overlooked the parking lot. They ordered cheeseburgers with fries and iced tea, then sat looking out the window where mud from the week before had dried to dirt clods. Those clods had broken down to fine dust now that eddied around passing vehicles like a brown current in a dry streambed. Having secured the perimeter, they peeled out of their outer jackets and waited.

"You first," Tubbe said when the tea was delivered. He pulled the faxed copy of Walter Folsom from the inside pocket of his blazer and laid it on the table, face up. "What more you got on this guy?"

Chitto studied Tubbe, the intensity in his eyes. Something about Folsom had triggered more than passing curiosity. "It's complicated," he said. "But I think I've got a bead on something and need to know everything I can about him. His service records would be useful."

Tapping his pocket again, Tubbe said. "Gonna cost you more than a burger. You can use the Jimmy this weekend, but I'm driving. Where do I pick you up?"

Chitto paused long enough to decide it would useless to argue with someone as pigheaded as Tubbe. Besides, what choice did he have? The man had something he needed. Service records and a vehicle perfect for undercover work.

"Pick us up at my place." Pulling his notebook from a pocket, he wrote his address down. "We'll need to sleep in the camper and haul our own food. Not a good idea to be seen in town."

"Us?" Tubbe asked, folding the slip of paper into an inside pocket.

"I'm bringing a dog."

Tubbe's eyebrows hiked up. "Must be a good dog."

"Not particularly."

Tubbe leaned back in the booth. "So why are you bringing it?"

"Because he can smell a certain county sheriff from a mile away."

"Um-huh." Tubbe's eyes narrowed to slits. "So, there's no cross-jurisdiction agreement in place."

"That, and I don't want to involve my guys in that district."

"Because . . ."

Chitto rested his elbows on the table, fingers tented. "Because this whole thing could end up a wild goose chase."

Tubbe laughed softly. "Pick you up 'bout eight Saturday morning. Bring your own sleeping bag and a blanket for the pooch. I don't sleep with dogs."

Chitto nodded, grinning. "And don't wash the Jimmy. It'll blend in better." He paused, the grin fading. "Rifle with a scope might come in handy, too."

Tubbe rubbed his mouth, blinking eyes indicating he was considering the implications of this disclosure. "I'm providing the wheels. You provide the grub."

"Done." Negotiations finished, Chitto nodded at Tubbe's pocket. "The service records."

Removing another folded piece of paper, Tubbe tapped it on the edge of the table. "Brief me first," he said. "I like to know exactly what I'm letting myself in for."

Chitto's jaws dropped, not believing Tubbe would stoop to blackmail. Part of him wanted to wipe the cocksure grin off his face, while another part admired him for having connections that could deliver military service records without the usual rigmarole. The fact was, Tubbe had him between a rock and a hard place. Folsom's service record, when compared to Crystal's birth certificate, could prove or disprove a certain parable that was keeping him awake nights.

Sighing, Chitto leaned forward and gave Tubbe a quick summary of the last week's events, including the meeting with Dr. Ray Reeves at Southeastern University.

"A Bible story?" Tubbe said. "Now that's a new one."

"For me, too."

"What about Folsom's car? You check with the DMV?"

Chitto glanced through the window at traffic on the highway. "Cars still right where he left it. His mother's held out hope all these years that he'd come back."

"Thirty-some years . . ." Tubbe shook his head.

"Hand it over." Chitto held out a hand, palm up. "And fill me in on what those ribbons told you."

Tubbe gave him the service records. "Ribbon bars didn't reveal much. Folsom saw a lot of the world and was an A1 sailor. Seaman third class, good conduct and all that, and a hell of a marksman."

"Marksman?" Chitto mulled this over as the cheeseburgers and fries made an appearance. As soon as the waiter was gone, he looked at Tubbe again. "I picture sailors swabbing decks, not being good marksmen."

Tubbe took a timeout for a bite of cheeseburger, washing it down with iced tea. "That didn't surprise me as much as that little piece of metal on his chest." He attacked the cheeseburger again.

Chitto bit into his burger, studying Walter Folsom's picture as he chewed. "That thing there?" He tapped a spot on the photo. "What is it?"

"Not sure, but I had to guess, I'd say this guy did some joint service work with another branch of the military. My gut says it was the Marines."

Chitto tried unsuccessfully to pull together the pieces of the puzzle Tubbe was handing him. "So, what would a sailor that could shoot the wings off a beetle at a hundred yards be doing with the Marines?"

"Six hundred," Tubbe said, "and that's conservative." He leaned back in the booth, staring out the window. "I had to bet, I'd say a gunner on a helo and his record confirms a reason for it." He nodded at the piece of paper he'd delivered to Chitto. "Last service he saw was in Nam in '75, aka the fall of Saigon. More than likely, an exercise dubbed *Frequent Wind*. For good reason. Our government was hauling ass to get people out of there, both ours and nationals, before the North overran it."

Chitto had finished his burger and fries and now worked on the tea. "I recall reading something about that." He looked at Tubbe, eyebrows knit. "Raised quite a stink but can't recall why just now."

Tubbe laughed without humor. "Turned out to be a pretty expensive rescue mission. Had to shove fifty helos overboard to make room for small aircraft to land. Rats deserting a sinking ship. The locals flew anything they could get their hands on to where the carriers were waiting. It was a pretty clean mission from a loss-of-life standpoint, but our government had to pick up the ticket, to the tune of billions. Helicopters don't come cheap."

"In other words," Chitto said, "a quick decision had to be made. Ditching budget-busting war machines, making for bad PR, or letting refugees take a nose dive into the China Sea."

Tubbe turned to stare out the window. "When push comes to shove, you deal with the situation."

Situational again, Chitto thought. His tea glass empty, he swirled the ice cubes to hurry their melt. "You think that's the reason Folsom had a strong need to go to the river to drink coffee?"

"Didn't say it was his only mission." Tubbe nodded at the service record. "Saw lots of others and not all of them without bloodshed." He looked away again, staring at a sky grown cloudy. "Those boys could paint the ground red in a hurry."

"So, the trips to the river were . . . what?"

"Probably therapy, accounting for the regularity." Tubbe finished off his tea. "You said he went every day at the same time?"

"Mornings, and again Friday evenings. I figured it had something to do with the murdered woman whose coffin his head was found in." Chitto clasped his hands behind his head, frowning. "Thought there might be something between the two, but the connection didn't pan out. I learned last weekend she had a thing for the guy that was murdered. This Billy Robb Niles, not Folsom."

Tubbe pulled a narrow notebook from his pocket and wrote something in it. Reading upside down, Chitto saw it said Billy Robb Niles. "You think this Niles is connected somehow?"

Tubbe tucked the notebook back into his pocket. "Lotta times, therapy's done with a buddy."

Chitto let out a sigh as more pieces to the puzzle came together. The girl wasn't what drew Folsom to the river. It was the man she was dating. As a utility lineman, Niles would've been working the rural areas and could've planned his day so he could meet up with Folsom for coffee in the morning, and again on Friday night when he had his girl with him.

He turned to Tubbe, head shaking. "How could I have overlooked something so simple? These guys were getting together to work through the traumas of war."

Tubbe's eyes turned as opaque as smoky quartz. Rising from the booth, he walked toward the front counter, moving with the speed and grace of an animal in the wild.

Knowing he'd put his foot in his mouth, Chitto followed Tubbe to the cash register where he was paying out. "I said I'd buy, Frank."

"I pull my own weight."

Chitto knew better than to argue. Paying his tab, he followed Tubbe outside. "Appreciate you're going with me, but . . ." He stood next to the driver's window, leaning against the sill. "If you've changed your mind, I'll understand."

"Oh, *hell* no," Tubbe said. "You're not getting' rid of me that easy. Consider me invested." Tubbe keyed the ignition and sat while the GMC idled, eyeing Chitto's arm on the sill.

Chitto leaned closer. "I, uh, I'm sorry for whatever I said back there that made me out to be a fucking asshole."

The hint of a grin appeared. "Don't worry, professor. I don't hold inexperience against virgins." Shifting into reverse, he looked Chitto in the eye. "Who knows, I might just teach you a few things this weekend."

Chitto watched the dusty GMC merge with traffic and disappear. You already have, he thought, knowing where he'd erred. People that had seen war never got over it. It was a log chain they dragged behind them the rest of their lives.

CHAPTER FIFTEEN

Chitto lowered his window to absorb temperatures hitting sixty degrees. As he drove back toward Durant, he chewed on the information Tubbe gave him. With it, he could verify that Crystal had been conceived out of wedlock. The birth certificate Jasmine found would show her birth weight. That, in turn, would indicate whether she'd been a full-term baby or a preemie. Walter Folsom's service record would prove or disprove he was her father because a man couldn't be in two places at once. In short, he could produce a string of events, called a causal chain by some, confirming what he had already suspected. Crystal was not Walter Folsom's child. All of which spawned another question.

Who *was* Crystal's birth father?

Nearing the city limits of Durant, he thought about the picture of Walter and Glenda Folsom taped to his kitchen wall. The way he hadn't questioned that dark-eyed parents could've had a light-eyed child. Why? Because logic told him it was possible. It boiled down to a simple rule of genetics. Blue eyes, or in this case, gray eyes, would be recessive to brown eyes, and everyone had two genes for each trait. One from the mother and one from the father. Depending on which genes the baby inherited, its eyes could be different from either of its parents. The bottom line? The

161

color of Crystal's eyes wouldn't help lead him to her birth father.

Meaningless stats that only led to more questions, he thought, tapping the brake as traffic slowed. Such as, had Glenda Folsom abandoned her infant daughter? Or had someone felt a need for her to disappear? He frowned again. That would imply she was a danger because . . .

"She was seen as a threat," he mumbled, feeling the frustration of one lost in a maze. "Why would Glenda Folsom be considered so dangerous she needed to be eliminated?"

Stopping at a traffic light, he pulled up Glenda Folsom's image in his memory. He looked again into the eyes of the round-faced girl whose husband was away serving his country. Her driver's license indicated she lived in Antlers. An apartment, probably. Small and plain because they were living off Walter's service pay. Had she become so lonely or bored that she succumbed to the advances of another man? Or had her child been the result of non-consensual sex?

No, he thought. Non-consensual sex would've been classified as rape. A child conceived from rape was not the same as a child conceived in adultery. Adultery meant the relationship was consensual. Involuntarily, he shook his head. Women, especially Indian women, didn't bother to report rape because the cases got buried in bureaucratic nonsense. Would Glenda have bothered to report rape, if that was the case?

"Besides," he mumbled, "parables don't have to be completely accurate. They're situational."

He frowned as these questions kindled others. His thinking went back to the visit with Quince Winters. Who was the whoring bastard he spoke of? And why was he so reluctant to reveal what he knew? Only one answer made sense: to protect the child. To prevent what happened to the mother happening to the daughter. In this case, that meant keeping Crystal ignorant of her birth because . . .

Because Daddy wouldn't like it if someone spilled the beans, whispered the voice in his head.

Drawing a breath, he pulled Glenda Folsom's picture from his memory again. That straightforward look held the answer. She would've told Walter who the father was, but waited until it was time for him to come home. Why?

Because he would've gone AWOL, the voice whispered again.

Chitto rubbed a hand across his mouth, thinking of a promise he'd made Mary when they married. "I promise to protect you through whatever life may bring," he'd vowed. That was the husband's duty, to protect his wife. But he hadn't protected Mary. How do you protect someone from something as insidious as cancer? And Walter hadn't protected Glenda either. Someone had disposed of her before he could, preventing him from doing his duty, too.

"Damn," he mumbled through numbed lips. "That girl was raped."

The question now came down to who. Someone in a position of power or who had friends in high places? Someone who was still close enough to pose a threat? Given the fate of Glenda and Walter Folsom, Leona Mann and Billy Rob Niles, that someone had to be as insidious a disease as cancer. His thinking went again to the sorry excuse for a trainman Quince was reluctant to name. If that man was still in the area, he was overlooking something. More to the point, someone.

A honking from behind pulled Chitto out of the dark meditative state he'd fallen into. Stepping on the gas, he waved a hand out his window as an apology and resumed his trip to tribal headquarters.

As he gained speed, his thinking went again to a trainman, one covered in what appeared to be dark grease and oil that just happened by when the sheriff was loading up the bodies—and whose identity old Ben King had omitted from the case file. Circumstantial?

In a pig's eye.

His next thought went to Peony Folsom and the incident that crippled her so badly, she could no longer drive. He'd bet a dollar to a donut the intent was to eliminate her because she was raising a stink about the picture in the paper. With her gone, the rendering of the skull would die, too. But she hadn't died. The old girl was tough, and that meant, he had another clue. He needed to look for a vehicle painted in camo colors that was big enough to roll a passenger sedan down a steep incline. Who would have the time, resources, and reason to do such a thing?

Sonofabitch . . .

A name popped into his head just as another honk came from behind. Glancing in the rearview mirror, he realized he was holding up traffic again. Filing the Kiamichi murders into a mental file, he focused on immediate priorities. He had a boss waiting for a report of his current cases and that meant he needed to get his ducks in a row.

∞

The call came from dispatch. A fight at a cookout, address on the west side of Durant. *Any officer in the area, report in. Possible injuries.* As the address was repeated, Chitto responded that he was en route and turned on his light bar and siren. Glad he was wearing his duty jacket, he pulled up to a low-slung yellow brick ranch just ahead of a city cop. A woman met them on the curb, mid-forties to fifty. Mother of one of the guys in the fray, she said her son was being killed. Looking the direction she pointed, Chitto heard voices and barking sounds.

He beat it to the backyard, instinctively gathering data for a report. A flat cake on a picnic table, words piped in red that said Happy Birthday, Joe. The smell of charcoal briquettes, burgers and wieners on a grill. Crushed beer cans scattered like billiard balls across the grass.

A half dozen screaming women on the periphery of a circle held barking dogs by their collars. Dog breeds? A blonde poodle and standard boxer. Female breeds? Given the sweaters bearing Greek letters, sorority girls attending Southeastern University.

Pushing through the outer circle, he saw half dozen young men. Some on the ground, some standing. Male breeds? Bat-shit drunk frat boys.

Chitto looked at the city cop. The city cop shrugged slightly and dove in. Chitto dove in after him.

"Police. Break it up—" He didn't know which hurt worse. The kidney punch that straightened his backbone or the sucker punch that collapsed his midsection. He watched what appeared to be a partially digested cheeseburger and fries fly through the air, heard chimes ringing an unfamiliar tune, saw stars flickering overhead. Just before the stars went out, he decided the sucker punch hurt worse.

When he opened his eyes again, he was lying on a gurney in the back of an ambulance looking up at a man with a stethoscope around his neck.

"Don't think they're broken," the man said, pressing against his ribs, "but I'll wrap them for good measure."

Chitto sucked air as the medic pulled the bandage tight. "I could use some aspirin," he mumbled. The EMT shook three into his hand and gave him a bottle of spring water.

"Helluva way to break up a fight," the city cop said when Chitto exited the ambulance. "Step between two guys slugging it out." He sucked spit from between his teeth. "Worked, though. Nothing more effective in breaking up a brawl than laying out a cop. You wanna press charges?"

"Against who? I don't even know who threw the punch."

"Punches," the town cop said.

Chitto thought the town cop's name was Jones, but right then, he couldn't care less. "No charges. I have to get to a meeting."

Another man showed up, the picture of youthful health with a few minor blemishes. A shock of blonde hair textured with coleslaw. Robin's egg blue eyes, except for the blood-streaked right one. Lips girls longed to kiss, which would be twice their normal size in a matter of minutes. Breath that would gag a maggot.

"My name's Joe," Picture of Youth said, thumping Chitto on the back. "How y'doin', man? You, uh, you gonna press charges?"

"No," he mumbled, wishing Joe would stop the thumping. "I have to get to a meeting."

"Oh, man, that's cool." Joe looked around the backyard, coming to rest on a cooler. "Beers made it through. Lemme get you a six-pack."

"No," he managed, wishing the beers were cigarettes. "It's against regulations. Besides, I don't drink."

"No shit?" Joe looked perplexed. "How 'bout cake. It made it through undamaged, except maybe the boxer took a couple licks."

"Regulations," he repeated.

More thumping. "You, uh, you sure you're not gonna file charges."

"Positive," he said, teeth clenched. "Happy birthday, Joe."

∞

"Long lunch," Jasmine said when Chitto codgered through the front door.

"But productive," he said, one arm supporting his ribcage. "Got a little more on our case in Antlers. Need to see that copy of Crystal Folsom's birth certificate you dug up."

166

"*Our* case?" Rummaging through her bottom drawer, she retrieved a file folder and pulled a photocopied document from it. "When did it become our case?"

"By reason of *de facto,* I hereby proclaim you invested." Hurriedly, he looked at Crystal's birth weight. Seven pounds three ounces. Full-term.

"I'm honored." She raised her head, giving him the once-over. "Why are you walking funny? You assist on that call about a picnic in the backyard?"

"It was a birthday barbeque for Joe. Hamburgers and weenies."

"Joe?"

"Palooka." He fingered his abdomen gingerly.

"*Humph,*" she snorted. "You're not old enough to remember Joe Palooka."

"My dad was a fan. Credited Joe for helping establish his ideology."

"Which was?"

"Be a gentle knight. Defend the little guys but avoid fights."

"Appears you didn't listen too well. What's that god-awful smell?"

He bent his head, looking at his jacket and pants. "Beer and beans, I think. But there were dogs present."

She frowned over her glasses. "You all right? You're a little green around the gills."

"More or less." He took a deep breath, winced, and glanced toward Blackfox's office. "I'm late for a meeting with Dan. Supposed to update him on cases I'm working on."

She lifted an eyebrow.

"*Official* cases."

"Didn't say anything to me. But then, he never does. I figure it's because I'm a temp."

Though it hurt like hell, he laughed. "Being a temp has nothing to do with it. He's teed off because you won't make a pot of coffee for the office like Wanda used to."

"Spoiled brat."

"And because you're not the most civil person in the world." Emphasis on civil.

"Ignorant brat." She lifted both eyebrows. "He ever hear of the civil rights movement?"

"Not that kind of civil."

She paused, thinking. "As in uncivilized?" She looked toward Blackfox's office. "Snotty brat."

"As in hard exterior," he said. "Which I figure is a defense mechanism."

She turned to look at him. "So now you're Dr. Phil?"

"Oh, hell no. Just a cop that needs a couple minutes to get his act together." He gave Blackfox's office another glance. "But I've got a strategy. If you can't convince them, confuse them."

"What dumbass told you that?"

"I was quoting someone," he said, sinking onto the corner of her desk. "Can't remember who right now."

Truman, said the learned voice in his head. *Harry S., not Capote.*

"Get your dirty behind off my desk," she said, flicking away grass and dirt that fell from his clothes.

"I just remembered," he said, rising from the desk and lifting an index finger simultaneously. "It was Harry Truman."

"Oh, that makes *all* the difference. Truman also said the atom bomb was a weapon of righteousness." She pulled off her glasses and looked at him. "Look, Sam. Dan's a smart man. He'll find out sooner or later, better from you than someone else."

Chitto shook his head, remembering the ultimatum Blackfox had given him about his job. "Believe me, that is not a good idea."

She leaned back, making the *humph* sound again. "Custer ignored his scout's advice, too."

"You don't know the whole story."

"Well," she said, nodding toward the new cafeteria. "You've got a few minutes to reconsider that strategy. He's having coffee with some guy from another agency that dropped by."

He exhaled, relaxing a bit. "Give me a whistle when he gets back."

Batting her eyelashes, Jasmine smiled. "Pardon me, sir, but would you mind fucking off . . . *please.*"

"Atta girl," he said. "The journey of a thousand miles begins with one step."

She shook her head, mumbling something uncivil under her breath.

Reaching his desk, Chitto slipped out of his jacket. Settling into the familiar and comforting grooves of his chair, he thought about the meeting with his boss. If Blackfox wanted an update on what he was working on, he was about to get a dump. Two domestic violence incidents that required mediation with social services. An underage runaway boy hitchhiking to Louisiana so he could join the Marines; more social services intervention. An assist with an interview after a lie detector test. A Choctaw stallion that jumped fence because it took a shine to a non-native registered quarter horse mare, ruining the bloodline. As added weight, he pulled a few miscellaneous files from a drawer and put them on the bottom of the stack, increasing its volume. If all else failed, he'd throw open his shirt and show him the wrapped ribcage.

Just as he finished putting together his defense, he heard a whistled tune coming from Jasmine's desk. He laughed softly, recognizing the tune as the old cavalry call to charge.

Raking up his pile of folders, he rose stiffly and aimed his body at Blackfox's office.

Pushing through the door, Chitto's well thought-out strategy dissolved into the ether. FBI Agent Ramon Rodriguez sat across from Blackfox.

"Perfect timing." Blackfox waved Chitto to a chair, eyeing his stained clothing in the process. "Agent Rodriguez dropped by today to return something to you."

In front of Rodriguez lay three manila file folders with Confidential stamped across the front. On the top file was a stain that an imaginative person would think looked like a howling wolf.

Sucker punched twice in one day, Chitto thought. He listened to Blackfox clear his throat, a cue that he was supposed to say something.

"Right . . ." He sighed, thinking it was a hell of a time for Sheriff John Skrabo to start working with other jurisdictions. Rubbing a hand across his mouth, he mumbled, "Thanks."

"What?" Rodriguez leaned forward, an ear aimed in Chitto's direction.

Chitto closed his eyes, wondering if there was a record for the number of sucker punches a person could survive in an afternoon. He mumbled "Thanks" again.

"Sit down." This time, Blackfox's words were not uttered as a polite request.

Chitto sat, trying to gather his wits. Unconsciously, he reached for the pack of gum in his pocket. Seeing Blackfox's eyebrows hitch, he replaced it and looked at Rodriquez instead. "How'd you get hold of those files?"

The agent said, "Pushmataha Sheriff's Department couriered them to our office."

"And how'd you know they belonged to me?"

"Business card clipped on the top one. When word got out whose, I volunteered to return them."

"Business card?"

Rodriguez tapped the top file. Clipped to it was one of Chitto's cards with the department phone number replaced with his cell number.

Clutching the stack of folders meant to redeem him with his boss, Chitto tried to sort out the questions stacking up in his head. How many of those cards had he handed out? Who had he given them to? Where had Skrabo gotten this one? What did that card signify? He reached for the personnel folders, hoping a closer look would help identify the pocket it ended up in.

"What were you doing over on that part of the rez," Rodriguez asked, holding the folders just out of his reach. The grin had disappeared.

"We're not reservation Indians," Chitto said, snatching the folders out of Rodriguez's hands.

Rodriguez's eyes narrowed to slits. "It's all in how you look at it."

"I'm interested, too." Blackfox leaned forward, frowning. "How'd the Push County Sheriff get hold of our confidential files?"

Chitto went silent, time spinning backward. "I, uh I took my dog over to the Kiamichi Wilderness for some training and took the files with me. I planned to review them at night. The last time I laid hands on them was in a motel there at Antlers. I left them on the foot of the bed and . . ." He shrugged, leaving his two inquisitors to fill in the gap.

Blackfox was still frowning. "*Your* dog?"

"Well . . ." He swallowed. "He's more my neighbors than mine. We've sorta worked out a deal. The pup stays with her, but I'm training him. He, uh, he chases chickens."

Rodriguez snickered.

"That would be Hattie George," Blackfox said, blinking. "Didn't know she had chickens."

171

"She doesn't. Belonged to the neighbors that live behind her. They went on the warpath because the dog ate some of them."

Rodriguez laughed outright.

"Look," Chitto said, feeling blood rushing from his neck to his eyeballs. "It's my business what I do on my time."

Blackfox turned to the FBI agent. "He's got a point. Thanks again for returning our goods." Standing, he gestured both of them toward the door.

Rodriquez and Chitto exited the office in silence. Chitto watched the FBI agent walk out the front door, then hauled the two stacks of folders to his desk: those he'd carried into Blackfox's office and the ones Sheriff John Skrabo had couriered to the FBI. As soon as he was seated, Chitto pulled a business card from his wallet. Dialing quickly, he counted the rings. Two. Three. Four . . .

"Come on, come on," he muttered. "Pick up."

"You better not tell me you're not coming," Crystal shouted in his ear. "I told Grandma you'd be here Saturday."

"Chill out, I'm still coming." He sank back his chair. "You, uh, you still have that business card I gave you?"

A hesitant-sounding "Yes" came over the line, followed by "Why?"

"Just checking. Anything new since I was there?" He assumed any deaths would make the front page of the *Antlers American.*

"No," she said and again asked, "Why?"

"No reason," he said, knowing when less was more. "I'm coming in from the north this time to avoid town but not sure when we'll get there. Might make a stop or two on the way."

"We?"

"I'm bringing a sidekick."

"Where else you going?" she asked. "We went everyplace there was to go."

"We didn't make it by Bud King's place." Chitto had decided the old sheriff was the logical one to have the time, resources, and a reason to keep interest in the murder investigation from rekindling.

"Are you crazy?"

"Just give me the address, Crystal. I'm working."

He listened to the sound of a phone receiver being laid down, the sound of pages turning, the receiver being retrieved. Crystal read off an address on a county road and asked, "Why you need to go see that old devil?"

"Just compiling information. See you Saturday."

Disconnecting, he eased back in his chair. The fact that Crystal was still alive was reassuring, but he'd given four more people his business card. Even though no deaths had been reported, he couldn't shake the feeling that one of the four hadn't been as lucky as the child conceived out of wedlock.

∞

Blackfox appeared at Chitto's desk, unannounced, and sank into the guest chair. "Hear you did an assist this afternoon." He eyed the stains on Chitto's shirt.

"Who'd you hear that from?" he asked.

"Our temp turned over a new leaf. Said you needed the afternoon off." Turning contemplative, Blackfox said, "Hell of a thing, isn't it? Just when it's time for her to shuffle off to Buffalo, she gets friendly."

You go, Scout, Chitto thought.

"Need a couple days off?" Blackfox asked. "You look a little peaked."

"I'd just as soon stay busy. And besides, we've got that last interview tomorrow afternoon."

"You're off the hook for that one." Blackfox stared through the window at mushrooming clouds. "I'll handle it myself."

"Oh, no you don't. As old as you are, you won't have to live with Wanda's replacement as long as I will. I'm in on this to the bitter end."

Blackfox chuckled, shifted in the chair, made no move to leave. "No more snow jobs," he said a minute later. "How'd our confidential personnel files get into the hands of a county sheriff that's blown me off every time I tried talking to him about cross-department cooperation?"

Chitto slumped in his chair. "Believe me, Dan, I'd like to tell you, but I can't."

Splaying his hands, Blackfox said, "Why not?"

A few months ago, Chitto was ready to leave the force, to return to his first love, geology. That was before he made the acquaintance of a pissant kid with the eyes of a dead fish named Leon Messina. In a routine interview, the kid had let it slip he had knowledge that Chitto's father and Bert Gilly had been executed by men trained to kill. It was confidential information not shared beyond a few, and never to the press or public. There was only one way he could've known about it: from the person who put the hit out. Though brief, the meeting with Leon was enough to reaffirm to Chitto that he'd made the right move to abandon a career in geology for one in law enforcement where he'd have a better chance of finding the killers.

He rubbed his face. "I can't tell you because you're a man of your word. I do, you'd be obliged to fire me."

It was Blackfox's turn to become introspective. "It that important to you?"

"It is."

"Well . . ." Blackfox blinked several times. "Maybe if I heard the whole story, I'd reconsider that ultimatum."

It took Chitto mere seconds to spread the contents of Peony Folsom's envelope in front of Blackfox. It took a half hour to fill him in on the double homicide, the lack of police action on either the murders or a missing Navy veteran, and the forensic artist's determination about the skull found in Leona Mann's coffin. He described the extreme measures Campbell, Bradshaw, and Winters had taken to avoid unnaturally shortened life spans and closed with how Peony Folsom had been deliberately run off the road. He chose to omit the part about *Hatakachafa* and his pal the wolf—and being appointed Folsom's Bone Picker.

"One more thing," Chitto said. "This Walter Folsom would've been related to my wife Mary."

Blackfox scrutinized the artist's rendition of the skull and Walter Folsom's Navy picture. "After all this time, how you planning to prove this Folsom was murdered?"

"There's people still alive that know things."

Dropping the picture back on the desktop, Blackfox looked at him. "Who'd that be?"

"The old coroner, the former sheriff, and the mystery man who assisted at the crime scene I've yet to ID."

"Wouldn't count on that old sheriff," Blackfox said.

"I know, but I got the feeling the coroner is ready to clear his conscious. He's top of my list, if he lives that long. He's old and pretty feeble."

"Tape record it. Just make sure he knows you're doing it." He exhaled. "And you know for sure the killer's still alive?"

"Confirmed by one who would know."

Blackfox made a guttural sound in the back of his throat. "Sounds like you need someone to ride shotgun. Got some family things planned this weekend, but I can beg off."

"No need. Mary has family there." He grinned. "Good old boys."

Blackfox nodded. "One thing still puzzles me. I can't believe you'd be brainless enough to leave confidential files in a motel room."

"Didn't." He filled Blackfox in on the near arrest at the motel and the files Skrabo confiscated.

"That sorry bastard," Blackfox said. "Who the hell he think he is?"

"There's more." Chitto squirmed in his chair, trying to find a more comfortable position before beginning the next chapter of the melodrama he'd become the leading star in. Fifteen minutes later, he'd covered the mystery of Crystal's birth father and the disappearance of Glenda Folsom. He chose to omit the part about the old tavern being haunted. With a pencil pusher like Blackfox, facts spoke louder than fiction.

Blackfox sat quietly, absorbing the discourse like a two-hundred-pound sponge. "You think the skull is Folsom's?"

"No doubt whatsoever." He leaned forward painfully, elbows on his desk. "It just didn't seem right to do nothing. Folsom and that murdered couple deserve justice."

Blackfox's eyes clouded. "You should know by now you can't fix everything." Leaning back, he folded his hands over his stomach and sighed. "All right, follow through with it on the QT, just keep me informed on how it's going." He eyed Chitto directly. "This better not come back to bite me."

"It won't," Chitto said, relief making him limp as a dishrag.

"Now go home." Blackfox rose from his chair. "You're stinking up my department."

"I'm out the door."

Blackfox paused, looking down at him. "I knew that chicken-eating dog story was a crock of shit."

Chitto found the energy to grin. "Actually, that part was true."

"Ate the neighbor's chickens?"

"Chicken parts, to be exact. Some hens stopped laying, so the neighbors butchered them and buried the scraps. Dog dug them up and ate them."

The muscles pulled at the corners of Blackfox's mouth. "Similar thing happened to me once. Had a pup that killed three of my mama's chickens and ate one of them entire, feathers and all. The dog was sick as a horse and my dad whipped the tar out of me."

"You? Why?"

"Because it was my dog and I was in charge of teaching it better." Blackfox looked down at Chitto again. "I ever tell you that you're like a son to me?" He walked away, not waiting for a response.

Chitto dropped his forehead to his desk and moaned.

CHAPTER SIXTEEN

A half hour before the alarm was to go off on Thursday, Chitto kicked the covers back, still exhausted. Before heading home the night before, he'd changed into sweats he found rolled up in the cargo space of his unit and dropped his shirt, jacket, and slacks off at the laundry. He'd stopped at a Walgreen's next, to pick up something for stiffening muscles. The clerk had recommended a deep-heating rub.

"How do I do this?" he'd asked, unable to focus his eyes enough to read the fine print on the tube. She read him directions warning against using with a bandage or a heating pad.

"And it smells good," she's said. "Healthy."

He'd bought two tubes. After the verbal abuse he'd gotten at the office, he felt a deep need to smell good.

Skipping supper, he'd peeled the bandage wrap off his midsection and camped out under a pulsating showerhead. Following that, he'd rubbed the deep-muscle ointment into his abs and lower back muscles and gone to bed, an extra blanket on top to hold in the heat. The blanket also held in the smell, menthol so strong his nose leaked like a faucet.

You can't have everything, he thought now, gimping to the bathroom. Washing his face, he decided to look on the bright side. For one, his encounter with Joe at his birthday party had kept his mind off the Kiamichi dilemma. For two, it was a day for milestones. Even though he still couldn't straighten to his full six foot one, he would have a clear head for the Leon Messina hearing mid-morning and the interview with the last candidate that afternoon. The thought invigorating him, he rubbed more healthy-smelling ointment into front and back muscles before putting on a blue dress shirt, navy slacks, and a sports coat.

The morning grayer than the one before, he turned the car radio to the local weather report at Eaker Field Airport. Sunrise occurred at 6:14, CST, and the sun would set at 7:05, CST. The high was forecast to be in the low fifties, a little below average, with lows in the mid-thirties, also a little below average. Another front might move through that weekend. The forecaster, who referred to himself as a weather prognosticator, was an optimist, however. He was certain the front would swing either north or south, leaving the region in a sweet spot he called "downright equatorial."

Chitto smiled to himself. If he'd had a cup of coffee in his hands, he'd be in paradise. With that thought in mind, he pulled into a drive-thru and ordered a coffee, high and dry.

"What's 'at mean?" the voice on the speaker box said. Given the static and traffic noise, gender was hard to pinpoint.

"Black." Chitto translated. "No cream."

"We don't have cream," the speaker squawked. "Just milk. No fat or low fat. Soy if you're lactose intolerant."

"No problem," he said, deciding the speaker box was of the male persuasion. "I want it black."

"You want sweetener? We got the kind in the little pink packet, the kind in the little yellow packet, and the kind in the little white packet."

Chitto paused, deciding the speaker box was feminine. "What's in the little white packet?"

"Sugar."

"No sweetener."

"You don't want sugar?"

"No."

"What size?" the speaker squealed.

He sighed, deciding the talking box was a robot. "Big a cup as you got," he said.

"So, one large black coffee?"

"Right," Chitto said. "Coffee. High. And. Dry.

"Oh." A crackling pause. "I get it."

"Don't blame yourself," Chitto said, his head starting to throb. "Eating that one lousy apple screwed us all up. A little knowledge is a dangerous thing."

Speaker Box hesitated. "I, uh, I don't think I saw that movie. Pay at the first window. Pick up at the second."

So much for paradise, Chitto thought.

Eden is a state of mind, said the voice in his head.

He pulled into the parking lot at Tribal Police Headquarters and parked next to a yellow Corvette Stingray. He paused a moment, admiring it, then put his mind on the milestones he needed get past that day.

The asphalt in the lot had dried but still looked like a spider's web. Noticing a few crows milling around the trees, he recalled the night another flock, maybe the same one, tried to warn him about *Hoklonote'she*, a shapeshifter that stalked hunters. The crows had been overwintering then but should have migrated to Canada for breeding by now. He stood outside his car, listening to the grating call of the laggards, wondering why they hadn't left, if they were acting as messengers again.

The punch to his left kidney doing strange things to his gait, he did a stuttering sidestep to the front door. Even though the next interview wasn't scheduled until after lunch, he automatically looked toward the reception area. Seeing a woman sitting there, he stumbled to a stop. Early- to mid-twenties. Hair so black it looked blue. Dark-lined Cleopatra eyes. Full lips shiny with lip-gloss. Legs that lengthened as she stood. He stared, wondering how much of her height to attribute to the shortness of her skirt and how much to the shoes on her feet.

It can't be her, he thought. She's not due till one o'clock. The woman gave him a quick up and down. She smiled. She said, "I came early."

Hurrying to Jasmine's desk, he said, "Follow me."

"You didn't say please," she said, falling in behind him.

"Please," he said. Setting his coffee and briefcase down, he planted his palms on the desk and looked at her.

"You still look terrible." She folded into the chair across from him. "Sit down before you fall down."

"I'm working up the nerve. Give. Why's she here so early?"

She hunched her shoulders. "Ask HR. I'm just a temp."

"I don't have time to BS with HR, Jasmine." He sat down and pulled a bottle of aspirin from his top drawer.

"Wouldn't do any good anyway. She didn't tell HR she was coming early either. They didn't know what to do with her, so they gave her to us."

"What're we supposed to do with her?" He shook four aspirin into his hand.

"You and Dan are supposed to work her into your schedule." She leaned forward, sniffing. "You still stink."

"But it's a good stink," he said, chasing the aspirin with coffee. "Healthy."

"You're making my eyes water."

He gestured in the general direction of the reception area. "What is she? A model?"

"She'd like to think so."

He sank back in his chair. "I thought miniskirts went out in the sixties."

"They did, but those with the body to wear them, wear them any time they feel like it."

"Well, she does have the body to wear them."

"And obviously, she felt like it. Bet you know the color of her underwear before the interview's over."

He ignored the comment. "I thought red dye in lipstick was determined hazardous to your health."

"It was. Contains lead but it's cheap. Check out the markdown bins at Walmart."

"And she's so tall."

"It's those platform Mary Janes."

"What?"

"Those heels she's wearing. The kids call them fuck-me shoes."

"I'm not ready," he moaned, leaning his head on the desk. "I haven't looked at her file."

"Two copies and you couldn't look at *one* of them?"

He wondered how Jasmine would know that bit of information, given FBI agent Ramon Rodriquez only returned the lost files the previous afternoon. He turned his head to one side, giving him a partial view of her face. "Tell me Dan's up first."

"He's in a Public Safety meeting. That means you're on first."

The Choctaw Nation Public Safety Department consisted of four departments. Tribal Police, Tribal Security, Casino EMS, and Dispatch. Tribal Police covered the ten and a half counties in the Nation, a force including over thirty patrol officers on tribal lands within jurisdictional boundaries and about ten officers stationed at the hospital at Talihina. Tribal Security was charged with providing security at the Nation's gaming facilities, and Casino EMS provided medical assistance to the Durant casino's customers and employees. Dispatch channeled calls for service among all the groups. Bottom line: Public Safety meetings could go on for hours.

"Said he'd hurry back soon as he could," she added as if reading his mind.

Chitto returned to the facedown position.

"You're snorting."

"I'm trying to smother myself."

"You eat breakfast?"

He lifted his head. "I have to back up Four in court on that dog-baiting hearing this morning. I don't have time to interview her."

"You've got time. Hearing's not until ten. Four called and said he was on his way down."

"Oh." He blinked. "I didn't eat breakfast . . ." He paused. "Or supper last night . . ." More blinking. "And I think I lost my lunch at Joe's barbeque."

"I'll be right back."

He eased back in his chair, settling into the most comfortable rut. Minutes later, Jasmine returned with two donuts.

"Bless you," he said. "How much I owe you?"

"They're on the house, compliments of Joe Palooka."

"You're shittin' me."

"I don't shit in public," she said.

He stopped eating the donut. "But it's against regulations."

"To shit in public?"

"To accept gratuities. How'd you know it was him?"

"Nordic giant. Split lip. Black eye."

He eyed the second donut. "I told him it was against regulations."

"Junior and Jake were not aware of that rule. They finished off a half dozen already. I hid the rest in my bottom drawer until the others show up." She glanced across the office to where the K-9 officer and his dog resided. "Want me to go reprimand them?"

"Take my advice," he said, biting into the second donut. "Never reprimand those two. Now, give me the scoop on Candidate Number Three."

"Name's Madeleine Culpepper, but she goes by Maddy. She went to school with my kids there in LeFlore County."

He brushed crumbs off his desk. "I didn't know you had kids."

"Now you do. Maddy had a rough childhood, rougher than most. Dropped out of high school, started working as a stripper in nightclubs, fell in with the wrong crowd . . ." Jasmine stared out the window. Seeing nothing. Saying nothing.

He tried to read the silence. "Sounds like she's trying to make something of herself."

She looked at him, eyes clouded. "With any other kid, I'd say yes. But out of the blue, she began doing strange things."

"Strange how?"

"Out of character. Up and enrolls in the local business college, which she showed no aptitude for in school, then applied for a job working for the Nation—and got on."

"I can't imagine why," he said, remembering the legs that went on forever.

Jasmine blinked behind the thick frames. "I gotta say, she's one I never expected to see working for any law department, much less someone who'd apply for *this* job. Person who works here has to handle a lot of things—confidential things."

"And I gotta say, I'm having a hard time reading you. Are you for this girl or against her?"

"Oh, I'd be a hundred percent for her, except . . ." She looked out the window again, frowning.

Situational . . . Chitto's thinking went to the three people from LeFlore County in town that day, wondering what the chances were that would happen.

Quickly, he cleared the clutter off his desk calendar, looking at changes to his schedule that week. The first was for a court date for Leon Messina on Friday morning, but it had been changed to Thursday afternoon at one o'clock, then that morning at ten o'clock. Next, he checked the changes that had been made to Maddy Culpepper's interview schedule. Friday morning first. Then Thursday afternoon. And now she shows up unannounced to anyone, not even HR. Then there was Wayne Drumright, aka Four, the field officer who was to testify at the hearing. His schedule, of course, had changed to fit with Messina's.

"Here's the thing." Jasmine leaned forward, her brow still furrowed. "I can't stop thinking about that crowd Maddy fell in with. They weren't good people, but they had money. Someone had to pay for business school, and trust me, you don't pay for tuition and buy designer clothes on our salary." She glanced out the window again, blinking. "Who was it said there's more here than meets the eye?"

He followed her gaze through the window, recalling a poem that mentioned a corpse, a ghost, and a lady who danced. "Auden," he murmured. "The poet, Auden."

"Of course," she sighed. "How could I forget."

"Listen close, Jasmine," he said, voice low. "As soon as that woman's in here, call Dan and tell him to look at the calendar. Have him compare the changes made to the court docket for Messina's hearing and the changes to Maddy Culpepper's interview schedule. And remind him that they're both from LeFlore County. Then tell him to get on the mic and make sure Four reaches the courthouse. Got it?"

She looked at him, eyes wide. "Oh, my lord. What's that girl got herself mixed up in?"

"No time to waste, Jasmine."

"I'm ready." She rose to her feet, eyes narrow slits. "You ready?"

"The pump is primed," he said, pulling his pocket-size tape recorder from a drawer. "Send in the lady who danced."

∞

Maddy Culpepper's underwear was black. Black lace, to be exact. Chitto discovered those facts the first time she crossed her legs.

"Okay to tape our interview?" he said, clicking the On button. "Since you came early, I'm not as prepared as I usually am." Not a lie, actually.

"Oh, sure," she said, again crossing one bare leg over the other.

He picked up one of his worry stones, a diversion from a skirt that inched up every time Maddy Culpepper performed the leg-crossing ritual.

"What in your experience best qualifies you for this job, Miss Culpepper?"

"I learned lots of skills in business school," she said, uncrossing and crossing her legs again.

"Like what?"

"Oh, you know. Secretary stuff."

He waited for more to come. When none did, he modified his approach. "List some examples of cases there in LeFlore County you assisted with that would help you with this job?"

"I didn't help with no cases."

"But you'd know the kinds of cases the officers worked on."

"Oh, sure. It's my job to keep the files. I learned all about filing in business school. I redid all the files on my last job." She uncrossed her legs, crossed them again. "Well, actually, I guess it's still my job because I don't have this one yet." Her smile was dazzling. "I can do the same thing here. You know, redo the files."

He rubbed the worry stone, thinking how to channel her from business school, the one strength on her resume, to the real reason she was sitting in his office. "But you also kept the calendars for the field officers, right?"

"Oh, sure." Her favorite response, obviously. "I keep track of where they are and what they're working on."

Of course, you do, he thought. Since his father and Bert Gilly were ambushed, Dan Blackfox made that a requirement in all offices.

"What, uh, what person influenced you the most in your life?" He looked at her, keeping his gaze from the neck up. Her teeth were perfect, the kind that comes from lots of dentist visits and lots of money.

"Like, what do you mean?" she asked, switching her legs the other direction.

He sighed, deciding it was time to change tactics again. As he stared at her, he noticed a wayward look in her eyes. Rebellious, almost. She hated having to act so meek. So compliant.

Without warning, a loud raucous commotion caused him to turn toward the windows. The contrary crows had decided it was time to muster for the trip north.

"Holy fucking shit," she said, looking out the window. "What got into those damn crows? They scared the crap outta me."

Chitto grinned as the real Maddy made an appearance. "They're forming up to head for Canada," he said. "They winter down here, breed up there."

"Breed? Like, make babies?" She looked out the window again. "That's a long way to go to get laid."

Laughing, he rose and walked behind her. "Lift your feet," he said. "We're going for a ride."

Obediently, she lifted her feet, removing the heels in the process. He wheeled her chair next to his, facing the window.

"Why're we looking at crows?" she asked a couple minutes later. Like magnets to metal, her eyes followed the large black birds as they dipped and swooped.

"You ever hear the Choctaw legend of how crows got to be black?" He gave her a sideways glance. "My grandma used to tell it to me at bedtime when I was a boy."

"No one ever told me any fuckin' bedtime stories."

"It went this way. See, in the beginning, when the Great Spirit made all the peoples—the Bird People, the Animal People, the Insect People, and the Human People— the world was still dark, but Great Spirit forgot to give them fire. That meant they ate their food raw and shivered when it was cold. Now, somehow or other, the people that lived to the east got hold of fire, but they wouldn't share it."

"Why not?" she asked, glancing at him.

"Because . . . they were control freaks."

"I hate fuckin' control freaks," she said, looking at the crows again.

He picked up the story, his attention on the window. "So, the animals got together and made a plan to steal fire from these control freaks. Different ones were chosen to go, based on their strengths. Because he was clever, Crow was one of those picked. The crow was white back then, pure white, and had the sweetest singing voice of all the birds. But when he got to the fire, he took so long standing over it, trying to decide which piece to take, his white feathers smoked black. And he breathed so much smoke that it turned his voice shrill and rough sounding."

"Did he get the fire?"

"Nope. Flew back without it."

"The fuck up." She turned steely eyes to the crows outside the window. "All that cawing prob'ly woke up those control freaks."

"Could be." He paused, sighing. "You know, I bet Crow wishes he could rewrite the past, just like a lot of us do."

She stared at him.

He drew her eyes to the window again. "But look out there. He didn't let it keep him down. All his ancestors are getting ready to fly north to make a fresh start."

Silence.

He looked at her. "Let's pretend you could start over again, Maddy. What if you hadn't dropped out of high school or gone to work doing lap dances in those joints? If you could rewrite your past, what would it look like?"

She turned a graceful neck to look at him, her eyes glistening. "I knew I was in trouble when I saw Mrs. Birdsong."

"What would you do, Maddy?" he said softly.

Her mouth opened but it took a long time for words to come out. "Move as far away from this fucking place as I could." She sat with feet flat on the floor, knees locked like a kindergartner on the first day of school, platform heels clutched in her hands like a lunchbox. "So far they'd never find me."

"Would *they* be spelled, Messina?"

She stood, a platform Mary Jane in each hand. "I tried to tell them you were too smart. I tried to tell them I heard things 'bout you."

Chitto watched as she skirted his desk, then rose to follow her. He passed one fuck-me shoe midway across the office, then the other. As he reached the reception area, he saw a glistening blue-black hairpiece on the floor.

"She left you something." Picking up the clump of dark hair, he tossed it to Jasmine.

"Not my style." She walked to the window, watching Maddy Culpepper's hasty exit. "What'd you say to that girl?"

"Told her a story. Four okay?"

"Yes," she said, still staring out the window. "Couple of other field officers took him in tow and are escorting him to the courthouse." She glanced over her shoulder. "Where's she going? Dan left the meeting early so he could get back here. What am I supposed to tell him?"

"Tell him Elvis has left the building."

She looked out the window again. "Was her underwear black?"

"Um, could be. Why?"

"She must've liked you a lot."

He reached the window in time to see Maddy Culpepper glance at a flock of crows sweeping north, climb into a yellow Corvette Stingray, and burn rubber out of the parking lot. A Choctaw Tribal Police cruiser pulled into the lot right behind her, taking the parking space she'd vacated.

"Doesn't matter," she said, returning to her desk. "Dan's bringing whatever she left under your windshield wipers inside with him."

∞

"I guess you know the HR manager's gonna be on my back." Blackfox rewound the tape in Chitto's recorder. "Wanting to know why that last candidate walked out of your interview."

"Tell her she should screen her candidates better."

"Gonna have to fire her, you know. Can't let her continue to work for the Nation."

"Don't think that will be a problem. Something tells me Maddy Culpepper's headed for the border."

"Mexico?"

Shrugging, Chitto picked up the black panties and opened his bottom drawer.

"What're you doing? That's evidence."

Chitto held the thin, lacy fabric to the light. "Trust me, Dan, you're not gonna get any fingerprints off these." He dropped them into the drawer.

Blackfox shook his head, sighing. "I'll put out an alert on that Stingray. It'll stick out like a sore thumb. Where'd you get the info on her dropping out of school, stripping in clubs?"

Chitto lifted his chin the direction of Jasmine's desk. "Our admin's from LeFlore County."

Blackfox looked Jasmine's direction. "Well, at least you avoided the don't-ask questions." He pushed the On button on the tape recorder, letting the interview tape play again. When it was done playing, he removed the small cassette and tucked it into his pocket.

"What're you planning to do with that?"

"Use it to sic a certain FBI agent on Victor Messina. It could just be the thing to light his fire." He looked at Chitto, a satisfied look on his face. "Good job, Sam, but you better lay low for a while." He looked at the stack of case files on Chitto's desk. "Stick around the office today, clear out some of that stuff . . ." He paused. "And stay close to home this weekend."

"No can do." Standing, Chitto slipped into the sports coat. "Told Four I'd be at the hearing on Messina. What're you gonna do about a replacement for Wanda?"

Blackfox stood up, face thoughtful. "We got those other two."

"They wouldn't work out," Chitto said. "You know they wouldn't. This place is the hub for all the other districts. Neither of them had the right disposition to handle that kind of pressure."

Blackfox nodded, sighing. "Well then, I have no choice. HR will have to repost the position."

"Does that mean we interview more people?"

"It does."

"Can you put a bug in that HR lady's ear about doing a better job with this next batch?"

"I can try. I swear, that woman was to smile, her face would break."

Chitto laughed. "That's just what Jasmine said."

Blackfox looked at him.

"Her exact words, I swear."

Blackfox turned to leave, then paused. "Never heard that old story about Crow told quite that way."

"I might've embellished it a bit."

"I like your version better," Blackfox said.

CHAPTER SEVENTEEN

Remembering the weatherman's prediction for a "downright equatorial" weekend, Chitto ignored Friday morning's gray sky. He scanned the trees for crows as he walked across the department parking lot but they had left for parts north, accompanied by a dark-haired, dark-eyed young woman named Maddy Culpepper. Lucky bastards, he thought, feeling a twinge of envy. He quickly retracted the thought. The dark-winged messengers had saved his butt once. The least he could do was pay it forward.

He stopped at Jasmine's desk, listening to the sound of a click-clacking on her keyboard. He waited a minute, then said, "You ignoring me?"

"No . . ." The keyboard continued its click-clacking. "Just didn't smell you come in."

"I have moved beyond smelling." He breathed deep, feeling only the slightest pull on his midsection. "You need some menthol rub? I bought an extra tube."

"Hold on to it." She handed him several message slips. "Joe Palooka will have another birthday next year."

"Something to look forward to," he said, flipping through slips. "What's the word on the street?"

"Best time to plant corn's in March, between the eleventh and twenty-first." She handed him a folded paper. "I

195

checked in case something new came up *off* the rez. Wouldn't want it to interfere with planting corn."

He chuckled. "Anything new *on* the rez? He inserted the folded paper into his shirt pocket, wondering why her remarks about being reservations Indians didn't bother him in the same way Ramon Rodriguez's had.

Might it be the source? came the taunt in his head.

She glanced up at him, the bottom of her eyes opaque slivers of white. "Rumor going 'round that Maddy's car was found at Will Rogers International."

Oklahoma City . . . Chitto felt a sinking in his stomach. He thought she'd make it further—hoped she'd make it further. "That rumor say which flight she took?"

"No one matching her description on any flight. Of course, that girl struck me as a master of disguise. They're wondering if she ditched the car there and took another form of transportation to wherever it was she was going."

"Would *they* be named Ramon Rodriguez?"

"For a quiet man, he can talk real loud when things aren't going his way." She began typing again. "Dan was surprised to find the car up in Okie City. He figured she'd go to Dallas or points south if she was aiming to go to Mexico." She hit the Print button on her computer and waited for the printer to kick in.

He rubbed the corners of his mouth, defusing a smile. "All kinds of ways to reach the border."

"All kinds of borders, too." The tortoise-framed glasses turned his direction. "Rumor goin' round that Seven's resigning to take a job with ODOT."

"Damn. Our loss, Department of Transportation's gain."

"Um-hmm. Seems his wife was concerned about the mortality rate in District Seven."

He tilted his head, thinking about Pushmataha County being in District Seven. "Might be a valid concern."

"And you're going back over there."

Hearing reproach in her tone, Chitto decided it was time to move from rumors to facts." I guess you also heard that Dan's reposting this position."

"No . . ." Removing her glasses, she stared at him. "Bet that's what HR wants to talk to me about. That lady left me a message."

Chitto translated "that lady" to mean the one whose face would break if she were to smile. "You're well broke in now. Should give some thought to applying for the job yourself."

"Broke in? What am I, a horse?"

Chitto felt his neck turning warm. "What I meant was . . ."

"Oh, hush." Putting her glasses back on, she pulled the Antler's file from her bottom drawer. "You interested in what I've found *off* the rez?"

"Hell, *yeah*." Looking around, he noticed both Nate and Junior were in the office. Nodding the direction of the cafeteria, he said, "Coffee time."

They sat at the secluded table by the windows. Jasmine stirred hazelnut creamer into her Styrofoam cup and took a sip. Making a satisfied grunt, she looked at him. "Checked that list of fifty names. You know, the original suspects?"

He frowned. "Why? Most of them are dead or gone."

"Yes, they are, and a lot of them shared something in common." She tapped a plastic spoon on the edge of her cup. "Might be nothing, but the majority died in their sleep."

"Like old Edgar Guthrie?"

"Yes, indeed. Seems he started an epidemic. I placed a checkmark next to the names of the unlucky ones." She pulled a sheet of paper from her file folder and slid it across the table.

He studied it, then looked at her. "What do you think it means?"

"It means you should not sleep while you're there."

He felt the hair on the back of his neck rise. "Forewarned is forearmed. Anything else?"

Her brow puckered. "There is an amazing lack of information on Glenda Folsom, that sailor's wife."

"Still MIA?" He stared out the window, watching clouds scudding across a murky sky. "Any records showing when she checked out of the hospital?"

"Didn't check out. Apparently took off the same day the baby was born. Left the poor little thing in the nursery there at the hospital, where it stayed until grandma got a court order to take it home."

"That would be Grandma Folsom."

"Yes. Glenda's parents died in a car crash some years before."

"What kind of woman would walk out on a newborn baby . . ."

Chitto watched a flock of small gray birds landed in the trees behind the parking lot. The trees were showing a hint of green, a sign of spring. Rebirth. Unconsciously, he shook his head, thinking of the round-faced, level-eyed young woman in the photo on his kitchen wall.

"Woman who's just given birth, especially with the first child, wouldn't be inclined to walk anywhere too far." Jasmine stared into her coffee cup as if trying to read the grounds at the bottom.

He made eye contact with her. "Think she died in her sleep?"

"Occurred to me." She resumed the spoon tapping.

He rubbed the back of his neck, pausing. "Who could walk into a hospital and not be seen as suspicious?"

"Someone above suspicion." She looked at him, a wry smile on her face. "Or is that not obscure enough for you?"

"No, my thinking was running along the same lines." He leaned forward, resting his elbows on the table. "Here's something else to think about. Walter Folsom got out of the

Navy right after the baby was born and apparently flew straight home. I figure Glenda was waiting for him to get back to name the baby."

"Well," she said, dark eyes blinking. "That would account for the name being written in later."

He rocked back in his chair, hands laced behind his head. "You think Grandma named her?"

"Or Daddy."

Chitto nodded, looking thoughtful. "He did have an interest in rocks. Brought some back from the walks he went on every day. Peony called them diamonds, but they could've been crystals."

"Hmmm," she said, head cocked, "From pictures I've seen, they look pretty much the same, especially when they come out of the ground." She moved from her spoon machinations to the Styrofoam cup, moving it so it left an overlapping ring of circles across the tabletop.

"They do at that," he said, studying the duplicated rings. "How many of those who died in their sleep were trainmen? I'm interested in those that didn't, and *very* interested in any that stayed in the area."

She looked out the window, following someone walking toward the front entrance. "Let me do some more checking." Picking up her coffee cup, she stood to leave.

"Who'd you see coming our way?" Swiveling in his chair, he looked the direction she'd glanced but saw no one.

"The Exec. And he's dressed for battle."

"Damn." Chitto pulled his car keys from his pocket, deducing the SWAT team had a practice planned. "I need to follow up on some things. Might be out of radio reach and phone service today."

"Um–hmm." Eyebrows arched over tortoise-framed glasses, she said, "Ever hear of an all-points-bulletin?"

CHAPTER EIGHTEEN

Chitto jerked awake on Saturday morning, listening to a thrumming sound on the roof. Stumbling to the window, he pulled the blinds apart and watched fat raindrops sluicing down the pane. Making offensive remarks about a weather forecaster with the analytic ability of a rusty weathervane, he made for the bathroom. Hot water pulsed on his back and abdomen, liquid massage fingers. A glance at his fore and aft in the mirror above the sink revealed bruises the color of mustard and eggplant. The colors of healing. He dried off quickly and dressed in faded jeans, a long-sleeve tee, and flannel shirt. While not a hundred percent, he was close. The thought energized him enough to think about the trip to the Kiamichi Valley that weekend.

He'd spent most of the previous day out of the office. In part to avoid a swat team recruiter in camo, aka the Director of Law Enforcement, and in part to pick up things for the weekend. Food mostly, the kind that could be eaten cold. He'd decided a campfire wouldn't be smart. As big game season had come and gone and game birds weren't in season, he and Tubbe couldn't pretend to be hunters. Two men and a dog doing incongruous things would arouse the curiosity of mountain-hardened outdoorsmen and one sheriff who had the nose of a hound on the hunt.

Fixing a pot of coffee, he drank a cup and poured the rest into a thermos. Betting Tubbe ate before leaving or picked up something en route, he fried bacon and eggs and stuck two pieces of white bread into the toaster. As he waited for the toaster to bump the bread, he studied the map on the wall. One green sticky note in particular caught his eye.

"Well, hell," he mumbled and transferred Glenda Folsom from the Pending area to the town of Antlers. Four victims now. He hoped it was the last such move he'd have to make.

He'd just finished rinsing dishes when he heard the sound of a vehicle pulling into the drive. Walking to the door leading to the garage, he hit the opener button and watched a dark green GMC emerge in increments.

"Damn," he mumbled. Thanks to Mother Nature, the Jimmy was now clean as a pin. So much for camouflage. Watching Tubbe pull a rain slicker over his head, he met up with him at the garage entrance.

"Bet you were a boy scout," Tubbe said, studying the stack of items on the garage floor. "We need all this stuff?"

"It's mostly food and sleeping gear. A backpack, couple of guns."

Tubbe picked up two zippered cases. "What kind of guns?"

"Remington 879 and Colt AR 15." Lifting the back of his jacket, he revealed the Glock at his back. "Plus my service weapon."

Tubbe whistled. "It bear season?" He gestured toward his GMC. "I just brought the one, and . . ." He patted the back of his jacket.

Chitto didn't ask what "the one" was, figuring it would out power any of his. "If you want to start loading this stuff, I'll go get Boycott." He paused as he slipped into a slicker. "That's the dog's name."

"I'm not even gonna ask," Tubbe said. "Bring a towel to dry off his feet. I don't hanker to sit in a puddle."

"Hanker?"

"What? You forgot how to speak Okie?"

Groaning, Chitto resumed his trek. He'd never been caged up with Tubbe in a tight space, so the weekend promised to be interesting. On the recent undercover case, they'd taken turns leading and following as they'd driven around the Chickasaw and Choctaw Nations. On this trip, he might just get a peek at the man inside the flesh.

Hattie had Boycott ready to go, including a new reel-type leash. "I'll leave that with you, Hattie." He snapped Boycott's training leash to his collar. "He's minding pretty well."

"Might be minding you, but he drags me around like a yo-yo on a string." She held her pointer finger under Chitto's nose. "Yet one more reason why you should take him off my hands permanent."

He kissed her on top of her gray head. "I could use something to wipe him down with."

Grumbling, she walked to a hallway closet and returned with a frayed towel. "This one's seen its better days, like someone else I know." Before he could respond, she closed the door.

"Come on, boy. Hattie's in a mood." Boycott took up a hip-hopping gait beside him. "You need to meet someone new, and he's not a pushover like Hattie. So mind your Ps and Qs." Boycott responded with a rumbling bark, cheeks flapping and tail wagging.

Tubbe had finished loading the gear under the camper shell and shed his slicker. He sat behind the steering wheel, a black hoodie covering a navy-blue pullover.

Chitto gave the dog's feet a quick wipe before letting him in the truck. Boycott reciprocated with a vigorous shake, shedding water like a fish flopping on the bank.

"*Holy moly.*" Tubbe wiped his face with his sleeve.

"You said feet." Chitto tossed his backpack on the bench seat next to Boycott. "I'm a literal person," he said, stealing a line from Jasmine.

Tubbe responded with a cold-eyed stare. "Well, literal *this*. He sleeps with you.

As Chitto slipped out of his slicker and stowed it behind the seat, he noticed a large gun case and huge Bowie knife on the floor. Picking up the knife, he held it to the light. "What's this?"

"A knife," Tubbe said, looking at Chitto like he was missing a few nuts and bolts. "You forgot something."

Eying the gear, Chitto said, "What?"

"Bodybag."

Chitto's heart skipped a beat. "You, uh, you think that might be a bit premature?"

Tubbe shook his head, sighing. "We have to assume Folsom's not ambulatory. If we find his remains, we need something to carry them in."

A sigh. "Valid point. I've got some heavy-duty garbage bags."

Tubbe hiked an eyebrow. "Poor ending for a warrior."

"As would be a bodybag." He opened the car door.

"That's true." Leaning his head out the window, Tubbe yelled, "Bring more than one."

Chitto turned, seeing a dark head behind a rain-streaked windshield that looked otherworldly, and said, "Why?"

The head appeared at the window again. "Odds and end."

"Odds and ends . . ."

Tubbe's head appeared a third time. "Folsom's dog? The murdered woman's head?"

Odds and ends. Retrieving the box of garbage bags from the shelf, Chitto tossed it behind the seat and hooked his seat belt. Noticing Tubbe staring at him, he said, "Now what?"

"We'll leave as soon as you become literal. Which way?"

Chitto sighed. "East on 70, north on 271. We'll take off down a back road before we reach Antlers, circle around from the north."

The rain continued as they left Durant, Boycott occupying the middle of the bench seat in the GMC. The wipers flung water off the windshield dutifully, but the rain was insistent, sweeping down the glass in waves. Semis added to the deluge, creating breakers that swamped the pickup.

Two grown men and a hound in a closed up cab can put a lot of humidity in the air. The GMC might handle bad roads like a dream, but its defroster was a nightmare. Periodically, Chitto and Tubbe wiped sleeves across side windows and windshield. Boycott supported their efforts with enthusiastic panting.

"Sure we can't hole up in a motel?" Tubbe asked some miles down the road. "It could get close, we're forced to sleep under that camper shell."

"Won't need to. I have it on good report that the weather will be good this weekend. It'll stop before we reach Antlers."

Tubbe glanced at him. "So now *you're* a prognosticator?"

He looked at Tubbe. "Is that Okie speak?"

"I listened to the weather on the way over. Weatherman described himself as a prognosticator. Said something about a front making a surprise move."

"Damn," Chitto growled. He paused to assess this development. "We can't go to a motel, at least not in Push County." A stare bordering on glare prompted Chitto to relate his near-arrest experience the previous weekend, ending with, "John Skrabo cruises his kingdom 24/7."

205

"Okay . . . How 'bout the people who pulled you into this? The sailor's mother and daughter would probably put us up."

"They offered, but I didn't want to put them at more risk. Someone's already tried to kill Peony, and her granddaughter has the whole family taking turns watching over her. That means you, me, and Boycott are on our own."

"Well, then . . ." Tubbe inhaled, exhaled. "Could you at least dry him off? It reeks of wet dog in here. And while you're at it, tell me what the plan is." He shot Chitto another look. "I'm assuming you have one."

Chitto rubbed Boycott down and briefed Tubbe on getting George Forsyth out of the nursing home and into a safe house where he could tape record his testimony.

Tubbe looked at Chitto. "We're supposed to kidnap an old man out of a nursing home."

Chitto nodded. "I met a guy up in the hills who'll let him hole up for a while." He looked at Tubbe. "I think you'll relate to him." He recounted the preventive measures Quince Winters had put in place to prevent trespassing. Encountering another look, he decided to stick with the mission. Tubbe wasn't ready to reveal the man inside the flesh.

"And after Forsyth's safe, we need to look for a vehicle that looks like trees." He told Tubbe his theory about the vehicle that forced Peony Folsom off the road. "I figure it's painted camo colors, and to push a full-size sedan down an embankment, it would have to be big. An SUV, maybe a Hummer. If we can find who owns it, maybe we'll have our missing trainman."

Tubbe focused on windshield wipers moving at breakneck speed. "And how does this help us find Walter Folsom's remains?"

Chitto sighed. "I'm hoping the mortician will fill in that blank. If not, this guy I told you about saw Folsom on a hillside there by the campground back when he was working as a switchman. He was planning to pin down where that was exactly."

"You think the body's buried near the campsite where those two sailors drank coffee?"

"It makes sense. I figure the killer took the quickest way out, buried him close and shallow. According to Winters, there's all kinds of dump spots on those hillsides."

"Hillsides . . ."

"Yep, more than one," Chitto said, deciding it was a time to speak literal.

"And he observed Folsom on *one* of them more than thirty years ago."

A pause. "I know. It's a long shot, but . . ."

They were quiet for several miles. Tubbe broke the silence when a semi veered over the centerline. When he was through giving the trucker a piece of his mind, he turned to Chitto. "It seem strange to you that a trainman known around town could remain anonymous all this time?"

"Like something out of a sci-fi novel. I figure it has something to do with people dying in their sleep." He pulled Jasmine's report from his pack, indicating those she'd marked. "The guy's still around, has to be. My, uh, my informant is checking to see what trainmen survived, and any that remained in the area."

"Your informant?"

"Our admin, but she prefers to be called Scout." Chitto grinned at him. "She's hung up on Custer, who didn't listen to his scouts."

Tubbe flashed his cockeyed grin, then gave Chitto a serious look. "You've changed," he said, turning back to the windshield.

Chitto stared at his profile. "How so?"

"Not so uptight." Tubbe's eyes remained glued on the highway. "I figure it was that redhead that did it. Women are known to work the kinks out of a man."

The redhead Tubbe referred to was named Dr. Leslie Anderson, a cultural anthropologist who'd spent time researching social and cultural variations in Oklahoma since the Removal. She *had* reached Chitto, in more than one way. Showing him that his obsession was keeping Mary from completing the final leg of her journey. Showing him that he still could feel for a woman. Her involvement in the last undercover case, however, caused her to leave the checkerboard prematurely and decide not return. He'd gotten that word recently that she'd taken a full-time position at the college where she taught.

"That didn't go anywhere." Chitto stared out the side window at trees submerged in what was quickly becoming a very large swamp. "She, uh, she held herself responsible for how that last business came about. You know, teaching the old ways and all."

Tubbe made a grumbling sound in his throat. "You could've stopped that last killing and didn't."

"Yup," he sighed, lapsing into Okie speak. He swiveled his head from the gray landscape to the dark profile at the wheel. "Why you bringing it up?"

Tubbe continued his highway vigil. "You don't seem much affected."

Minutes passed, with Chitto exchanging frequent glances with Tubbe. Sighing, he said, "I did a cleansing ceremony. Old Sonny Boy Munro does that kind of thing."

"You're joking." Tubbe rubbed the corners of his mouth with a thumb and forefinger to keep from smiling.

"Indian warriors used to go through one after they got back from killing the enemy. It prepared them to be accepted again by their own people." He looked at Tubbe. "If you think about it, it's not a whole lot different than going to the river to drink coffee . . . or a fourteen-thousand-foot mountain to freeze your ass off."

Tubbe swiveled his head towards him, eyes steely.

"Maybe that was a poor example," Chitto said.

Tubbe's head swiveled back toward the struggling windshield wipers. "An Indian sauna, huh? Too bad no one told the VA. Would've saved the government a shitload of money." A minute passed. "And a lot of wasted time."

The windshield wipers made shadows that advanced and retreated across Tubbe's face. Chitto studied the man, wondering if he'd just gotten a peek inside the flesh. From the back of his mind, a thought took shape, and he started looking at road signs.

"Pull off at the next exit, the one to Bokchito," he said. "I need to talk to a man about bacon."

∞

Tubbe pulled to a stop in front of a house with a pyramid roof. "That the old singer, Munro? The prayer man?"

"And pig farmer." Chitto glanced at him. "He's a man of many talents."

Sonny Boy Munro sat in a folding lawn chair on his front porch, a cap with earflaps tugged low on his head, a canvas coat several sizes too large draping his thin frame, metal snaps on galoshes hanging open. Recognizing Chitto, he smiled a toothless smile.

Chitto and Tubbe donned their rain slickers, Boycott was snapped to his leash, and all three made a dash for the porch. The old man was on his feet by the time they reached it.

"Your pig is growing," he said to Chitto. "Pretty soon, you will be eating fresh bacon."

"That's just what I was checking on. What you figure, another month?"

"Two weeks." Sonny Boy held up two crooked fingers.

"What're you doing out here?" Chitto secured Boycott's leash to a porch post. "It's too wet, too cold."

"Waiting for you. Many people have needed prayers." He slapped where his shirt pockets hid under the oversized coat. "I am out of smokes."

209

"Figured you would be." Chitto pulled a pack of Marlboro Reds from his jacket pocket and handed it over. "Keep it. It's a spare."

Sonny Boy smiled again. "You come in, dry off by the stove."

A gas heater toasted the front room of the little house. The smell of a boiling bean pot drifted in from the back room and a bare-bulb lamp cast a glare across the plank floor. Shedding their rain gear at the front door, they followed Sonny Boy to the kitchen.

"You sit down. Coffee is ready." Sonny Boy took three cracked mugs from a cupboard and filled each with boiled coffee.

"We can't stay long," Chitto said. "We're headed to Antlers."

"*Ahhh*. The Nameless One has found the monsters . . ." Sonny Boy pointed with his chin toward Tubbe. "And Wolf goes with you to kill them."

Tubbe looked at Chitto. "What'd he say?"

Chitto shook off the question. "I told you before, Sonny Boy, I'm not this *Hatakachafa*. And my friend here isn't a wolf. He's an off-duty cop, just like me."

"No, he is Wolf." Without warning, Sonny Boy reached across the table and pushed up Tubbe's shirtsleeve, revealing a mark on his forearm.

"I'll be damned." Because he was looking at it upside down, it took Chitto a few seconds to identify the tattoo as the head of the wolf.

"What the hell's he talking about?" Tubbe said, jerking his shirtsleeve down.

"Later." Chitto turned to the old man again. "Anything new since we last talked?"

Sonny Boy blinked several times, his eyes trained on a rain-spattered window. "It is too wet to plant corn." He held up a thumb and two crooked fingers. "In this many weeks, the ground will dry out."

Except for the boiling bean pot and raindrops on the windowpanes, the room went quiet.

"Okay, then," Chitto said, draining his cup. "Time to hit the road."

"Yup," Tubbe said, downing his coffee, too.

At the front door, Sonny Boy laid a hand on Chitto's arm. "You have forgotten what I told you, my son."

Shuffling through memories of the last visit, Chitto came up empty. "Tell me again, Grandfather."

"A man can be many things. You look with blind eyes."

"Meet you at the truck," Tubbe said. Pulling the hood of his slicker over his head, he stepped off the porch.

"Wait." Sonny Boy walked to where Tubbe stood and pushed back the hood. "When it is done, you come back. We will have a cleansing ceremony to remove the shadows from your head . . ." He tapped Tubbe's forehead. "Put them at your feet where they belong." He pointed toward the ground.

Tubbe looked at Chitto, a look on his face that said, Let's get the hell outta here.

"Yup." Chitto unhooked Boycott's leash and stepped off the porch, noticing Tubbe was halfway to the GMC. "Take it easy, Sonny Boy."

Sonny Boy bumped a cigarette from the pack of cigarettes. "I will send up a prayer," he said, striking a stick match on his pants leg. The flare illuminated his face and a plume of smoke worked its way skyward.

∞

"And our reason for stopping there was . . ." Tubbe let the question hang.

Chitto took a minute. "Something just told me I needed to."

Tubbe gave him a cold stare, then nodded at Boycott. "He's wet again."

Pulling the towel from under the seat, Chitto gave the dog another rubdown. The sky had lightened some, but the humidity was heavy.

Back on the highway, Tubbe glanced his way. "How the hell did he know I had that tatt? And what's this Nameless One business? Something tells me you left something out."

"It didn't seem relevant at the time." Chitto wiped the towel across the windshield. "Sonny Boy's a mystic of sorts. Sees things, knows things. My grandma's the same way." He leaned back in the seat, stroked Boycott's head, and told Tubbe the old story about *Hatakachafa*, The Nameless One, and his wolf that taught dogs to howl.

"So we're these guys in this old story?"

"No. I don't take this stuff seriously. Except . . ."

Tubbe looked at him.

Sighing, Chitto told him about the monsters his grandmother told him about, the ones the Nameless One and his wolf supposedly killed.

"A one-eyed monster," Tubbe repeated. "An evil medicine man, and a shapeshifter who stalks hunters."

"There might've been others. Grandma was giving me the abbreviated version."

Tubbe was quiet a minute. "You said *except*."

Pulling a deep breath, he told Tubbe about Ben King being blind in one eye and George Forsyth having questionable mortician practices.

"Okay. So you think you've identified the one-eyed monster and the evil medicine man. That leaves the shapeshifter." He turned the wipers on intermittent as the rain let up. "Who would be the trainman you can't see because you're blind?"

"I don't know." Chitto lifted his hands, let them drop.

Tubbe let out a grunt. "And we're supposed to not only kill these guys but find Folsom's bones and bring them back to his mother?"

"No— *Hell*, no. I'm not even holding out hope we'll find Folsom's bones, much less kill anyone. We're just two off-duty cops snooping around. Nothing more."

"And don't you forget it," Tubbe snapped.

The miles clicked past, most of them in silence. As they exited onto Highway 271 north, Chitto said, "I'm overlooking something."

"Could it be you're looking with blind eyes?"

Picking up on Tubbe's sarcasm, Chitto said, "I'm serious, Frank. I've missed something."

Tubbe drove another couple of miles, then sighed. "You know the drill. When you're done and there's nothing there, go back to the beginning."

Chitto did, telling about the botched investigation and Walter Folsom's disappearance. The campground where the two ex-sailors met for coffee and its proximity to the murder scene. The case files that walked out with Bud King when he retired. The witness, Edgar Guthrie, who died in his sleep a week later. The deputy who died around the same time, a gunshot to the head. The fifty suspects that had been questioned, an obvious snow job. His interviews with the three remaining suspects that led nowhere.

"You left out the nameless trainman," Tubbe said.

"It's easy to overlook a ghost."

Tubbe looked at him. "We're getting' close to Antlers. Where do I turn off to avoid running into this 24/7 sheriff?"

Chitto looked around, taking a read. "About a mile ahead. It's not paved, but new gravel was put down on the county roads last fall. Most of them."

As Tubbe turned onto the county road, Chitto noticed a frown on Tubbe's face. "What did I overlook, Frank?"

"Maybe nothing. But didn't you say this trainman had an uncle that was protective?"

"Right . . ." Chitto paused, then mumbled, "Oh, damn . . ."

Tubbe glanced at him. "A light just come on in the closet?"

"Maybe. See, Crystal Folsom and I had lunch at this place in Antlers and old Bud was there. He waved Crystal over, rubbed her arm affectionately, and referred to her as 'his girl.'"

"Affectionately. And you think that was relevant?"

"He just seemed . . . possessive."

"And you're wondering why so many people have died in their sleep or took one behind the ear, and this Crystal's been lucky."

"Something like that."

Tubbe dropped his speed as the newly laid gravel turned to slippery clay. "How old is this Ben King?"

Chitto leaned back, studying a rip in the headliner. "Don't know for sure. I read up on the new sheriff, Skrabo, on the internet. He's been in law enforcement over thirty years, sheriff half of that. Assuming he went to work right out of school, that would make him fifty-five, sixty now. That would put the old sheriff in his eighties, and from the looks of him, they were not kind years."

Tubbe wiped the windshield with his jacket sleeve. "If those assumptions are good, thirty-five years ago, King would've been . . . what? Forty-five, fifty?"

"Right," Chitto said, sighing. "So, it's possible old King is Crystal's birth father."

Tubbe took a minute to steer the GMC out of a slide that almost put them in the ditch, then said, "Where we going? This road's turning to something that belongs at the bottom of a Port-A-John."

"Quince Winters' place. The county conveniently runs out of gravel just before they reach him. He was one of the suspects on the sheriff's list."

"And what do you need to talk to him about?"

"Bringing the old undertaker there for safekeeping." A few minutes later, he looked at Tubbe. "You were thinking something else back there. What?"

Tubbe shrugged. "Just seemed strange to me that the old sheriff didn't call Skrabo to assist at the murder scene. Would've been good training for a new deputy."

Chitto blinked, considering the idea. "It's a big county. I assumed Skrabo was off duty or working somewhere else."

Tubbe made a noise in his throat.

"What?"

"You do a lot of assuming."

Shaking his head, Chitto reached for his cell.

"Who you calling?"

"Scout."

CHAPTER NINETEEN

After calling Jasmine to have her check on John Skrabo, Chitto dialed Crystal. Both calls were challenges, given cell phone reception was questionable in the best of times.

"I can't hear you, Crystal," Chitto repeated for the third time. He put his cell on speaker and moved it around the truck's cabin.

"I said, where the hell are you? Grandma's pacing the floor."

"So. you're at the house now?"

"No. I had to show this frickin' piece of property to some frickin' Californians. I'm going home soon as I'm frickin' done."

"We'll be there soon."

"Well, hurry the frick—"

As static filled dead air, Chitto noted the grin on Tubbe's face. "Crystal's the impatient type," he said, "not to mention impulsive."

"Would it be a fair assumption to say that's why Winters didn't want her to know the truth about her real father?"

It was Chitto's turn to grin. "Now I know why Chata kicked Chiksa out of the tribe."

Tubbe feigned an injured look, then turned sober. "Something tells me we're here."

Before Chitto could confirm they'd reached Quince Winters' place, Tubbe pulled in at a locked gate bearing a sign that said Trespassers Will Be Shot. Shutting off the engine, he pointed his chin toward the thermos on the floor. "It'll be a while before he reaches us."

"How would you know that?" He poured the last of the coffee into their mugs,

"He's a cautious man," Tubbe said, taking a drink of tepid coffee.

Chitto scanned the fencerow and culvert area. "What? I'm not seeing anything."

"He knows how to do it right."

Chitto scanned the area again, letting his eyes rest on irregularities on the ground. "Deadfalls? Trip wires?"

"You're getting better, professor. Except for this stuff." Lowering his window, he dumped his cup. "Next time I bring the coffee."

Chitto cranked his head around so he could see Tubbe's face. "There's gonna be a next time?"

"I'd bet money on it," Tubbe said, sighing.

Quince Winters' arrival mimicked his last, with the addition of an olive-green rain slicker. Rolling down his window, Chitto called over the barking of his dog pack, reminding Winters he was Crystal's cousin.

"Yeah, I remember." Winters' voice echoed across the short expanse like a rumble of thunder. "Tried calling you from the washateria when I was in town."

"That right?" Chitto's curiosity meter went off the charts.

"Your phone's not working," Winters said.

"Poor reception out here. Can we talk at your place? I need a favor."

The ATV's idle ricocheted off the heavy air, sounding like a Boeing preparing for takeoff. "Who's that with you?" Winters yelled.

Tubbe opened his door wide enough to hold up two empty hands. "A friendly," he called out."

Killing the ATV's engine, Winters unlocked the padlock, swung the gate open, and looked inside the GMC's cab. He gave Chitto a quick once over, rubbed Boycott's head, and held Tubbe's eyes in a stare. "Don't step where I don't," he mumbled, waving them through.

They didn't.

"Coat hooks inside, to the right of the door." Winters shook the water off his slicker before entering the cabin. Chitto and Tubbe followed suit. Boycott immediately made for a spot in front of a wood-burning stove.

Once inside, Tubbe looked over the armaments, the food stores, the books, and mumbled, "Holy moly . . ."

"Coffee's hot." Winters indicated the pot on the wood stove.

"Hot coffee would be appreciated." Tubbe sat down at the plank table. "Nice place. Stayed in one pretty much like it once."

"Except in snowier country," Chitto said, sitting down next to Tubbe. The remark earned him a look that would curdle milk.

"You first." Winters filled three mugs and sat down across from them. "What can I do you for?"

Chitto filled him in on the plan to free George Forsyth from the nursing home. "Yours is about the safest place I know of."

Winters stared at the table, fingers on one hand doing a drum roll across its top. "Why would you want to do that?" he said, raising his eyes to meet Chitto's.

"Forsyth knows who killed Niles, Mann, and Crystal's dad."

Winters spooned powdered whitener in his coffee and stirred it slowly. "And you know this how?"

Chitto gave him the whole story, ending with the old mortician's need to clear the air about what happened that night.

"Well, that explains that." Winters rose from the table, picked up a newspaper off the table next to his reading chair, and laid it before them. It was folded to an obituary notice.

"Shit," Tubbe mouthed. "That him?"

"One and the same," Chitto said, reading George Forsyth's obit. "Says he died in his sleep." He looked at Winters. "This is why you tried to call me?"

"Figured you'd want to know."

"Well, hell," Chitto mumbled, rubbing his mouth.

"What?" Tubbe stared at him.

"Just wondering if someone let it slip we were there. That receptionist was the talkative type."

"We?" Winters said.

"Crystal was with me." Lowering his gaze to the tabletop, Chitto did a drum roll of his own. Feeling Winters' eyes on him, he looked up. "What?"

"You sign that register there at the home?" Winters' eyes had hardened to steel.

"We did," Chitto sighed. Hearing his cell phone ring, he pulled it from his pocket and looked at the number. "I need to take this"

"That who I think it is?" Tubbe asked.

Chitto nodded. Remembering Crystal's example from their last visit, he walked to the front door. "You two reconnoiter," he said over his shoulder. "I'll be a couple minutes."

Chitto didn't take time to slicker up. He walked from one end of the sodden plank porch to the other, looking for a place where he could get a signal. At the end nearest the pole shed used for skinning wildlife, he found the sweet spot.

"I've got you, Jasmine. Can you hear me?"

"Barely," came the weak response. "So start listening 'cause I'm gonna talk fast."

When she finished her report, Chitto mumbled, "Well I'll be hornswoggled."

"Did you get all that?" she said after a long silence hyphenated with static.

"Yup."

More static. "You need me to check on anything else?"

"Nup."

Static again. "Am I talking to Sam Chitto or some redneck that stole his phone?"

"I am feeling my neck start to redden. You done good, Scout."

"Aw, shucks."

Disconnecting, Chitto pushed through the cabin door. He found Tubbe and Winters examining what appeared to be a long-handled knife. Grabbing his coffee mug from the table, he turned his backsides to the stove and looked between them. "I know it's some kind of knife . . ." He nodded at the long blade. "But what kind?"

"Vintage Marine sword knife with an eighteen-inch blade." Tubbe ran his fingers along the well-oiled steel.

"Army used it first." Winters replaced the long bladed weapon into a leather sheath and looked at Chitto. "That Crystal?"

"Scout," Chitto said.

Winters looked at him.

"His informant," Tubbe interceded. "Professor here likes to use language no one can understand."

"That right?" Winters filled his cup from the pot on the stove. "Up till now, I haven't had any trouble."

"Our friend here is the one who uses language no one can understand." Chitto made eye contact with Winters. "But we can all stop talking in riddles now. I now know the name of the sorry excuse for a trainman and worst kind of whoring bastard God ever made."

"Took you long enough." Winters cracked a smile. "Blind man could've seen the resemblance."

Tubbe leaned against the wall, smothering a laugh in the crook of his arm.

∞

"A man can be many things," Tubbe said, imitating Sonny Boy Monroe's ancient croak.

"Shuddup," Chitto growled. In the last quarter hour, he had transferred the information dump from Jasmine about the current sheriff, John Skrabo, being employed by the railroad at the time of the double murder and disappearance of Walter Folsom. He was appointed deputy immediately after a convenient opening occurred in the sheriff's department, facilitated by a bullet to the brain of the deputy that assisted at the murder scene. After his uncle retired, he'd filled the vacancy and continued to do so, year after year. Unopposed.

"That would explain old Bud King being possessive of Crystal," Chitto said. "Assuming Skrabo's Crystal's father, she'd be a blood relative."

"Probably walked right up on the deputy," Winters commented. "Knowing he was Bud King's nephew, he wouldn't have thought anything of it."

"Wouldn't surprise me if old King did it," Chitto said. "Something tells me that man has the morals of a pissant."

"I get the motive for the double homicide," Tubbe said. "An obsession can turn to jealousy, and if someone's twisted enough, revenge. But why Folsom?"

Winters gave Tubbe an approving nod. "The man knew how to say it, didn't he?"

Tubbe looked at Chitto, eyebrows hiked.

"It's a quote from Johnson. 'Revenge is an act of passion, vengeance of justice. Injuries are revenged, crimes are avenged.'" He paused, grinning at Tubbe. "Samuel, not Lyndon Baines."

Winters chuckled.

"Can we get back to business?" Tubbe fed a stick of firewood to the stove. "If I'm understanding this right, Skrabo decided to seek revenge for Leona Mann jilting him."

"That'd be my guess," Chitto said.

"So, how'd Walter Folsom figure into this need for revenge?"

"Didn't." Chitto sighed. "I figure he was in the wrong place at the wrong time. Probably at the campground, either waiting for Mann and Niles to arrive or still there after they left. At any rate, he would've heard the gunshots and when he investigated, found Leona's body." He looked between Tubbe and Winters. "Her, uh, her groin area had been covered. From what I hear, Folsom was an upright guy. If I had to guess, after he found her, he went looking for his buddy."

"Makes sense." Winters frowned. "But why didn't Skrabo leave Folsom at the scene, too?"

"We'll never know." Chitto rolled his coffee cup between his hands. "Like Tubbe said, the guy was twisted as a corkscrew."

"Not that slick bastard." Tubbe walked to the window and pulled back the shutter. "He killed Folsom's dog, so he was covering his tracks. It was a deliberate act."

Chitto lapsed into silence, wondering if the King-Skrabo consortium was betting on a returning vet that conveniently disappeared becoming the suspect.

"So, Skrabo's the shapeshifter." Tubbe looked at Chitto "Think he killed the evil medicine man, too?"

"How's that?" Winters stirred a pot on the cooktop, then retrieved a pan of cornbread from the oven.

"He's referring to Forsyth. I thought the old guy was safe, locked up like that." Chitto gave his head a shake, feeling more tired by the minute. "How could anyone know he'd talked to me?"

"Someone there at the home must've spilled the beans," Tubbe said. "That or the sheriff's department has the whole county wired."

"Guest register." Winters set a cast-iron stewpot holding venison stew in the middle of the table, a skillet of cornbread alongside it. He filled three bowls and pushed two toward Tubbe and Chitto. "You mentioned you and Crystal signed in at the home." As he sat down, he cast cold blue eyes on Chitto. "Surely you used fictitious names."

"We did." Chitto paused eating. "More or less."

"I told you." Tubbe held his spoon up like a pointer to Winters. "Language no one can understand."

"Explain," Winters said to Chitto. More an order than a request.

Chitto mentioned the poet's name he'd used. "I doubt anyone caught it." He gave his head a shake. "But Crystal used the name of one of George Forsyth's granddaughters, a schoolmate that died in grade school."

"And the girl's last name was Forsyth," Winters said. More a comment than a question.

"Yeah," Chitto muttered. "And with the renewed interest in the murders, Skrabo's probably keeping a close eye on his old cronies. Obviously, he felt Forsyth wasn't trustworthy, even in his demented state."

Winters nodded. "Two men can keep a secret if one of them's dead."

Tubbe looked between the two. "Crystal must not know about Forsyth, or she would've said something this morning."

Chitto told Winters about the brief and static-interrupted call from Crystal. "Even if Skrabo figured out Crystal visited the nursing home, it doesn't mean he suspects she knows his identity."

"And if she's to live, she's *never* to know that," Winters snapped. "So, go get Folsom's remains and get them back to Peony, then get the hell out of town so we can return to what is considered normal in these parts."

"Go get . . ." Chitto stared at him. "You son of a buck. You found where Folsom's buried."

Tubbe rose from the table. "You pinpoint location while I take that dog of yours for a walk." He looked at Winters. "Those other hounds leave him alone?"

"They'll tolerate him. Can't swear what they might do to you."

"I'm not worried." Pulling on his jacket at the door, Tubbe snapped Boycott's leash to his collar and stepped outside.

Winters made a grunting sound. "Where'd he see duty?"

"Doesn't talk about it."

"Probably for good reason." He stared at Chitto. "He has the bearing of what was known in my day as a Snake Eater."

Snake Eater. Frowning slightly, Chitto said, "Special Forces?"

Winters nodded. "Door Kicker. Did a lot to level the playing field."

A pause. "Thought those guys were in the business of training, acting as advisors."

"Propaganda. Had the capability to do more than help us win hearts and minds. Could do things and in ways that were not attributable to anybody in particular, and that tended to terrify the terrorists."

Chitto breathed deep. Then he remembered some talk in grad school among veterans who had used a similar term: Meat Eater. His recollection was the expression referred to a type of Special Operations Forces soldier whose job was bloodshed, usually violent bloodshed. But he had not heard the talk directly from one who had actually performed those duties, only from those that had heard it from someone who had heard it from someone.

"Well, that would explain why he doesn't talk about it." Chitto waited a minute, absorbing the full impact of Tubbe's service duty, then looked at Winters. "Where'd you find Folsom's remains?"

"Didn't say I found them. But I'd bet my bottom dollar someone else had a look at them."

"Go on . . ." Chitto nodded, encouraging Winters to continue.

"Walked the old track yesterday. At that trestle by the campsite, I saw someone on the hillside. Appeared to be digging around in the brush about halfway up the hill. Back was to me the whole time, so couldn't get a clear look at his face."

Chitto exhaled loudly. "Too bad you couldn't ID him. Was he alone?"

"He was. You had something belonged to the guy and a dog with any kind of nose could find the spot easy."

A thoughtful pause. "Yeah, makes sense."

"I could loan you Lolo Four. She's got a killer nose."

"Thanks, but I have a good dog."

"Good enough." Winters turned to face him, grinning. "Want to know what kind of truck he was driving?"

Chuckling, Chitto said, "You had to ask?"

∞

A pale, watery sun was making an effort to clear the sky when Chitto, Tubbe, and Winters donned their slickers. Winters laid a hand on Chitto's arm at the door. "It's time someone shut this business down, once and for all. This county's entitled to a little peace. Let me know if you need a hand." Pulling the door closed behind him, he said, "I'll get the gate."

"Guess we can scratch another one of your monsters off the list," Tubbe said as Chitto climbed in next to Boycott. He maneuvered the GMC back down the narrow track, then out onto the country road.

"Monsters killing monsters," Chitto said, giving a wave to the gaunt man locking the gate behind them.

"Get literal on me again," Tubbe said, driving away. "Which way to the Folsom place? "

"One more stop first." Chitto dug an address out of his pack, then a map. "King's the linchpin in this deal. Let's see what's parked in his barn."

Tubbe corrected his course at the next crossing, heading in the easterly direction Chitto indicated. "So the current sheriff is this woman's father, making the old sheriff her uncle."

"Sounds right." Chitto's skin crawled, remembering Bud King's scarred face and missing eye. "And Winters is right about not letting her know."

Tubbe eyed him. "The sensitive type, huh?"

"Oh, hell no." Chitto paused a minute, waiting for Boycott to settle his head on his thigh. "It's just that she's had a hard go of it, believing her mother abandoned her and her father had a few shingles missing. She was never fully accepted because of it. Her history in Antlers has left a bad taste in her mouth." He shook his head, focusing on greening buds on the hardwood trees. "Bad as that is, the truth would be worse." He looked at Tubbe. "Even if Peony Folsom isn't her real grandmother, Crystal believes she is. I don't know what it would do to her if she learned otherwise."

"What about her mother?" Tubbe took an unexpected curve fast, his rear tires spitting pasty muck into the barrow ditch. "All kinds of ways to find missing people today."

"Not this woman." Chitto scanned the rough hillsides surrounding the valley floor. "Something tells me no one will ever find her bones."

"You mean . . ." Tubbe inhaled, exhaled. "Speaking of bones. Where'd Winters find Folsom's?"

"Didn't, exactly. " He leaned back in his seat, stroking Boycott's head. "He walked the old railroad track yesterday, just to refresh his memory. Crazy thing is, he saw someone poking around one of those hills."

"You're kidding!"

Chitto laughed softly. "What with the underbrush and all, he couldn't get a clear line of sight on him, but he didn't need to." He looked at Tubbe. "I ever tell you what kind of vehicle the sheriff drives?"

Tubbe grinned. "No way in hell."

"Yeah. A beet-red pickup. Just like most killers, he felt a need to revisit the burial place. Probably wanted to make sure George Forsyth didn't spill everything."

"Winters follow up, track him to see exactly where we should be looking?"

"Nope. But he offered to loan us Lolo Four." He looked at Tubbe. "One of his dogs that has a killer nose."

"Dog?" Tubbe gestured outside the window. "As wet as it is?"

"Rain wets the scent, refreshes it. That's why morning's best time to go, when there's dew."

Tubbe took his eyes off the road briefly to look at Chitto. "You read that in a book, didn't you?"

Chitto just grinned.

A few miles later, Tubbe glanced at him again. "You sure he said Lolo? Not Lola or Lulu?"

Chitto laughed quietly. "In case you didn't notice, Winters is into precise language."

"He is that. Of course, you took him up on the offer."

"Didn't need to. We've got our own dog."

Tubbe came close to putting the GMC in the ditch. Pulling straight again, he said, "You have got to be kidding."

Chitto stroked Boycott's long ears. "This pup doesn't have a lot going for him, but he does have a hell of a nose, especially for John Skrabo. We just need to get something

228

with the sheriff's scent on it. A glove maybe. He wears these expensive kid leather ones, the soft kind with a design punched in the back. We let Boycott have a sniff and turn him loose in that campground."

"That's *all* we have to do, huh? Steal one of his sexy gloves."

"Well, actually I had someone else in mind for that project. If I know Crystal, she's just aching to pay old John a visit. I'm betting she hasn't bitten his head off this week. Should be easy enough to pick up a glove at his office."

Tubbe drove another mile. "That's where the skull would be, wouldn't it? The one mentioned in that newspaper article you showed me."

"Probably. Skrabo confiscated it as evidence." He swiveled his head slowly, studying Tubbe's profile. "You ask because . . ."

"If she's going in, might as well kill two birds with one stone. We need a diagram of the office, especially the location of the evidence locker."

"Right," Chitto said, nodding. "Can't return Walter's bones *sans* head."

They drove in silence for another ten minutes, with Tubbe turning where Chitto indicated. Chitto held his hand out suddenly, indicating Tubbe should pull over. "Let's see what we can see," he said, pulling binoculars from his pack.

Leaving a window cracked for Boycott, Chitto led the way through a clump of mixed pine and hardwood, underbrush and thick grass. Five minutes later, the two peered over the top of a pile of boulders.

"That's a helluva compound." Chitto examined the low-slung house, barred windows, two barns filled with hay, corrals to one side holding three quarter horses, and a four-stall open shed containing equipment and vehicles. "I knew it." He handed the field glasses back to Tubbe. "That camo painted Hummer's in that shed."

"Place looks impressive, but it's laid out poorly." Tubbe lowered the field glasses, looking at Chitto. "You satisfied now?"

"Not quite." Chitto took another look through the glasses. "What did you mean, 'poorly laid out'?"

"You serious?"

"You said I might learn a few things from you on this trip. Enlighten me. I don't have your skill set."

Tubbe moved a branch aside. "See that propane tank next to the shed where the Hummer's parked?"

Focusing the glasses again, Chitto mumbled, "So?"

"A well-placed shot would turn everything inside it to shrapnel."

"Uh-huh," Chitto murmured. "Well now, that would create quite a diversion, wouldn't it?

"Do we need a diversion?"

"You never know." Retracing his steps, Chitto said, "We need to hurry. Crystals probably having a hissy fit about now. Oh . . ." He paused, looking over his shoulder at Tubbe. "If you haven't figured it out yet, Crystal's attitude suffers when she gets agitated."

"Does she agitate easily?"

"I've never seen her any other way," Chitto said, sighing.

CHAPTER TWENTY

"How did you know about this road?" Tubbe put the GMC in a lower gear to navigate the old access road alongside County 271. The rain had turned it to a mire, and time had allowed Nature to begin reclaiming her own.

"It's the way Walter Folsom went on his daily walks."

Tubbe let out a swearword as the Jimmy's front bumper snapped the trunk of a small tree. "Where he and Niles met up to listen to the river?"

"And drink coffee."

"Bet it was better than yours." He glanced at Chitto. "Maybe someone will give you a coffee grinder for Christmas."

"Never took you for a coffee snob, Frank."

"Like Williams said, 'One man's crutch is another man's wing.'" Tubbe grinned at Chitto. "Hank not Vanessa."

Chitto's laugh was cut short as the truck bounced through a hole.

"*Holy shit,*" Tubbe mumbled. "How long's it been since this thing was maintained?"

"Decades." Chitto studied the overgrown road, envisioning how it would've looked thirty-five years before. "Skrabo worked for the Frisco line before it pulled up stakes. I figure he was in charge of maintaining this section of track. Probably lived in a maintenance house north of the campground we came in through. The same road runs past the tavern where he got into it with Robb Niles the night he and Leona Mann were murdered." He looked at Tubbe. "His own private shortcut."

"Slick bastard."

"Pull up here. Let's scope out Peony's place to make sure we're in the clear. We're only a half mile to the highway. Skrabo could spot us if he's using glasses."

Taking field glasses from the glove box, Tubbe climbed out of the truck. "I'll take Boycott and check the road. If he's as good as you say he is, he'll pick up Skrabo's scent. You check the home place."

Chitto watched man and dog merge with the scrub brush, then turned his attention to Peony's house. It looked the same as it had the previous weekend: curtains downstairs open to let in light, window upstairs still dark. A newer model SUV was parked near the back door, a magnetic sign for a real estate company on the side. Returning to the GMC, he watched Tubbe and Boycott weave their way through the trees.

Tubbe let Boycott inside and crawled in beside him. "Road's clear." Peering through his field glasses, he looked at the house. "The SUV?" he asked, looked at Chitto.

"Crystal's. Let's head on in."

Tubbe pulled into the drive leading to the Folsom place. Crystal was outside before he turned off the engine. Her short denim jacket barely reached the waist of floral-printed leggings that accentuated a trim, muscular frame.

"*Holy moly*," Tubbe murmured, giving her an admiring look. "You didn't mention that she was a looker."

Crystal's long hair stuck out the back of a flattop ball cap. Hands on her hips and fury on her face, she watched Tubbe climb from behind the wheel. "Oh," she said. "You're the sidekick he was bringing."

Tubbe stuck out his hand. "Call me Frank. You must be the Crystal I've heard so much about."

She ignored his outstretched hand. "Don't believe anything he says," she snapped. "He lies." She walked up to Chitto. "You said you'd be here early."

"Needed to check out a few things." He hooked Boycott's leash to the fence post.

Rolling her eyes skyward, she led the way to the back door. "I'm still gonna punch you out one of these days," she said over her shoulder.

Inside, she hung their jackets on a coat rack and pointed them toward an inner room. "Grandma fell while I was gone. She took a notion to visit Dad's old room and tripped on the bottom step." She turned her glare on Chitto again. "If you'd been on time . . ."

"Hurt bad?"

"No, just scraped a knee. I've threatened to strap her to a chair if she tries it again. She fixed dinner for you, even made fry bread."

"We, uh, we ate already," Chitto said, exchanging glances with Tubbe.

"Well, you're gonna eat again," she replied, walking to the kitchen.

Either Peony Folsom was thinner than Chitto remembered or she'd lost weight in the last two weeks. Lines wrinkling the rugged face appeared deeper; eyes darker, more sunken.

Crystal handled the quick introduction of Tubbe, describing him as Chitto's sidekick. He responded with, "It's an honor to meet Walter's mother, Mrs. Folsom. Please call me Frank."

Peony sat at the table, her walker parked next to her. "You are a policeman, too?" she asked Tubbe.

"Yes ma'am, with the Chickasaw Nation." He flashed a grin at Chitto. "Sometimes we team up."

"You call me Peony," she said, addressing both Tubbe and Chitto. She pointed to a kitchen table and said, "*Pashofa*, and bread and butter*.*" A square wooden table had been set with plates and napkins; a pot of thick soup and basket of bread held center place. "You sit now. Eat. Tell me when you bring my boy home."

"Soon," Chitto sat down next to her and held the breadbasket close so she could take a piece.

"Not hungry," she said, waving it away.

"*No.*" Crystal filled Peony's plate with the hominy and pork stew. "You don't eat, I'm not letting these guys have any. And you know I'll do it, too."

Peony looked between Chitto and Tubbe. "She has always been a bossy child." Quietly, she picked up her spoon. "When is soon?" Her voice barely carried over the clinking of dishes and cutlery.

"Hopefully before the weekend's over." Chitto laid down his spoon, looking at her. "You do know Walter's not coming back of his own accord."

She nodded. "I make arrangements."

He glanced toward wooden stairs in the corner. "Why did you go upstairs?"

"To look at Walter's things."

"Would you mind if Frank and I took a look?"

"Everything is the same." She turned to stare out the window.

Tubbe cocked his head toward the stairs, indicating they had been given permission to leave.

"I'm coming, too," Crystal said. Turning to her grandmother, she said, "Don't lift a finger down here. I'll take care of things when we get back." She cranked her head toward Chitto and Tubbe. "And they'll help."

"Peony looks thinner," Chitto said when they reached the top of the stairs.

"Hope does *not* spring eternal," she said, sighing. "And when she's gone, I'm gone. This frickin' real estate job's made me into a pariah."

She looked back down the stairs, an ear cocked for noises from the kitchen. "It'll be hard to leave her, even after she's gone." She glanced between them. "She's the one who keeps the weeds pulled around the family graves, puts lilacs out on Memorial Day. Those dumb-assed cousins of mine wouldn't know a weed if it bit them in the butt—unless it was marijuana." She laughed quietly. "But hell, I'd even miss them."

Chitto rubbed his mouth, remembering something Jasmine mentioned. "What if you could get another job, something that would help the people here?"

"Here? In Pushmataha County? Yeah, *right*."

"No, listen. The district field officer is planning to move on, took a job with ODOT. You could apply for the job."

The tenseness in her face eased. "Become a policewoman?"

"They're called officers." Tubbe grinned at her. "Simplifies the gender crap."

"Cop is even simpler." She looked at Chitto. "You serious?"

"You know the county upside down and inside out, and you've got the grit for it. Maybe a hair too much. You'd need to learn to shoot."

"Learn to shoot—? Boy cousins, remember?" Her eyes glinted with excitement. "I'd get to wear a uniform, wouldn't I?" The glint faded. "Oh crap. Your uniforms are those gray and black things." She looked at Chitto, frowning. "How come you don't wear a uniform."

"Detectives have that choice. Only thing is, you'd be stationed in Hugo."

"Oh." She glanced away. "Wouldn't be optimal, but not a bad commute." She looked at him again. "You think I'd stand a chance? Of getting on, I mean."

"You can use me as a reference. Now, how about you leave Frank and me to look around on our own. You know, less distraction while we—"

"*Observe* things. I know." She walked toward the stairs. "You find something I overlooked, you better tell me. Especially if it deals with diamonds."

As Crystal disappeared down the stairs, Chitto looked at Tubbe. "So now we're a team?"

"By chance, not plan. What's this about diamonds?"

Chitto shook his head. "Don't get your hopes up."

They turned to the small room, containing a full-size bed and chest of drawers, a library table shoved under the window, a closet in the corner.

"I take it the boy cousins aren't really boy cousins?" Tubbe walked toward the desk.

"Honesty is not always the best policy," he said.

Tubbe picked up a framed picture off the chest, studying Walter and Glenda Folsom as newlyweds. "She doesn't favor either of them much, which means Winters was right. She must favor the real one."

Chitto made a grunting sound. "Eyes, maybe hair. Skrabo's hair's faded now and turning gray, so the resemblance isn't as obvious as Winters made it out to be."

"And she never suspected anything?" Tubbe returned the picture to its former place.

Chitto shook his head, walking around the small room. "I think she sensed something. Said Skrabo made her feel prickly." He knelt beside the bed and looked underneath. "You know, uncomfortable. And Bud King gives her nightmares."

Tubbe opened the closet door, held up a retro Navy uniform for inspection, then replaced it. "If Skrabo's ego's as big as you say it is, had to be hard for him to keep the secret."

"I suspect there's a couple of reasons for that." Chitto exhaled slowly. "I don't think he would've blinked twice at getting rid of the baby at the same time he snatched Glenda Folsom out of the hospital. But his Uncle Bud believed in taking care of his own, and the baby fit in that category. I also suspect it wasn't consensual sex, which for a law officer could mean the end of a career. Not to mention old Bud's dynasty."

Tubbe whistled softly. "That would help explain Winters' concern about Crystal never finding out Walter wasn't her father."

Chitto rummaged through the desk drawer on the library table, closed it again. "It's a little more complicated than that. I also suspect Winters had a crush on Glenda." He let out a short laugh. "And Crystal said she often wished he'd been her father. Strange little triangle."

Tubbe snorted. "More like a warped cube."

Chitto looked around the room, hands on his hips. "Where you want to start?"

"Let's find his personal stuff. I'd like a look at his medals."

"And I'd like a look at his rock collection."

"Rocks?"

"Aka diamonds. Rocks tell a story."

"So do medals." Tubbe opened the top drawer of a narrow chest and rummaged through undergarments yellowed with age. "Bingo . . ."

Chitto watched Tubbe raise the lid on a battered cufflink box. Protected from light and air, the ribbons had held their color like miniature rainbows. The small pieces of metal Tubbe fished out had developed a deep patina with age. "Can you tell what it is?" he asked, watching Tubbe examine one medal in particular.

"Wings. Like I thought, Walter flew with the Marines. And with his training as a sharpshooter, they'd make him a gunner." He watched Chitto walk to the closet. "Any luck with his diamonds, aka rocks?"

"Maybe." He pulled a shoebox off the top shelf of the closet. "I used to keep my rock collection in a box just like this." He laughed softly as he removed the lid.

"They diamonds?" Tubbe said, peering inside the box.

"Not exactly. When double-terminated quartz crystals were found over on the Pecos River in New Mexico, amateur collectors started calling any kind of crystal they found a Pecos diamond."

"Crystal? You mean, like her name?" Tubbe chuckled. "The sailor had a sense of humor."

"Or irony." He glanced at Tubbe. "Lot of people use crystals in meditation. Belief is, if you hold them a certain way, they'll stabilize the emotions."

"Yeah?" Pulling back a faded curtain, Tubbe held a large specimen to the light. "Worth anything?"

"Not like diamonds, but these resemble those found in Arkansas, which are some of the best quality quartz crystals around. A collector might be interested." He rummaged through the box. "It's a hell of a collection, some of the finest specimens I've seen."

Tubbe placed the piece he held back into the box, then turned a slow circle taking in the room. "Might as well give it the once over for good measure. By the book?"

"Leave no stone unturned," Chitto murmured.

∞

By the time they returned to the kitchen, Crystal had the dishes draining next to the sink. Peony sat at the end of the table, hands folded.

"Took you long enough," Crystal said, pulling the plug on the drain. "Don't think you're fooling anyone. You stalled

238

just to get out of kitchen duty, didn't you?" She paused, looking between them. "You found something . . ."

Tubbe set the cufflink box on the table in front of Peony. "Your son's ribbons and medals." Opening the box, he placed the medal shaped like wings in her hand. "This says he was assigned to the Marines at one point. More than likely, he was a gunner on a helicopter in South Vietnam when Saigon fell. Probably responsible for hundreds of people getting out of the country alive." He held up another medal. "And this one was presented to all those who did honorable duty there. He was a helluva warrior."

Crystal said, "You're saying my dad was a hero?"

"He was."

Peony returned the medals to the box. "I have always known my boy was brave." She looked at the box Chitto held.

"This is his rock collection," he said, setting the shoebox in front of her.

"Yes," Peony said, removing the lid. "His diamonds."

"Let me see." Looking over her grandmother's shoulder, Crystal picked up a large crystal and held it to the light. "These are diamonds?"

"Lot of people call them diamonds," Chitto said, "but sorry to say, they're not."

"I knew it," she said, her jaws clenching. "Just rocks."

He paused. "Well, in fact, they're crystals."

"Crystals? You mean, like my name?" Walking to the window, she stared at the overcast sky. "That's just swell. He named me after a fake diamond."

Tubbe joined her at the window. "Look at it this way," he said, voice low. "To him, you were something pretty priceless."

She let out a bitter laugh. "That's all I need. Another frickin' poet."

"Hey—" Tubbe made a guttural sound. "Don't turn this into a joke. The man deserves better."

"Easy, Frank." Chitto moved toward them.

"No, he's right." Looking at Tubbe, she said, "I'm sorry." Sighing, she turned to Chitto. "So, where do we find his remains?"

"We don't," Tubbe said. "While we recover his body, you'll be on another mission."

"Mission?" Her eyes widened. "You mean, like a police investigation?"

"More like covert operation. I hear you've visited the sheriff's department before. Right now, we need a sketch of the inside, down to the last nut and bolt. Your goal's to locate the evidence locker."

"Oh . . ." Her shoulders sagged. "It's that skull, isn't it? It *is* Dad's and you need to get it back."

"We also need something personal of Skrabo's," Chitto said. "Glove, one of those fancy hatbands, something that would have his scent on it."

"Scent? Why? He's not the one you're looking for."

Chitto exchanged a glance with Tubbe, then looked at her. "So we can keep track of him. Don't want the good sheriff surprising us."

"Think you can handle it?" Tubbe asked.

"Piece of cake." Her grin resembled a wild panther baring its fangs. "Old John spends his days driving around his kingdom. His goofball deputy's the one who mans the office, and he's had a crush on me since high school."

Chitto shook head, frowning. "Don't do anything that will bring suspicion down on you later. This has to be handled discretely."

"Hey, I can be discrete." Walking to the kitchen cupboards, she opened a drawer and pulled out a pad and pencil. "I'll draw the office, at least as much as I can remember."

Rising slowly, Peony motioned to Chitto. "You come with me."

He followed her to the front room, leaving Tubbe and Crystal working on a sketch of the sheriff's department. As she sank into a chair near a wood-burning stove, he walked up close. "Sorry to be the bearer of bad news, Peony, but at least, you have closure."

"Yes, Walter will finish his journey now." She motioned him closer. "There is something you should see. In my bedroom closet . . ." She pointed her chin at a door on the other side of the room. "A blue box."

Chitto found the box and, returning to the front room, placed it in her hands.

"□□□□□□l has not seen this." Pushing aside letters and papers, she removed a yellowed envelope and handed it to him.

The stationery inside the envelope crinkled like a dried leaf as Chitto unfolded it. He read the date at the top first, a Sunday in early March 1975, then, *Dear husband . . .*

In the following lines, Glenda Folsom informed her husband that she was pregnant.

"I have waited to tell you this because where you are, you could do nothing. I am pregnant with another man's child. The child in my belly is of my blood, my body, so I could not bear to kill it. When you come home, I will tell you everything. But what is done is done. It is my hope you will accept the child as yours and bury your anger. I am afraid if you pursue this wicked man, it will end badly for you, for me, and the baby . . ."

"All this time," he said, returning the letter to Peony. "You knew all this time."

"Glenda disappeared like a ghost." Peony shook her head slowly. "The letter, not knowing where she was, the name of the evil man. It made Walter's sickness worse."

He nodded, remembering how he felt when Mary became ill. "Because it was his job to protect her."

She nodded.

Chitto paused, frowning. "Did you mention this letter to anyone?"

"Not to my granddaughter."

Chitto took a minute, reading between the lines. "But you did tell the sheriff that day."

She nodded, sighing. "I told him I knew things . . . that I had saved letters." She closed her eyes, pausing. "I think that was a bad idea."

Chitto looked away, thinking that finally, all the dominoes had fallen in place. Peony telling Skrabo about the letters had made her a threat.

"You will keep the secret?" she asked, looking at him directly.

"Yes, but you need to destroy this letter. If you don't, Crystal will eventually find it."

Looking toward the wood stove, she nodded. "Yes, the time has come for all this to die."

"Not everything, Peony. You can't leave yet."

She closed her eyes again, talking softly. *"Su tikahbi."*

"I know you're tired, but . . ." He moved closer. "Crystal still needs you." He waited, watching the dark eyes open. "You have to wait a while longer."

She considered this. "I have grown used to waiting," she murmured. Placing the letter in his hand, she motioned toward the fire.

∞

"Camp out?" Crystal said. "Are you nuts? It's a quagmire out there—and cold." She pulled on her jacket, preparing to make her covert run on the sheriff's department.

"Yes," Peony said. She sat down at the kitchen table again. "We have room."

"Too risky," Chitto said. "Can't take the chance."

"I'm not afraid." Crystal looked at Peony. "*We* are not afraid."

"I know you're not," Tubbe said. "But we can't have anything interfere with what we need to do. Maybe you can phone us with the location of the evidence locker. That's all that's missing from this sketch."

Chitto shook his head. "Won't work. We still need that personal item. We'll have to meet up somewhere."

Crystal picked her handbag up off a side table. "I know the perfect spot." She removed a key from a large ring. "There's a cabin up in the woods, just beyond Quince's place. It'll be private and dry." Picking up the tablet she'd used earlier to sketch out the sheriff's office, she ripped out a page. "I'll draw a map."

"That could jeopardize your job," Chitto said, looking at the drawing she had made.

"Screw the frickin' job." Smiling the panther smile again, she pushed out the door.

"We have to be going, too," Chitto said to Peony. "But we'll be back."

"I will wait," she said.

CHAPTER TWENTY-ONE

It was mid-afternoon by the time Chitto and Tubbe headed for the cabin in the woods. Thin sunlight had failed to burn off the clouds, meaning darkness would come early. The mixed pine and oak forests on distant hills had already turned indigo in color. Chitto studied the land to the side of the narrow two-lane, covered with a thick carpet of leaf and pine needles. Low grape vines were plentiful, as was brush, and common grass types interspersed the heavier growth. Without moonlight, all of it would become carbon black.

Tubbe slowed when they reached the spot where the gravel played out. "You indicated this stretch road was left unmaintained for a reason. What?"

"Punishment. Winters doesn't kowtow." Chitto reached for the grab handle above the door as GMC groaned its way around a curve. "Neither do the other two survivors on that original suspect list."

"They pay with bad roads, too?"

"No," Chitto said. "Their drives exit onto paved roads, state not county, but they've paid in other ways." He glanced at Tubbe. "Ranchers are cautious by nature, but these two top them all. I've never seen better-armed cowboys in my life. Lot of the other suspects that were questioned chose to leave. Those that stayed, died prematurely."

"Hell of a deal, retreat or pay the consequences." As they pulled past Quince Winters' driveway, Tubbe raised a hand in greeting.

"You think Winter's is watching us?"

"You deaf?" Tubbe tapped an ear. "That fool sheriff did Winters a favor by not fixing this road. Engines have to work overtime just to make the climb, much less hold the road in these conditions. He doesn't hear it, those dogs of his will." He glanced at Chitto. "You said he named one of his dogs Lolo."

As the GMC lurched up an incline, Chitto put an arm around Boycott to hold him steady. "That's right. Lolo Four."

"Four . . ." Tubbe steered the truck around another curve "You figure this Lolo's the fourth in the line?"

Chitto glanced at him. "According to what Crystal told me, that would make sense."

"Don't suppose his other dogs would be named Liz and Sophia."

Chitto hesitated. "She might've mentioned it. Why?"

"Winters must like those names a lot."

Chitto hunched his shoulders. "Sometimes people get attached to names."

"And sometimes names get attached to people." Tubbe slowed, rubbing his side window with a forearm to clear it. "This where we turn in?"

Chitto checked the number painted on a fence post. "It is. I'll get the gate."

The log cabin was small, but a smokestack and well-stock woodshed promised a warm night. A propane tank promised hot food and an outhouse eliminated the need for night sorties through damp, unfamiliar brush. The chinked walls inside were tight, with two bunk beds positioned on opposite sides of the room.

Tossing his sleeping bag on a bunk, Chitto took stock. "There's even water." He pointed to two five-gallon containers sitting along a counter marking off the kitchen: a small cabinet, complete with an aluminum sink, and small table surrounded with four folding chairs.

"Log rack's full, too." Tubbe dropped his sleeping bag on the opposite bunkbed and walked to the stove. "All the comforts of home," he said, laying a fire.

Releasing Boycott from his leash, Chitto said, "I'll get the grub." He returned with a cooler under one arm and a brown grocery bag under the other. Setting a plastic container holding coffee and a jar of creamer on the table, he said, "Let's start with this."

Rummaging through the grocery bag, Tubbe said, "This is the best you could do? Oklahoma tenderloin?"

"I thought we'd be dry camping. Sandwiches made sense." Chitto shot him a look. "What's wrong with baloney sandwiches?"

"If it's the same caliber as your coffee, a lot."

Chitto shook his head. "It's from the deli, not that packaged stuff. Good cheese, too."

"White bread, I suppose."

"I like things simple."

Tubbe snickered, "Five-star dining."

Chitto paused, studying him. "You didn't acquire that gourmet habit in the military. What is it, some kind of passive aggression?"

Ignoring the question, Tubbe found an enamel coffeepot in the cupboard and spooned coffee into the basket. Smelling the coffee, he said, "What kind is this?" The pot clunked when he set it on the stovetop.

"I just buy whatever's on sale . . ." Chitto's voice trailed off as Boycott walked toward the door, growling.

Hearing a knock, Tubbe drew his gun. "It's too soon for Crystal to come. Think Skrabo followed us?"

Chitto walked to the door, his forehead pinched. "Skrabo's not the polite type." As a louder knock sounded, he waved Tubbe behind the door and lifted the latch.

"Thought that was the sound of your Jimmy." Quince Winters' deep voice reverberated around the sparse cabin. "I'm assuming these accommodations are compliments of Crystal."

Exhaling loudly, Chitto ushered the lean-faced man inside. "That is a good assumption."

Eying the gun Tubbe held, Winters raised his hands and said, "I'm a friendly." Slipping a 30.06 off his shoulder, he set it in the corner and walked to the stove. "I'm also assuming this move is part of an overall strategy."

"Bring Lolo, Liz, and Sophia with you?" Tubbe quipped, holstering his gun.

Winters paused, eying Tubbe. "They follow me everywhere unless I chain 'em up. You got a problem with my dogs . . . or me?"

"You talk like an officer. Enlisted men talk tactics."

"One comes after the other." Winters removed his mackinaw and laid it on one of the bunks. "Appreciate a good cup of hot coffee and hearing what the plan is."

"Can guarantee the coffee will be strong," Tubbe said. "Nothing more."

"Some creamer then, if you've got it. Stomach's gotten cranky in my older years." He eyed them again. "You do have a plan."

Chitto searched out three mugs in the cupboard. "We do," he said, facing Winters and Tubbe. "And I'll tell you what it is as soon as you tell me about Lolo, Liz, and Sophia. And I'm not talking dogs."

Tubbe made a slight bow, aimed at Winters. "You've got the floor."

Winters paused, then pulled a folding chair close to the stove. Eyes distant, he recounted a mission late in the Vietnam conflict.

"You see, Nixon was still pushing for peace with honor, which involved phasing out our involvement, turning everything over to the South Vietnamese." He opened the door on the stove and worked another log into the blaze. "We started pulling our troops out by the thousands, and the Vietnamese were given their first real mission. To take a town called Lam Son. The column made it halfway and bogged down." Closing the stove's door, he leaned back. "So, Nixon got bighearted, decided to help our allies." He paused, accepting the cup of coffee Chitto handed him. "The strategy was to jump-start the advance again, involving armed U.S. chopper crews in three key areas."

Tubbe carried the jar of powdered creamer to Winters and watched as he spooned the white powder into his cup. "Three missions called Lolo, Liz, and Sophia."

Winters looked up at him. "You weren't even born then."

"You hear things." Tubbe pulled a chair up next to the stove and propped his feet against the wall. "You were an officer?"

Winters' nodded, his eyes on the glowing stove. "For a while. Gave up my commission a couple years after the peace agreement was signed in Paris, giving Nixon his *peace with honor*." He grimaced, as if the words left a bad taste in his mouth. "Came back home and went to work for the railroad. It was more to fill time than anything. My daddy had sold the ranch by then and what was left when he died came to me. Not a lot, but enough to get by." He inhaled deep, exhaled slowly. "And that brings us to now. Today, I'm just a man warming old bones by a fire, drinking slop coffee."

Tubbe laughed unceremoniously.

Shaking his head, Chitto dragged up another chair. "I'm a curious man, Quince. Just what was your rank?"

"Rank doesn't matter anymore."

"But you flew choppers, didn't you?" Tubbe held Winters' eyes.

Winters nodded slowly. "And directed others to fly them."

"Commander of an air combat unit?"

Winters stared at the fire, saying nothing.

Chitto looked at Tubbe. "What was your rank, Frank?"

"Not nearly as high as his." Tubbe looked at Winters again. "You fly with Folsom and Niles? We've learned they were helo gunners, in Nam about the same time."

Winters leaned forward, rubbing his eyes. "Hell, I don't know. Things got crazy in those last years." He raised reddened eyes, looking between Tubbe and Chitto. "Now what's the goddamn plan?"

They filled him in on getting the skull out of Skrabo's office. Crystal's role in locating the evidence locker. The retrieval of Folsom's bones.

"I want in." Winters held out his coffee mug for a refill.

Tubbe shot Chitto a glance as he retrieved the pot.

"Well, thanks, Quince," Chitto said, "but we can't involve you in this."

Winters laughed softly. "Hell, I've been involved in this my entire life."

"If you're caught, it could go bad for you."

"*If* he's caught?" Tubbe looked at Chitto and chuckled.

Resting his elbows on his knees, Winters looked at Chitto. "Appreciate your concern, son, but I will not put you in jeopardy. I'll get the skull. You boys will have your hands full with finding the remains."

"Trust me," Tubbe said before Chitto could protest again. "He will not put us in harm's way."

Chitto ran a hand over short-cut hair, sighing. "All I'm interested in is returning Folsom's bones."

"And Rosebud's," Winters said. "She's probably stuffed down the same hole."

Chitto and Tubbe exchanged another look.

Winters stirred the fire again. "Wouldn't be right to separate a man from his dog."

∞

The barking of Winters' dogs woke Boycott from a lazy sleep in front of the wood-burning stove. Bounding to the door, he began to bark, too.

Chitto pulled back the shutter of a front window, peering into fading light. "It's Crystal." Opening the door, he waved her inside.

"Hey, Quince." She gave Winters a kiss on the cheek. "What are you doing here?"

"Just being neighborly." He helped her out of her coat and pointed toward the woodstove. "Tubbe, get the lady a mug."

"Yes sir," Tubbe said, walking to the cupboard.

Opening her bag, Crystal removed two Ziploc bags holding a headband and a glove. "I didn't touch either one so my scent would get on them. I used a paperclip to rake them in. How'd I do?"

"You get an A in burglary," Tubbe said.

"I'm not even gonna ask how you managed it," Chitto said, studying the bag's contents. "Sure Skrabo won't miss these?"

She made a snorting sound. "They're old ones. Found them in a bottom drawer, right next to a whole box of *new* gloves and headbands. Invoice was there, too. Arrogant bastard spends more on ego toys than we do for a month's groceries."

"He's always been a dandy," Winters said, watching Chitto inspect the bags. "What're you thinking, Chitto?"

"That these would be good messengers." Noticing the room grow quiet, he shrugged. "Riley Campbell and Harry Bradshaw wanted me to let them know they'd been absolved from being suspects. Campbell mentioned his badge, Bradshaw, his hatband." He looked at the Ziploc bags again. "Too bad we don't have his badge."

"Wouldn't the glove work? Tubbe said. "How many men in this county wear hand-tooled kid gloves?"

Chitto laughed. "Trust me, there won't be much left when Boycott gets through with it." Looking at Crystal, he said, "You better get back home. Peony needs you right now. She's dealing with a lot."

"Yeah, I know. What're you gonna do now?"

"Proceed with the mission," he said. "Locate and retrieve the body. Quince is in charge of getting the skull out of the evidence locker, so fill him in before you go."

"Quince?" Crystal pulled a hand-drawn map from her shoulder bag. "Why Quince?"

"He pulled rank," Tubbe said.

"And soon as it's daylight, Tubbe and I will head for the hillside to get the bones," Chitto said. "After this many years, they couldn't weigh much. We'll use the old railroad maintenance road to get to Peony's place."

Winters turned to look at him. "What if Skrabo goes back to the hillside for another look?"

Chitto frowned, considering the possibility.

"Good point," Tubbe said. "Might be time for a diversion." He told them about scoping out Bud King's shed and the propane tank. "I brought a gun that can handle it."

"That could work," Chitto said. "You could drop me off on the way, and I'll hide out until I know it's safe." He paused, looking at Tubbe. "How will I know when you've made your play?"

Tubbe shook his head, looking weary. "Watch for my smoke signal, professor."

"What about me?" Crystal said. "You're not leaving me out of this."

"You need to stay with your grandmother," Winters said. "You have guns at the house?"

"God, yes." She laughed softly. "My dad had this thing for guns. Shotgun, deer rifle, pistols . . .."

"There's one more problem we need to discuss," Chitto said.

"What?" She stared at him.

"Skrabo. When he finds the skull is missing, he'll figure you had a hand in it. That deputy is bound to fill him in on your visit."

"Not a problem," Tubbe said, feeding more wood into the stove. "He'll hightail it to old Bud's place once it goes up. I'll be in the right spot to, uh, cut him off."

Chitto and Winters exchanged glances. Tubbe's meaning was slow in coming for Crystal.

"You mean . . . Oh, hell no. I'm not scared of that jerk. He shows up at our place, I'll blow him to kingdom come."

"I'm sure there's another way to handle it," Winters said.

"Like what? Tubbe asked.

Winters locked eyes with him. "I'm in charge of strategies, remember? Leave it to me."

"What am I missing?" Crystal looked between them. "I'm missing something."

"Nothing," Winters said. "You get back home. We'll meet up back at your place when it's done." Helping her into her coat, he walked her to the door.

"See you tomorrow," she called over her shoulder. "*And don't be late.*" With a wave, she was gone.

"I need to head out, too." Slipping into his jacket, Winters paused at the door. "Don't dally once you finish up, Tubbe. Soon as that tank goes up, you disappear." He looked at Chitto. "And don't wait around to fill in the grave site. Just beat it back to Peony's."

Tubbe said, "I'd appreciate you sharing your strategy with us."

"I'd like to know, too," Chitto said.

"Gentleman . . ." Zipping his coat, Winters pulled the hood over his head. "That is above your pay grade."

∞

Chitto found a cast-iron griddle hanging from a hook, set it on top of the wood-burning stove, and covered the bottom with a thin layer of vegetable oil. He glanced the front door as Tubbe walked inside, Boycott by his side. "Everything okay out there?"

Tubbe gave him a sideways look. "Outhouses are pretty much the same, Sam." He unsnapped Boycott from his leash.

"You were gone a half hour, maybe a little longer."

Tubbe paused, grinning. "I decided to take Boycott for a little hike." He removed his jacket and dropped it on his bunk. "And yeah, I checked the road. It's quiet, no movement either way."

Chitto grinned, too. "How many sandwiches can you eat?"

"Couple."

Chitto made X-shaped cuts in the center of six rounds of bologna and laid them on the griddle. "There's paper plates and plastic knives in the paper sack," he said to Tubbe, who was washing up at the sink. "Some chips, mayo and mustard, too. Didn't know which you'd want."

"I get choices?" Tubbe walked to where he stood and looked over his shoulder.

"Smells pretty good, doesn't it?" Chitto looked at him. "You want cheese?"

Tubbe nodded. "Anything would taste good to a starving man." He walked to the brown paper bag and dug out tableware and sandwich spreads. Popping open the bag of chips, he poured some on three plates, then hesitated. "I'm assuming the two extra sandwiches are for Boycott."

"A good assumption." Chitto flipped the slices of bologna, then topped six slices of white bread laid out on a cutting board with thick slices of yellow cheese. Three minutes later, he removed the bologna and laid one on top of each slice. "Wanna haul the plates over here? Cheese is melting"

Complying, Tubbe set two sandwiches in front of the dog. "Eat slow," he said. "You're not getting any of mine."

At the table, Chitto watched a frowning Frank Tubbe spread mustard on slices of bread. "What's on your mind, Frank?"

Tubbe looked up at him. "Just thinking about Winters."

"Can you be a little more literal?"

"He was a pilot, not a ground fighter." Tubbe sucked a morsel of food from a tooth. "I'm having a hard time figuring out what kind of strategy he's gonna come up with to take care of Skrabo's counter-attack."

They ate in silence for several minutes. Licking his plate clean, Boycott proceeded to eat his.

"Hey—" Getting up from his chair, Chitto extracted paper from the dog's jaws. "Don't need you getting sick on me. You've got a job to do tomorrow." Opening the front of the stove, he pitched the paper plate inside and returned to the table.

"What do you think he's got planned . . ." Tubbe paused. "Let me rephrase that. You think he's even got a plan?"

"Don't have a clue." Finishing off his second sandwich, Chitto folded his plate in half, then picked up Tubbe's empty one. "He might not've had one when he left tonight, but I know one thing." Walking to the stove, he fed the paper to the fire. "By morning, he will."

CHAPTER TWENTY-TWO

Chitto and Tubbe left the cabin in darkness Sunday morning. The day was warmer and drier, but the county roads, at least those deprived of gravel, were a soup of brown slush. Tubbe fought to keep the GMC out of the ditch. Window partially down, Chitto surveyed the foggy hillsides. A riot of odors filled the air, boggy and cloying. Old grass, moss, rotted leaves. He noticed buds making a show on the hardwoods, a promise of spring in the fat spheres that tipped the branches.

The GMC quit its lurching as its tires found purchase on good road base. "How far?" Tubbe asked.

Chitto studied the map. "Turn south at the next crossroad onto Highway 271. The campground's a mile or two further on."

"Highway? You think that's smart? I figured we'd follow that old rail bed again."

"It'll be safe. Old John's at Mom's Café about now, stoking down biscuits and gravy." He glanced at Tubbe. "Just in case, I'll keep my eyes peeled."

"You had to mention real food, didn't you?" Tubbe said.

Chitto laughed quietly. "You have to admit, I make a helluva baloney sandwich."

Tubbe shot him a look. "I'll give you that, but I'm not accustomed to having them for breakfast, lunch, and dinner."

Wheeling onto Highway 271, Tubbe sped southward. Glancing at Chitto, he said, "Can you make it back to the Folsom place on your own? I might be delayed."

Chitto stared at him. "What're you thinking, Frank?"

Tubbe slowed as he spotted the sign for the campground. "I'm thinking I'm the one to take care of Skrabo. He'll come running, once he knows his uncle's place has been hit."

"Winters said—"

"Winters is a pilot—and old."

"You're gonna wait for Skrabo to show up, aren't you?" Chitto shook his head, eyes dark. "Don't screw things up, Frank."

Tubbe slid to a stop where the campground dead-ended at the old trestle. Nodding toward the door, he said, "Get out. It's time to see if that pup has a killer nose."

Chitto opened the door, letting Boycott out. Retrieving his backpack and shotgun, he stood outside the car door, staring at Tubbe. "Frank—"

"Climb high and wait for my signal," Tubbe said, revving the engine. "If you get done before I get back, don't wait around."

∞

The rocky ledge swelled from the hillside. Gray with algae and shaggy with moss, it crested from the scrub and trees like a bull buffalo resting on the ground. Breathing hard from the climb, Chitto perched on the crumbling hump, Boycott panting beside him. Digging his binoculars from his pack, he aimed them toward Bud King's place. From the height, he could see over the tops of hardwood trees and spires of pines to the rolling grasslands in the distance. Nervously, he looked at his watch. Seven fifteen.

Fifteen minutes later, he looked again, thinking thirty minutes was plenty of time to reach King's place. Ten minutes later, he was pulling his jacket sleeve up to check again when Boycott nosed his armpit, whining. The delayed blast came seconds later. The smoke didn't rise in round white puffs, as depicted in movies, but as an angry, churning plume, black and gray. A high wind carried the top of the plume toward the town of Antlers.

"Time for you to take the spotlight, boy." He replaced his field glasses to his pack and headed back down the hill, Boycott on his heels. Their objective, the old trestle.

Chitto was winded by the time he completed his less-than-graceful downward trek. At the bottom of the slope, he bent at the waist, catching his breath. He and Boycott panted in unison, their warm breaths comingling into mist.

Leading Boycott to the place where the road dead-ended at the river, he put him into a sit position. "Time to put up or shut up, buddy."

Boycott looked at him, his eyes bright. Quickly, Chitto dug the plastic bag containing Skrabo's kid leather glove from his backpack. Holding it out for the dog to sniff, he said, "Find."

Putting Boycott on leash, he began walking in a circular pattern. Boycott led him in a meandering route, nose to the ground. Suddenly, the dog let out a high-pitched sound, a mix of howl and bark, and lunged forward. Chitto stopped him long enough to unsnap the leash. Boycott went on the hunt, dodging scrub brush, sniffing the ground occasionally to find the scent, then spurting forward. Chitto did an uphill jog, digging boots into the soft, moist ground for purchase.

The search took fifteen minutes. Chitto grabbed the trunk of a tree midway up the hill, breathing hard, looking for the dog. "*Boycott,*" he called. Hearing a rustling in the brush, he turned to the left. Boycott emerged from a pile of brush, branches twisted and broken.

"What'd you find, boy?" He peeled out of his backpack and began pulling branches aside. A few minutes later, the broken face of a boulder pile emerged.

"Hold up," he said as the dog began a frantic digging. "Let me take over." He pulled the kid leather glove from his pack and tossed it to the dog. "Here, you've earned a treat."

Chitto piled larger rocks to one side. When he reached smaller size stone, he pulled a double-fold steel shovel from his pack and snapped it into place. He'd used the trenching spade as a geology student and found the serrated edge handy for any number of jobs. Ten minutes later, he hit pay dirt. A vault in the rock.

"I was right," he said to Boycott, who squatted beside him. "Skrabo didn't have time to bury them deep."

He began working with his hands now, raking his fingers through the loose-packed mix of dirt and mulch, pea gravel and mixed stone. Carefully, he cleared the earth and rock from three dry, shrunken bundles. A smaller bundle had once been khaki-colored canvas. Rotted now, it held what appeared to be the skeleton of an animal. Studying the skull, Chitto knew he'd found Rosebud's remains. He figured a larger bundle wrapped in a blue poly tarp was Walter Folsom. Through a tear in the third bundle, the size of a grocery bag and made of stiff plastic, he saw a mass of tangled, honey-brown hair. Leona Mann's skull.

He sat a while, staring at the burial place. With a geologist's eye, he identified pick marks in the walls of the natural crypt. There was no other answer. It had been Walter Folsom's crystal pocket. A low whining from Boycott helped him refocus.

"Yes, indeed," he said, pulling the box of heavy-duty trash bags from his pack. "Time they went home."

∞

"What'd you do, Frank?" Chitto met up with Tubbe where the walking trail intersected Peony Folsom's driveway. He was covered in dirt, tired from hauling a backpack and three trash bags on his back, and angry.

"Plugged the propane tank. Didn't you see the smoke?"

"And then?"

Tubbe cleared his throat, taking his time. "I waited and watched. Saw lines of dust heading toward King's place. I mean, they came from everywhere." He let a snort. "Half the county showed up. Fire department, sheriff's cars, police cars, an ambulance, cars, trucks. It looked like a damn war zone." He looked at Chitto. "But a red pickup did not show. So, I wound my way back around, which took a while given I didn't want to be seen, and here I am."

Chitto eyed him, wanting to believe Tubbe was telling the truth, fearing he was not.

"I'm leveling with you, Sam."

"Okay." Chitto wiped his face with his sleeve. "Help me load this stuff in the backend. I'm worn out." He opened the door so Boycott could jump onto the seat.

Tubbe followed him around the truck and opened the tailgate. "You find everything?"

"All three. Folsom was wrapped up in what was once a poly tarp. Rosebud in canvas. Leona Mann's skull in plastic. I put the remains in separate bags."

After loading the bones, they hurried back into the cab. "Boycott do his job?" Tubbe asked, putting the GMC in gear.

Angry as he was, Chitto couldn't help but grin. "You should've seen him." He pulled the dog into the crook of his arm and rubbed his head. "He made me proud." As evidence, he pulled the chewed kid leather glove from between Boycott's jaws. What was left of it.

∞

"Where *is* he?" Crystal had been walking the floor since Chitto and Tubbe pulled up to the back door. The bundles Chitto had collected now resided in plastic storage tubs inside the kitchen. Peony sat next to one of them, hands folded in her lap.

"Think he ran into trouble?" Chitto lowered the binoculars he'd had trained on the road the last hour.

"Hell, there wasn't anyone to interfere with him." Tubbe poured himself another cup of coffee. "They were all at King's place."

"Hold on." Chitto raised his binoculars again. "Someone just pulled in from the railway access road to the south."

"It's him," Tubbe said, looking through the window at the man getting out of the car. "And he's carrying something." He walked to the back door and held it open.

Winters paused as he entered the kitchen, eyeing the storage containers. "Which one's Folsom's?"

"The blue one, next to Peony," Chitto said.

Winters walked straight to her side and set a cardboard box on the plastic tub beside her. "Ma'am, your son's remains are now complete."

Peony looked around the room, making eye contact with the three men. Nodding her head, she said, "I am grateful."

Crystal was at her side in an instant. "C'mon, Grandma. You need to rest now—and they need to talk." Taking Peony by the arm, she guided her out of the kitchen.

"What delayed you?" Tubbe handed Winters a cup of coffee.

"Didn't see any need to rush. Could see the smoke from downtown, hear the sirens, too. Town emptied out like a balloon with a hole in it. Most of the men are volunteer firemen, and the women are moths drawn to a flame."

Taking a sip of coffee, he looked between them. "I take it everything went as planned on your end?" Seeing nods, he said, "Good. Now get the hell out of here. I can handle things here on out. I'm figuring the woman's skull is to go to Chuck Stovall."

"Right," Chitto said, "but that still leaves Skrabo and King. Soon as Skrabo finds the evidence locker was broken into, he'll know Crystal was involved . . . and me. I'm sure Skrabo kept Uncle Bud updated on anything that dealt with that murder case." He smiled ruefully. "One could say both their necks are on the line."

Winters shook his head slightly. "Half the men in the county had motive and opportunity to hurt King. Now that someone's made the first move, others will become braver—and he knows it. Which means he is no longer an offensive threat." He looked between them, eyes slitted. "And Skrabo is not a problem. Now, get going."

Chitto and Tubbe exchanged glances, looking doubtful.

Back ramrod straight, Winters said, "That was an order, gentlemen."

Chitto and Tubbe beat it out the back door. Arguing with reason was an exercise in futility.

CHAPTER TWENTY-THREE

Chitto rolled his car window down, enjoying the first signs of spring. Sunshine. Greening grass. Trees leafing out. Reaching the tribal police parking lot, he took his time walking inside. As had become the first order of business, he checked the reception area and was relieved to find no one waiting. Slipping out of his windbreaker, he proceeded to Jasmine desk. Finding her desk chair empty, he pulled to an abrupt stop. Except for neat stacks of mail and message slips lining the front edge, her desk was clean. He searched through his stack, then looked to see who else was in the office.

"Nine," he called to Nate White. "You seen Jasmine?"

Nine shrugged, his head shaking.

Chitto continued to his desk, eyes clouded. Hearing his cell phone vibrate, he checked the number and smiled. Swiveling his chair toward the window, he said, "You're up early, little brother."

A laugh came over the line. "I'm working a half day so I can start the weekend early." Tubbe's voice sounded tinny, but the static was tolerable. "Still nothing, huh?"

"Not a word."

"Damn. It's been a week."

"Well, Crystal's probably busy helping with the funeral. Leona Mann's brother and Chuck Stovall, too. But yeah, I

265

thought we would've heard something by now. All I can figure is the old ways take longer."

"How's that?"

"That day you and Crystal worked on the sketch of the sheriff's department, I had a talk with Peony." Chitto watched the traffic on the street, hoping to see Jasmine's car make a showing. "She said something about burying Rosebud with Walter. In the old days, a warrior's dog was sent with him on the trip west. Old Sonny Boy's doing a ceremony, too. Those things take time."

Tubbe made a grunting sound. "Well, speaking of olden times, I'll be out of touch for a few days." The sound of throat clearing came on the line. "Decided to take some time off."

Considering Tubbe's words, Chitto smiled. "You son of a buck. Old Sonny Boy got to you." The sound of people talking in the background came over the line.

"Hey, gotta go," Tubbe said. "Need to interrogate someone. Leave me a message on my cell, you hear anything."

"You're not allowed contact with the outside world once you shed your clothes. You'll be sweating out of pores you didn't know you had."

Tubbe chuckled. "Oh, before I hang up, Sonny Boy said you can pick up your bacon at the packing plant. Give you a call when I get back."

"Better than that, come up and help me plant my grandma's corn patch. We'll catch up on the drive north."

"Just leave me a message."

Chitto hesitated. "That might not be wise. Old Ben's probably had our phones tapped. See you Saturday week."

"Anyone ever tell you you're a smart ass?" *Click.*

"Frequently," Chitto said to dead air. Hearing someone enter the front door, he turned. Seeing Crystal Folsom speeding for his desk, he met her half way. "What're you doing here? Peony all right?"

"Grandma's great. I don't know why, but she's better. All I can figure is a big weight's been lifted. She sent this to you. A memento." She handed him a small, tissue-wrapped bundle.

He wasted no time unwrapping it. "One of Walter's crystals," he said, admiring the precise angles on the stone "A nice addition to my rock collection."

"You keep yours in a shoebox, too?"

"Not anymore." They walked to his desk where he sat down across from her. "You drove all the way over here to give me this?" He set the crystal in the center of his desk so it would catch the sunlight. The same sunlight ignited the flame in Crystal's hair.

"That, and more. You're not gonna believe what's happened."

"Skrabo causing trouble?"

"No." She pulled a copy of the *Antler's American* from her bag. "He's gone missing." She handed him the paper, which carried the news on the front page.

Chitto read quickly, gleaning that Sheriff John Skrabo had not been seen since the previous Sunday morning. According to his uncle, Ben King, he talked to his nephew early that day and was told he planned to have breakfast at a local restaurant, then make his routine run around the county. Skrabo's red pickup was found upside down on Wednesday in the Kiamichi River, at the bottom of a steep embankment. The end of the article reported that a search of the river was underway, but spring runoff was hampering efforts.

"What's your take?" she asked once he'd finished reading.

"From all appearances, he drowned."

"That's crap and you know it." She hesitated, swallowing. "You and Frank, did you . . ."

He gave her a direct look. "We drove straight out of town and didn't look back." For the first time, he noticed she was dressed in a dark green pantsuit. Low heels. Hair twisted neatly on the back of her head. "You here for something else. What?"

She tugged on her jacket to straighten it. "To turn in a job application. I put you down as a reference. You still all right with that?"

"You bet . . ." Pausing, Chitto picked up the newspaper again. "But maybe Fate has provided you options."

She stared at him a half minute, then opened her eyes wide. "You mean, go to work for the sheriff's department? Oh, hell no."

"Why not? King still pulls some weight, bet he'd give you a reference. Think about it. You could influence the way things are done, change things for the better."

She tilted her head to the side, grinning. "Now wouldn't that just be the frosting on the cake."

"Could get back in the good graces of your neighbors, *and* influence the way the department works with other agencies. Like ours." He folded the newspaper and returned it to her. "It's worth thinking about, Crystal. You'd be stationed right there in Antlers."

"Yeah, maybe I will." Glancing at her watch, she stood to leave. "Supposed to be in HR at nine." She turned to walk away, then looked at him again. "Someone still needs to punch your lights out."

He grinned again. "Guy tried that a couple weeks ago. Didn't do any good."

"Believe it or not," she said. "I find that comforting."

∞

By ten o'clock, Jasmine still had not shown. Chitto spent the morning fielding phone calls that came in, handling his mail, and wondering where she was. Hearing the front door open, he looked up to see Daniel Blackfox approaching his desk.

"Where's Jasmine?" he asked.

"She had an appointment." Blackfox motioned toward the red brick building visible through the east windows. "You're up. Last candidate's in the meeting room."

"Last candidate? Jasmine didn't tell me we had another candidate."

"Came about rather suddenly."

Chitto rose from his chair, grabbing a yellow pad and pen. "Fill me in quick."

"This isn't your first ballgame, just run the play. And no spitballs. We need to hire someone quick or that gal in HR's gonna nail my hide on her wall."

"I'm going."

"Oh," Blackfox said. "And given your recent experience requiring medicated ointment, I signed you up for some training with the SWAT team. Firing range practice on Saturday with the Exec. Defensive training on Sunday afternoon with Junior."

"*Junior?*"

"For a big man, he's remarkably light on his feet." Blackfox walked away leaving Chitto staring.

Mumbling unkind words, Chitto took time to go by the cafeteria for a cup of coffee. Opening the door to the interview room, he stared at a woman cradling a similar cup.

"Wipe that shocked look off your face," Jasmine said. Reaching out a hand, she moved a box of tissues on the table to one side, so they could face each other unobstructed. "Let's get this over with."

Recovering from shock, he sank into a chair across from her.

"Here's my file." She scooted a manila file his way. "Didn't have time to get it to you before Dan's interview. Won't find anything interesting in it, except I don't take dictation."

"I'm not a dictator." Still feeling stunned, he opened the HR file, Confidential stamped in bold red letters across the front. He glanced briefly at her work history, then shoved it aside. "Let's cut to the chase, Jasmine. Why?"

She took a breath, let it out slowly. "I been trying to figure that out myself."

The clock on the wall in the interview room ticked loudly. As Jasmine dropped her gaze to the tabletop, Chitto ticked off the minutes. As the first one passed, she started tracing a cup ring on the table with her right index finger. After the second, she moved to a deep scratch that cracked the smooth surface of the table. At the third, she looked at him.

"I've worked a lot of places, lot of offices, but this one makes me feel different." Shaking her head, she turned to stare out panes of glass that provided a view of the Choctaw Complex's wide front entry. She spoke without looking at him. "I got three kids, Sam."

Jostling his coffee cup, he watched coffee spreading across the table. "I'm not supposed to ask—"

"Oh be quiet," she snapped. "I'm the one taught you the rules. Just listen."

"I'm listening." He leaned back, listening to the chair creak like it had arthritic joints.

"Well, don't settle in. This will be short and sweet." She went back to staring out the window. "Daughter's a model in California. Sends a clipping when she's been featured in a magazine. Boy in the military sends an email to tell me what port he's doing shore leave in. Boy in jail calls couple of times a year, collect." She looked at him, eyes blinking. "There comes a time when a mother becomes an afterthought."

Chitto angled his head, staring out the window.

"If you're trying to come up with some sentimental mush that's supposed to make me feel better, don't—or I'll withdraw my application."

He held out his hands, palms up. "One thing I've learned, Jasmine. You are not the mush type."

"Okay." Straightening her shoulders, she leaned forward. "If I'm gonna do this, we need to set some boundaries."

He leaned toward her. "What kind of boundaries?"

"You don't stick your nose into my personal business and I'll do the same. If either of us asks the other a dumb-ass question, we have the right to tell them where to go."

"Deal. And I'm assuming you don't consider my outside activities of a personal nature."

"Police work is police work, whether you're wearing your badge or not. Which reminds me." She reached into her handbag and pulled out a small padded envelope. "This came for you today. Return address is Antlers, so didn't want to leave it lying around."

Chitto pulled open the envelope and shook the contents onto the table. "Judas priest . . ."

He stared at the brass badge a full minute, connecting the dots. Quince Winters' late arrival at Peony's house was because his strategy had involved resolving multiple issues: eliminating any threat to Crystal and Peony; clearing the names of the ranchers, Bradshaw and Campbell; and destroying the chokehold the sheriffs held on the county.

Hell, he thought, laughing softly. Maybe he'll even get gravel on his stretch of road now.

Leaning back, he rubbed his eyes with the heel of his hands, a mix of emotions turning his muscles to spaghetti. Relief. Satisfaction. A sense of justice. Then the cop took over. Grabbing a tissue from the box on the table, he began rubbing the package and its contents clean of fingerprints.

"I take it that means something." Jasmine folded her arms across her chest, following his movements.

"It and the hatband in my bottom drawer will mean a lot to a couple of ranchers in the Kiamichi Valley." Using another tissue, Chitto scooped the badge into the envelope, then looked at her. "I need a big favor, Jasmine. I want to get those items to them, but I'd rather not have our return address or a postmark on the envelope."

"Give me the names." Fishing a small notebook from her bag, she handed it to him. "Won't use a return address, and I'll drop them in a postal box on the way home. Mail goes to a distribution center now, so it won't have a Durant postmark." She handed him a pencil, saying, "Just tell me who gets what."

"You *have* to come to work for us," he said, scribbling down Riley Campbell and Harry Bradshaw's names. "Don't know their addresses, but I'm sure you can find them." Watching the notepad disappear into her cavernous purse, he said, "It's great to have you onboard, Jasmine."

"I still won't do coffee."

"That's what the cafeteria's for."

"I take it the interview's over." Standing, she tossed her paper cup into the wastebasket, wiped away her coffee stains with another tissue, then looked at the coffee he'd spilled. "That woman in HR will have your head, you don't clean up that mess."

When Jasmine said she didn't do coffee, she meant she didn't do coffee.

∞

Back at his desk, Chitto pulled his cell phone from his pocket and placed a call. The phone rang four times before a voice came on the line.

"Hey, Mama. What's going on?"

"I suppose you want to talk to your granny," Mattie Chitto said. "She's been wondering if you got the corn bought. I'll get her."

"No, wait— I, uh, I called to talk to you."

272

"Me? What's wrong?"

"Nothing, I just felt like checking in with you. You feeling all right? Lot of flu going 'round since that ice storm." He listened to the sound of breathing, a chair creaking in the background.

"Always a lot catching when the seasons change. I'm not sick. Grandma either. I make sure we both get plenty of vitamin C in the winter. Drink lots of orange juice, too."

"That's good. Make sure you keep it up." He listened to more breathing.

"You feeling all right, Sam?" she asked.

"I'm good. Just busy. But I'll be up to see you and Grandma soon as the moon's in the right phase."

"The moon . . ."

"Need to wait until the moon's waxing to plant corn." A pause. "I also need a dose of your home cooking. Fix plenty so I can bring home leftovers." He looked up, seeing Jasmine headed his way with a fistful of papers. "Someone's coming, so have to get back to work. Tell Grandma I have the corn."

"Okay . . ."

"You take care, Mom."

"Okay . . ."

Chitto cleared his throat. "I'm, uh, I'm looking forward to seeing you."

"*Sam* . . ."

"Yeah?"

"Stop at the store on the way home and pick up some orange juice." *Click.*

CHAPTER TWENTY-FOUR

The moon began a waxing stage on Monday, March eleventh. On Saturday, March sixteenth, Chitto watched Frank Tubbe pull into his driveway, parking next to the duel-wheeled Chevy.

"Am I to understand that we're taking your ride today?" Opening his door, Tubbe stepped to the ground and removed a rifle and his Bowie knife from behind the seat.

"Jimmy's earned a rest." Chitto nodded at the rifle and knife. "Think we need those to plant a corn patch?"

"One never knows." Tubbe deposited the weapons behind the passenger seat. "According to the news, Skrabo's body still hasn't been found. Until it is, I consider the 24/7 sheriff still on the loose."

"Well, hell," Chitto sighed. Taking his shotgun from the locker, he placed it in the gun rack.

"Not taking the rifle?" Tubbe said.

"Distance shots are your specialty."

"You're overlooking something." Tubbe nodded toward Hattie's George's house.

"Right. Boycott's the canary in the coal mine when it comes to Skrabo." Chitto did a slow jog next door and was back in minutes. The dog let out an excited yelp when he saw Tubbe.

"Let's roll," Chitto said, opening his car door. "According to the weatherman, it's supposed to rain tomorrow."

Tubbe retrieved a coffee thermos from his GMC and a sack of donuts. "That the same prognosticator that got it wrong last time?"

"One and the same." He shook his head at the sack of donuts Tubbe held open to him. "Can't believe you're so damn persnickety about your coffee, yet eat that stuff."

"What kind've cop are you?" Tubbe fished a glazed donut from the sack and laid it in front of Boycott. Fishing out another covered in sprinkles, he leaned back in his seat. "That's okay. Just leaves more for us."

Stepping on the gas, Chitto pulled onto the Indian Nation Turnpike, heading north. "I talked to Peony yesterday."

"Oh, yeah," Tubbe paused to pour a cup of coffee for Chitto, one for himself. "Fill me in."

"She said Walter's funeral went well. Buried Rosebud in the same coffin. Leona Mann's family buried the skull with her body, without fanfare to keep the authorities from snooping around." He paused, watching Tubbe feed anther donut to Boycott. "Oh, and Chuck Stovall held a séance at his place to see if Leona's ghost was still haunting it."

"And?"

"Spooks are gone." Thinking the Checkerboard could do with fewer ghosts, Chitto inhaled deep and emptied his lungs slowly.

"What about Crystal?" Tubbe asked. "She quit that realty?"

"Not yet, but she's put in her application with us and the sheriff's department."

"She's going after Skrabo's job?"

"Said old King almost fell over himself, giving her a recommendation."

Tubbe grunted. "Given his credentials, that could work against her."

"He's probably still got enough stuff on certain ones to have some clout. If she decides that's the job she wants, once she's in, she'll show him who's in charge."

Tubbe brushed crumbs onto the floor mat. "Only thing that worries me is those bastards' blood runs in her veins. You think evil's an inheritable trait?"

"Blood's not everything." Chitto glanced out the side window, seeing trees in spring dress, rivers running clean, farmers working hayfields. "Peony's upbringing's what shaped her."

Tubbe eased back in the seat, grinning. "She did a helluva good job with that."

Chitto chuckled. "I was talking about integrity, not moral turpitude." He gave Tubbe a sideways glance. "King's in a nursing home over there now."

Tubbe's jaws dropped. "You jerking me around?"

"Nope. He's pulling a George Forsyth. Crystal went by to see him and was told he didn't want any visitors. Hardly talks, just sits at the window and stares at the mountains. With his compound getting torched and his nephew disappearing, he's hiding out in the safest place he can find."

Tubbe laughed. "Well, we both know how *that* tuned out." He pulled his ball cap low over his eyes. "Wake us when we get there, professor."

The sound of a snoring man and a dreaming dog kept Chitto company on the eighty-mile trip to Krebs. It was enough. The sounds of inner peace wasn't a bad traveling companion.

∞

The trailer had been made from the bed of an old Chevy pickup. It sat next to the garden spot, a large plot of tilled ground fenced with chicken wire.

Pulling to a stop in his mother's drive, Chitto said, "Where the hell did that come from?"

Boycott began a frantic pawing at the back window, whining softly.

"I'm more interested in what's in it." Tubbe let the dog out of the truck.

Chitto smelled fish as soon as he opened his door. Beating him to the trailer, Boycott stood on his hind legs, scrambling to climb over the side.

"No you don't," he mumbled, pulling the dog away.

"Man, those are big carp," Tubbe said, giving Chitto a questioning look.

Hearing the back screen slam, Chitto turned to see his grandmother hobbling down a flagstone path. He made a quick introduction to Tubbe, then asked, "Where'd you get the fish, Grandma?"

She waved in an easterly direction. "That boy down there, he bring them. The corn will grow fast now."

Chitto stared at the fish cache again, estimating its weight. "What'd he do, use a net?"

"Yeh. He dammed up a creek over there at Eufaula. Catch fish fast that way."

"Fast, but probably illegal," Tubbe murmured.

"They're trash fish, too bony to eat," Chitto responded. "We're doing the fishermen a favor."

Tubbe grunted, arms crossed. "I take it we're supposed to dig holes, bury the fish, plant the corn on top."

"Yeh," Rhody said. "I will get the hatchet."

"That won't be necessary, ma'am. I have something that'll work."

Walking to the Chevy, Tubbe retrieved his Bowie knife. Spotting an old stump used for splitting firewood, he tipped it over and rolled it toward the trailer holding the fish. "You got a wheelbarrow?" he asked, eyeing the distance between the trailer and garden.

"I will get it," Peony said.

Chitto took her by the arm. "We can handle this now, Grandma. You go back inside."

"No. I wait here." She sat down on a weathered bench alongside the garden. "You must put three kernels in each one."

Knowing it would be useless to argue, Chitto jogged to a small shed and returned pushing a battered wheelbarrow.

Tubbe began sorting fish, tossing small ones in the wheelbarrow whole, hacking larger ones across in the middle. "If you're gonna keep up with me," he told Chitto, "you better get cracking."

Using a pointed spade, Chitto scooped holes into the well-turned and raked soil. Not planted for several years, the dirt was dark and rich and smelled of humus and worms. Now and then he glanced Tubbe's way. The Chickasaw was keeping pace with him, wheeling the wheelbarrow along the rows and depositing fish in the holes. Finishing at the same time, they took time out for a glass of iced tea on the back porch, then started planting. Tubbe mounded dirt over the fish and Chitto followed, depositing three seeds in each one.

They were finishing up when the two vehicles pulled into the driveway. Chitto recognized the Choctaw Nation unit right away, as well as the man behind the wheel. Dan Blackfox. He had no trouble identifying the occupant of the black SUV either.

Tubbe walked up to him. "What's that fed doing here?"

"Damned if I know." Chitto whistled Boycott to his side and put him into a sit position. "But we're about to find out."

Anchoring the spade end of the shovel in the ground, he waited for the two men to approach. Giving a sideways glance, he noticed Tubbe had recovered his Bowie knife from the chopping block. "Play it cool, Frank," he whispered.

Mattie Chitto appeared at the back door. Seeing Blackfox, she called out, "Dinner's almost ready, Dan . . ."

Spotting the dark, wiry man with him, she hesitated, eyes seeking out Chitto.

"Set a couple more plates, Mom." Chitto faced Blackfox again. "I take it this is not a Sunday drive, Dan."

"No, it's not. Agent Rodriquez here came looking for you. When he didn't find you home, he came looking for me. It, uh, it seems he's trying to puzzle through a development over in Push County." He lifted an eyebrow. "That sheriff that sent those HR files back came up missing a couple weeks back."

Chitto exchanged a quick glance with Tubbe, then looked back at his boss. "What's that got to do with me?"

"I'll take over." Rodriguez sidled up, looking Tubbe over. "Who's this?"

Grinning his lop-sided grin, Tubbe held out a hand smeared with fish guts and slime. "Sergeant Frank Tubbe, Chickasaw Lighthorse Police. Only today, I'm the man in charge of planting fish."

"Fish . . ." Rodriquez looked at the extended hand, the garden spot where fish tails protruded from mounds, and took a step back.

"Natural fertilizer," Blackfox said. Folding his arms, he looked at Rodriquez. "Go ahead, tell Chitto why we made this long drive up here. And make it fast. Mattie Chitto's 'bout the best cook in Pittsburg County and I missed dinner."

Eyes stony, Rodriquez turned to Chitto. "What was your relationship with John Skrabo?"

"Relationship?" Chitto laughed, then turned serious. "There was no relationship. Now cut the bull and tell me what this is about."

"I'll ask the questions," Rodriguez said. "When's the last time you saw him?"

"Aw, hell." Blackfox gave the agent a piercing look, then turned to Chitto and Tubbe. "Seems a deputy noticed something stinking up the sheriff's office. Thinking a rat curled up and died, he went looking. Traced it to the evidence locker in the back room, where he found a head in one of the cartons. John Skrabo's head."

"*Damn*." Tubbe's grin was so broad, his eyes crinkled. "Bet that did stink."

Rodriquez glanced at him, then turned back to Chitto. "Fill me in on your activities the last few weeks. Any contact you had with Skrabo, witnesses that can substantiate your alibi."

"Is this a joke?" Chitto looked at Blackfox.

Tubbe stepped forward, the Bowie knife an extension of his arm. "If that sheriff went missing a couple weeks ago, I can provide an airtight alibi for Sam. We spent the weekend in the mountains, teaching this dog here to hunt." Reaching down, he scratched the top of Boycott's head. "And I can guarantee neither one of us set eyes on anyone in the sheriff's department . . . or any other cracker imitating a lawman."

"Good enough for me," Blackfox said.

Without warning, a long, mournful howl echoed across the countryside. Lifting his head, Boycott responded with a deep, rumbling howl of his own. Pulling away from Chitto, the dog trotted toward the back fence.

Blackfox looked toward the hills. "Was that a wolf?"

"Couldn't be." Chitto followed his gaze. "Been extinct here for decades." He whistled Boycott back to his side.

"Enough of this." Rodriguez walked closer to Chitto. "I think maybe you need to come into the office with me. You keep turning up in places you shouldn't—and when you do, people die."

Blackfox placed himself between the agent and Chitto. "You're barking up the wrong tree, Rodriquez. Sergeant Tubbe provided an alibi for the time Skrabo disappeared. And I can vouch for him last weekend, even provide the name of witnesses. He was busy training with our SWAT group, one of which is the Executive Director of Law

Enforcement." He paused an effective length of time. "Sure you want to bring *two* Indian nations down on your head?"

Rodriguez looked between the trio, then turned toward his SUV. "I'm keeping my eyes on you, Chitto," he said over his shoulder.

"Tell you what," Chitto called after him. "How about putting that time into finding my dad and Bert Gilly's murderer? We've dropped clues as big boat motors in your lap and you've still got nothing?" He paused, watching Rodriguez turn slowly.

Edging up to him, Tubbe whispered, "Easy, Sam."

Rodriquez stood a minute, eyes blinking. "I'm handling my end. Just make sure you stick with yours." Climbing into the SUV, he keyed the ignition and spun gravel clear to the county road.

"Well," Blackfox said. "That went well, as usual."

Chitto turned as the back screen opened. "Time to drop the subject," he said, watching his mother approach.

A smiling Mattie Chitto joined them. "Come on in, Dan. Iced tea is waiting and the boys need to clean up." She looked to where Rhody sat on the bench. "You come, too, Mama. You forgot to put on your sunbonnet."

"Hurry up, boys." Helping Rhody to her feet, Blackfox led her toward the house. "I wasn't kidding when I said I was hungry."

As the yard emptied, Tubbe looked at Chitto. "You thinking what I'm thinking?"

"I am if you're thinking a wolf strayed into those hills back there." He scanned the country behind his mother's place, thinking of any number of places a man could be hiding. "Who you think he's been dogging? Us or the fed?"

Leaning on a fence rail, Tubbe stared at the hills. "I put my money on the fed. Probably been watching the sheriff's office for some sign his little present had been found. When Rodriguez showed up, he followed him to Durant and then up here." He glanced sideways at Chitto. "You fill in that hole you took the bones out of?"

"Nope. Unlike others present, I followed Winters' orders." Remembering a vintage sword knife with an eighteen-inch blade, he turned to face Tubbe. "That long sword, you don't think . . ."

Tubbe let out a snort "Now that's justice."

"Rough justice, but justice none the less. Hard not to like the man."

Tubbe nodded. "I did some checking. He was the real deal, a lieutenant colonel." He laughed quietly. "When he said Skrabo was no longer a problem, he wasn't kidding."

Chitto looked at the hills again. "Think he's got a scope on us?"

"You can bet on it."

"Well, maybe now he can let up a little bit, leave the war behind."

"The one in Push County maybe." Facing the hills, Tubbe snapped off a salute. Turning to Chitto, he said, "Where can I clean up? I'm tired of smelling like the bottom of a muddy lake bed."

"Sink in the laundry room, just inside the back door."

Chitto stood a while in the yard, searching distant shadows and finding nothing. Knowing when effort was wasted, he turned toward the house. As the call of a wolf echoed across the land again, he looked to the hillside. Removing his ball cap, he lifted it high overhead. "Peace with honor, Colonel," he said, and he gave the cap a wave.

ABOUT THE AUTHOR

Lu Clifton writes mystery that mingles Choctaw culture, science, and murder. She became interested in cultural traditions while tracing her mother's Choctaw roots. She was born in and spent her early childhood in southeastern Oklahoma, then moved to the Texas Panhandle with her family. She completed an associate degree at Amarillo Junior College in Texas and a B.A. and M.A. in English at Colorado State University. She now resides in northern Illinois.

Clifton writes fiction for both children and adults. *The Bone Picker* is the second book in her Sam Chitto mystery series. *Scalp Dance* (Five Star Mysteries), the first book, released in 2016. She also has three middle-grade novels in print.

Clifton is a member of the Oklahoma Writers Federation, Western Writers of American, Mystery Writers of America, The American Crime Writers League, and the Society of Children's Book Writers and Illustrators. Her middle-grade novel, *Freaky Fast Frankie Joe*, received a Friends of American Writers Award for Juvenile Fiction in 2012.

TOPICS AND QUESTIONS FOR DISCUSSION

Use this guide to facilitate your library group or book club's conversation.

1. Clifton includes elements of Choctaw myths and folklore in her Sam Chitto mystery series. This book opens with references to the Bone Picker and the Nameless One. Identify examples of other stories referenced, including biblical and cultural, and how they drove the action. How they influenced characters such as Sam Chitto and Frank Tubbe, Jasmine Birdsong and Maddy Culpepper.

2. The setting for the book is Pushmataha County, located in the remote Kiamichi Wilderness of southeastern Oklahoma. Over time, this area was utilized for different purposes: indigenous people used it for refuge, subsistence hunters for food, railroads to connect remote locations, ranchers to supplement grazing. Currently, its appeal is tourism. Describe how Clifton uses the setting to enhance the reader's understanding of not only the physical geography but also the characters that make use of it, i.e., the sheriffs, Skrabo and King; the ranchers, Campbell and Bradshaw; Quince Winters; Crystal Folsom.

3. The elders in the book, Rhody Pitchlyn and Sonny Boy Munro, appear as mystics and spiritual leaders representing the old ways of believing. Chitto and his sidekick, Frank Tubbe, are skeptics. Discuss how Chitto and Tubbe's attitudes change over the course

of the book. What do you see as the role of these two elders in the series?

4. The old mystic, Sonny Boy Munro, wants to cure Frank Tubbe of the shadow in his head. In contemporary terms, that "shadow" would probably be attributed to post-traumatic stress disease. PTSD is an important theme in the book. Several of the characters are identified as veterans. Name them and discuss what, if any, signs of PTSD they exhibit. Discuss how the prologue sets the stage for this theme.

5. Incidents in Vietnam play an important role. The United States Congress never declared war against Vietnam; it was classified a conflict, i.e., an open and armed hostility exemplified by active military operations. Discuss the fine line that distinguishes the terms war and conflict.

6. Clifton references two military operations: the evacuation of Saigon and the mission to take the town of Lam Son. The mission to take Lam Son appears doomed from the beginning. Why?

7. Coverage of the evacuation of Saigon appeared to focus on the financial losses, i.e., the cost to the government in scrapped equipment. Discuss other losses that resulted from these two operations, particularly to the three veterans in the story who served there.

8. Since there was no declaration of the war, the length of time operations in Vietnam lasted is sketchy. However, it is now widely accepted that it was from November 1, 1955, until April 30, 1975, or between 19 and 20 years. Would the long-term effects on those who served in a conflict differ from the effects on

those who served in an officially declared war? Discuss.

9. Justice is another prevailing theme in Clifton's mysteries, and it's often accomplished outside the official legal system. Discuss how the justice system had been handcuffed in Pushmataha County, preventing justice from being served. Consider Nixon's goal to achieve "peace with honor." According to the character, Quince Winters, the peace agreement signed in Paris accomplished, to Nixon's thinking, this goal. Identify the characters in the book you feel would disagree with this line of thinking. How was peace with honor accomplished at the end of *The Bone Picker*? Compare and contrast Quince Winter's need to see peace with honor achieved and Sam Chitto's need to see justice served. Do you think acting outside the system is ever justified?

10. Clifton tackles tough themes in her mystery novels. In *Scalp Dance*, the first in the series, she examines the effect of rape on women; in *The Bone Picker*, she examines warfare and its effect on men. Compare and contrast the two. Do you find the inclusion of such themes makes for a better mystery novel? Why or why not?

11. Ask the group to discuss their favorite character(s) in the book, both men and women. What did they find particularly appealing about them? Who would they like to see return in subsequent books?

Lu Clifton's website: http://www.lutricia-lois-clifton.com
Amazon Author page:
https://www.amazon.com/author/luclifton

CPSIA information can be obtained
at www.ICGtesting.com
Printed in the USA
LVHW101129160423
744489LV00017B/109